I0585919

THE CLAIRVOYANT'S GLASSES

VOLUME 3

HELEN GOLTZ

The Clairvoyant's Glasses Volume 3

PUBLISHED BY: Atlas Productions

First published 2022.

Proofread by Crystal L. Wren, COL Proofreading Service.

Cover design by Karri Klawiter, Art by Karri.

PLEASE NOTE: This book is written in British-Australian English.

Dedicated to Brian Goltz.

Kind, supportive, stoic, fun, my Dad.

CHAPTER 1

FOR JUST A MOMENT the lights in the *Optical Illusion* store dimmed in their brightness. It was such an unusual occurrence that Orli paused in her work and looked to the chandeliers and then to the leadlight windows with their diamond-shaped glass panels, to see if something had blocked the sunlight. As the tiny store wedged between *The Perfect Slice* cake store and *Just the Thing* gift emporium, a delivery van had, on occasion, momentarily cast a shadow as it visited the neighbouring stores. But there was nothing outside and within a few moments the shop returned to full light, the chandeliers beamed and the sun that entered during the day—and made the store gleam like a crystal wonderland—resumed in all its glory. Orli however, was not at ease.

'Uh oh,' she whispered. *An omen.* The thought filled her with trepidation.

Orli was in the store on her own, having left the company of her uncle, cousin and the small group that had gathered at the rambling residence of the newly minted clairvoyant, Sophie Carell. The very same residence that once belonged to Sophie's famous clairvoyant aunt, Daphne Shelby. Tension had mounted and her uncle suggested they all leave. Orli repaired the broken glass that had fractured along with tempers and departed. No one else did.

The young *Optical Illusion* optometrist had taken over from her uncle, Alfred, who these days was content to manage the shopfront and bookings, order the much-desired crystal figurines and do the books. He still looked into people's eyes for insights, but not professionally. Orli, with the lightest of blue eyes that ran in the family, saw more than most. Willowy of appearance and with her name meaning 'light', Orli radiated it and felt it keenly when it was dimmed.

Her cousin, Lukas, at 25, three years her senior, was the master clocksmith for the business. But neither Alfred nor Lukas were present and that's what worried Orli. Lukas had impulsively rushed off to reclaim his role as a protector of Sophie, and Alfred had gone in pursuit to save his grandson from starting a war.

Orli turned her face to the light as if absorbing its power and stilled. She sensed they were both in danger and it was connected to Sophie. And the Raven.

Melino Carter froze at her desk. Her fingers and nose were twitching which was not unusual since she came to work in the office space leased from renowned clairvoyant, Daphne Shelby. But since Daphne passed away and Sophie Carell, took up the reins from her aunty, Mel's twinges were all over the place. Just yesterday she raced around to Sophie's office to find black crows amassing on the windowsills and a witch inside talking with Sophie. A very handsome witch whom Sophie introduced as Detective Murdoch Ashcroft. That was definitely an improvement on some of the older guests the former owner, Daphne, used to entertain.

But now, this was not just a tingle Mel was feeling, but pins and needles like someone had turned her witch radar up to full bore. Mel was rarely still, but she sat for a moment, a little nervous. She ran a hand through her short dark hair, the pink streak in her fringe flopping back into her eyes and she waited, steadying herself trying to read her body's reaction.

Mel was from a long line of healers; her great-grandmother had the gift, second sight, the curse as some called it, and practised Tongan medicine – people came from all over the island to be healed by her. Mel's grandmother was the same, her mother ignored it; not Mel. She sensed things and worked with potions, creating herbal remedies and cures.

She looked at her fingers and opened and closed them. This was like something she'd never felt before. Beside her in the office of the community group *Sport for Every Girl*, her colleagues worked on oblivious. Mel stretched her fingers, trying to remove the pins and needles. She shivered with the onset chill and looked through the windows at the darkening sky. It was not just outside that the storm was building; it was brewing in the old manor in which she worked and the chill was coming from Sophie's offices.

CHAPTER 2

DETECTIVE MURDOCH ASHCROFT LOOKED shocked, and, and he was not a man easily shocked – Miss Sharpe had, on occasion, described him as too laid back for his own good. Not now. His dark eyes were affixed on Sophie waiting for her to say her announcement was a joke—that she hadn't chosen him, the Raven, the enemy, to protect her—but she didn't deny it.

Lukas Lens rippled with anger. His eyes narrowed, his lips thinned and he glared at Sophie through pale blue eyes. He had started this process and set the ball in motion but he never—not in a million years—could have guessed this outcome. That she would choose for a protector the very force they were protecting her from!

Nikolas Saggers stilled. His large, fit frame was rarely motionless which made him all the more fearful. His eyes studied the scene, waiting to see what would happen next but he would not lose out to the Raven, to the family enemy.

The eldest statesman in the room, Alfred Lens, stood dignified and reflective, ready for negotiation. He had not always been so calm under pressure but his years of experience and his power gave him the edge. He stepped forward, indicating with his hand for his grandson, Lukas, to calm himself and reinforced the sentiment in Lukas's mind without verbalising it. He had the respect of the inhabitants of the room, even the Raven, Murdoch. Alfred was, after all, the most powerful presence amongst them.

Miss Sharpe stood wary and concerned. A thin and wiry woman, gentle of nature, Miss Sharpe had amazing insight into all that went on about her, but she could not physically protect herself from the forces in the room. She need not worry, however, as Alfred Lens would lay down his life to protect her.

The last inhabitant of the room, Sophie, had brought about this meeting of the protectors and their enemy, the Raven. She looked contrite, not thinking for a moment that her selection of Murdoch as her protector would induce such passion. Naive perhaps, she realised now. Sophie ran her hands down her red dress, a nervous action, and wished she had worn flatter heels to work this morning – her legs were feeling shaky and it would have been easier to run in sneakers.

A crack of thunder startled Sophie and Miss Sharpe; the men did not flinch. Outside, the day had become night, darkened by the approaching storm. The glass in the windows rattled with the swell of wind. Fortunately, they remained intact thanks to Orli repairing and strengthening the cracked glass before she departed after Lukas's anger had caused major damage. The energy in the room shifted, the lights flickered out, leaving them all in darkness. For a moment the world around them stilled, but then the noise of the breaking storm increased and the lights flooded back on even brighter than before, as if catching them all in the flashlight of a camera.

'Is this really necessary?' Murdoch asked, raising an eyebrow in the direction of Lukas Lens and giving him the best disinterested look he could muster on his handsome and smug face, which only served to annoy Lukas more.

'No, it is not; on that, we agree, Detective,' Alfred Lens said and turned to his grandson. 'Still the storm, lad.'

Lukas's fists clenched and unclenched, but the storm did not lessen.

'I am sorry, this is my doing,' Sophie said apologetically and bit her lip.

Nikolas Saggers chuckled as if that was the understatement of the year. From where he sat, his large, toned body looking tense and coiled for action, he studied Sophie in disbelief. 'You have two protectors, both willing to continue the tradition, but you choose the enemy to protect you,' he said, trying to understand her choice.

The issue wasn't just about the choice, and Sophie knew it, it was ego. He and Lukas were rejected, and no one took kindly to being rejected. On the other hand, the detective—the Raven—looked like he was enjoying the show.

Another loud clap of thunder made Sophie jump and she braced herself for their reactions, something had to give. *Maybe Lukas would explode into little bits and scatter all around the room,* she mused. *So inappropriate,* Sophie scolded herself, but the theatrics annoyed her.

Men! What's the big deal?

She cleared her throat and voiced what she was thinking. 'It's truly not that big a deal... Lukas chose Lucy over protecting me.' She saw him flinch at her words but continued before he could defend himself, 'Nikolas was roped in by default whether he wanted to be or not, and Murdoch is on hand every other day, so why not put him to the task and keep him accountable?' She smiled at Murdoch as if it were the most brilliant idea, and surely he could see that.

Miss Sharpe, her trusted confidant and assistant, came and stood closer beside her. Sophie sensed she, too, was a little fearful.

Alfred raised his voice above the building cacophony of the storm and spoke. 'Sophie, this is rather unorthodox. Am I understanding you clearly? You want the family enemy, the

Raven, to be the one who protects you from his own line?' he asked, calmly, loudly, and clearly.

'You have got to be—' Lukas began, his grandfather cut him off with a wave of his hand. The young man was silenced.

'Please,' Alfred invited her to speak.

'You said I could choose my own protector, Alfred,' Sophie said, gently reminding him of his words and keeping her voice respectful.

'Yes, that is true,' he conceded. 'Perhaps I should have clarified that the protector should come from the generational line of protectors that have been linked to your family for centuries.'

Sophie frowned. 'So, I have to choose Lukas or Nikolas?'

Nikolas rose, angered. 'Enough.'

'It is not personal,' Sophie quickly added. 'It is not a popularity test, I promise you. I don't mean to be disrespectful.'

He glared at her and, like the three powerful men present, did not like to have his offered services declined.

'What exactly are you trying to achieve here, Sophie?' Lukas snapped.

Sophie ignored him, tired of Lukas's attitude when he put this show in motion in the first place by his own choices. She turned to Alfred. 'Has that ever been done?' Sophie asked, looking from Alfred to Miss Sharpe. 'Has anyone ever chosen the Raven as their protector?'

Lukas laughed. 'No. Why ask the enemy to protect you? What madness is that?' He looked to Murdoch who was sitting quietly, watching with interest. But no one was fooled. With a nod of his head, the Raven could tear down their lives and all around them. Not that anyone had seen a display of that nature from the cursed Raven line since early last century.

'Have you anything to say about this?' Lukas turned to Murdoch.

'Plenty,' Murdoch answered from where he sat on the edge of the windowsill, enjoying watching the drama play out; the ravens hovered outside the window like his guardians.

'Let's hear it then,' Nikolas said, crossing his muscled arms across his chest.

Sophie rolled her eyes. 'And yet again a man is asked to give his thoughts on my decision.' She shook her head at Lukas and Nikolas and noted Alfred's sympathetic look. 'Enough with the noise!' she yelled and the storm stilled.

Everyone froze in surprise.

'Woah, did I do that?' she asked, turning to Miss Sharpe.

'Most likely dear. I did say you were... well, let's talk about that later,' Miss Sharpe said. But Sophie recalled the conversation that she was destined to be the most powerful witch of her time, the top of the tree. With a glance at

Murdoch, she began to wonder if she needed any protector at all. His eyes narrowed.

Did he read my mind then? She wondered until Alfred's voice drew her attention.

'I admit Sophie, that since you had the curse thrust upon you and with so little preparation, we have sheltered you and not made you fully aware of your strengths,' Alfred said. 'It was not meant to be because we wished to shut down your voice, just protect you until you found your feet, and to be honest, we are not truly sure what you are capable of yet.'

'I understand,' she said and gave him a small smile. Sophie had a soft spot for the charming, most powerful witch in the room. She returned her attention to Murdoch. 'You needn't look so self-satisfied, Murdoch, given you didn't think to tell me that you were the enemy all the time we worked together, and everyone is trying to protect me from you!'

He shrugged. 'If you hadn't been told anything of the curse or who I was, you would have thought I was some crazy guy spinning a story.'

'So now that you know, Sophie, you have chosen Murdoch to protect you from himself,' Nikolas said and scoffed. 'Are you up for the job?' he asked Murdoch.

The men were not dissimilar in look—both dark in features and tall in stature—but Nikolas had the stance of a fighter and the scars to prove it. Murdoch was leaner and had an aloofness that only added to his mysteriousness.

'He's not going to protect you, Sophie,' Lukas sneered. 'You're just giving him legitimate access to you.'

Murdoch laughed, angering Lukas more.

'Say what you think about this,' Nikolas asked again of the Raven.

'No,' Lukas cut in before Murdoch could speak. 'I made a mistake.' He turned to Sophie. 'I am your protector, Sophie. You would not be taking this course of action if I had not walked away from the role. I am back. I am your protector.' He locked eyes with Sophie. She saw in her peripheral vision Nikolas bristled, given he had had the role for all of a weekend.

'I want Murdoch, the Raven, to be my protector,' she said again, slowly and clearly.

Lukas and Nikolas rose from their seats, the tension palpable. Alfred braced, ready to step in, Miss Sharpe stepped back towards the doorway. Sophie's eyes flitted from one man to the next. A chill descended over the room and she rubbed her arms to ward off the goosebumps. Miss Sharpe screamed and Sophie flinched as a bird hit the window, and then another, shaking themselves off and perching to stare in at the inhabitants.

'Hello, I thought I was going to get drenched, but I made it before the storm,' a voice said from the doorway and all eyes snapped to look at the entrance.

Mundanes!

Sophie heard Nikolas hiss the word as a quick warning. It must be the term for non-magical types or maybe just the uninitiated, she thought.

'Is everything okay?' another voice asked as a woman arrived beside the first guest. 'A meeting of suits anonymous!' she joked seeing every man was dressed for business.

Miss Sharpe could not help but smile and Sophie laughed, a little hysterically but enough for the room to dissolve of tension with the intruders. The rain began to fall, breaking up the clouds and the birds rose, flying away to find shelter in the trees.

Murdoch stood and clearing his throat, he addressed Sophie, 'I have a case. I came for your help but clearly you can't leave now.'

'Message me the address and I'll meet you there in thirty minutes,' Sophie said to him as he walked past and he nodded, bidding farewell to Alfred and Miss Sharpe.

'I am late for work,' Nikolas said as well and with a nod to Alfred and Miss Sharpe strode past Sophie, and through the gap of the two guests in the doorway to his waiting, very wet motorbike.

'You are leaving too, Lukas,' his grandfather announced, and Lukas angrily stormed out without the courtesy of farewelling the ladies.

'Something I said?' Blaine asked from the doorway and Mel laughed beside him, as the guests filed past.

Sophie looked at one of her dearest friends and grinned. 'On the contrary, Blaine, you are both a welcome sight to behold. And look at you, back from the Greek Islands, tanned and gorgeous.'

'That's me,' he agreed. 'Blaine Holmes.' Offering his hand and name to Mel, they shook and then extended the same to Alfred Lens. Blaine greeted Miss Sharpe. Everyone knew Miss Sharpe.

'I best be going too,' Alfred said.

'Won't you stay and have a pot of tea with me?' Miss Sharpe asked, needing the solace of a friend and a discussion on what to do next. 'I would be grateful.'

'Of course, I would be delighted. We'll leave you young people to it,' he said and, excusing himself, stepped away and they both left the room.

'What is going on?' Blaine asked.

'Is everything okay?' Mel asked, joining in.

'A meeting of the powers,' she said with a smile, trying not to convey her fear. 'All will be well.' She glanced at Mel, knowing she would understand.

Nothing was going to be well, not for a long time.

CHAPTER 3

Lukas Lens stood opposite the *Optical Illusion* store. He could not go any further forward; Orli had placed a protective barrier around the store... protective of him. He saw her through the small glass window frames as she stood at the counter with a customer. Sensing him, Orli looked up and indicated the back entrance to the store – the entry that avoided the glass windows and figurines. But Lukas stood in place, looking at the life work of his grandfather and his father before that, and then he turned and did not head to the back of the store, he walked. He walked until he disappeared from sight.

Alfred Lens saw the look of concern on his great-niece's face as he entered *Optical Illusion*. He greeted several customers, assisted Orli with sales and when the shop was empty again, she hurried toward him.

'Thank goodness you are back, Uncle Alfred,' she said with relief. 'Lukas returned but did not enter. Now, I don't know where he has gone. Can you read him?'

'Yes, do not fret,' he assured her. 'Lukas is trying very hard to not let me in his mind, but he's not strong enough to repel me. He's driving. He has been for some time.'

Orli frowned. 'What is he thinking?'

'He's angry at himself, at Lucy and Sophie. He believes Sophie chose the Raven to spite him.'

'Do you agree?' Orli asked.

'No. I think she likes and trusts Detective Ashcroft, and I think she's working on the adage, keep your friends close and your enemies closer.' He lowered himself onto his chair behind the counter.

'Hmm,' Orli mused. 'So, we don't know yet if the detective will agree to protect her... from himself or whatever else the Raven curse might entail.'

'No, he did not say either way if he would take the role, and I'm not sure what that would look like if he did. But Sophie is meeting with him now on a police case. That will be telling,' Alfred said and rubbed his temple as he tuned into his grandson's mind. 'I'm inclined to bring Lukas home. We need to talk this out.'

'Force him?' Orli said, biting her lower lip with concern.

'Yes. He needs to understand he has the best of all circumstances right now and to make something of it.'

'Has he?' Orli asked surprised. 'Perhaps you should explain that to me and I should go to him. He might be more forthcoming hearing it from a female perspective.'

'I think that's an excellent idea,' Alfred agreed. 'My calmness annoys him sometimes when he wants action, he'll be more at ease seeing you.' Alfred laid out his thoughts and when he had finished, Orli concurred with his reasoning. Moments later, she glanced around and ensuring no one was in sight, vanished.

'For the love of God!' Lukas snapped, his hand racing to his heart as Orli appeared in the passenger seat beside him.

She hurriedly grabbed the steering wheel and straightened him back on the road.

'You nearly gave me a heart attack,' he gasped.

'There is no easy way to announce I'm arriving,' Orli said matter-of-factly. 'It is better than standing in the middle of the road ahead and forcing you to screech to a halt.'

'Who said I would stop?' he asked and then smiled at her.

She laughed her light, musical laugh. 'I'm glad you haven't lost your sense of humour, Lukas.'

'Grandpa sent you,' he said, quickly reverting to his ill-humoured state.

'Yes, and no.'

'At least he didn't force me back with his mind control, I guess.' He glanced at Orli. 'Did he think about doing so?'

'You will have to ask him that,' she said discreetly.

'I'll take that as a yes,' Lukas said with a small, angry shake of his head. 'I'm okay, I'm not going to do anything stupid... I just needed some time out to think and—'

'—rage alone?' she finished his sentence, having read his anger and tension.

'And that,' he agreed.

Lukas's hands were gripping the steering wheel, his knuckles white from the tension of doing so, and his face was a mask of rigidity.

'Please,' Orli said with a nod to his hands, and Lukas released his grip a little and took a deep breath.

Orli continued, 'Uncle Alfred has a theory and I agree completely from a female perspective. Shall I give it to you?'

'Might as well since you dropped in and all.'

'Could you slow down a little? Pretend we are on a Sunday drive and you are enjoying my company,' she teased.

Lukas huffed. 'Sunday drive. I haven't heard that expression since Grandma would take me out Sunday afternoon for ice cream.'

'We can have ice cream when I finish, if you behave,' Orli said with a smile.

'Go on, give me your theory or whatever it is that you and Grandpa are conspiring on,' he said, slowing down and relaxing a little in the seat, his grip on the steering wheel easing.

'We believe you are in the perfect position to have Sophie as a friend and Lucy as your girlfriend, and you should take advantage of that.'

'Do you both? Go on.'

'Well Sophie will be coming into the store regularly to read the journals and visit us, so you two can develop a friendship. You get on well but you spar over power, that won't exist anymore. Lucy doesn't need to know when Sophie visits the store because Sophie's visits are legitimate and Lucy has no ground then to be jealous or demanding. You get to keep Lucy and keep her happy, and should it not work out with Lucy and you find yourself attracted to Sophie, you can pursue that because you are not her protector, still in her company, and Sophie and Lucy are no longer friends,' Orli said, smugly, finishing with a small shrug as if it would all work out for the best.

'And Grandpa came up with this theory?' Lukas said and then laughed out loud.

'What?' Orli asked.

'He just sent me a mental tap for that remark.'

'Deservedly so. Yes, and I agree with Uncle Alfred because that's what I would want if I were wearing Lucy or Sophie's shoes. Trust me, I know from a female perspective, you will be much more appealing to Sophie as a friend and—well let's just leave it as a friend— if you are confident, carefree and strong in yourself. Not angry, moping and jealous of anyone who has taken your protector role.'

'I'm not jealous,' he said. 'I just want to do that role and have Lucy as well.' He shook his head. 'Women.'

'Yes, fearsome creatures we are,' Orli teased. 'So, you should go to Lucy now, confirm you are one hundred percent hers, and then get back to being you, which will appeal to both ladies.'

Lukas smiled; his shoulders slumped in defeat. He slowed and when the road widened, turned the car around. He thought for a while, digesting Orli's words, and she did not speak, allowing him to think on it all, but she sensed his calmness.

After a while, Lukas said, 'There's one thing though, and best you are listening in Grandpa.' Raising his voice so that the word 'Grandpa' caught the elderly man's attention. 'If

Murdoch does become Sophie's protector, don't expect me to be happy about it. I shall still be protecting her and watching her like a hawk.'

'Then she'll have a hawk and a Raven watching her, won't she?' Orli said, and added under her breath, 'Two natural enemies.'

CHAPTER 4

SOPHIE TOOK THE FEW steps to the buzzer, pressed it, and pushed open the large glass door when the catch was released. She entered an impressive entrance hallway with a door on the left and right. Potted topiaries and mirrors adorned the entrance. The right door swung open and Murdoch beckoned her in.

In the lush apartment, Sophie recognised her – the blonde, tanned, taut woman wearing very fitted lycra that left nothing to the imagination, as Aunt Daphne used to say. She couldn't think from where she knew the woman, but she looked familiar. Murdoch grimaced at Sophie as if he hated every minute of being there; the scenery was good though, he couldn't complain about that. The apartment had a beautiful view of the river and the young woman was gorgeous. Sophie mused on Murdoch's grumpy partner, Detective Gerard Oakley, whom she recently solved a cold case with; he would have appreciated the client for sure but was nowhere to be seen. Several uniformed officers were talking to the woman in the corner of her apartment.

Without the brief from Murdoch, Sophie decided the crime can't have been too drastic given the woman was alive, no media was present, and the unit they were in was upmarket and in a good area. While the woman told the police officers what was missing, Murdoch pulled Sophie aside. She fished in her handbag for the glasses, which were a little more stylish since Orli had given Aunt Daphne's pair a modern makeover. Sophie slipped them on, pushing them back on her head, ready to pull into place to observe the scene when needed.

She turned her attention to Murdoch. 'I'm here.'

'Evidently, and thanks for that,' Murdoch retorted, giving her a smile that said he was pleased to see her given all the morning's dramas.

'Where's your partner?'

'Gerard's speaking to a witness who is just as attractive, so don't feel too sorry for him,' Murdoch said in a low voice and Sophie chuckled.

'She's still alive, so why am I here?'

'Because I'm suspicious and I'm hoping you can confirm something for me,' he said with a glance at the woman to make sure she was still occupied and not overhearing them. 'She's an influencer, apparently, and claims she has a stalker.'

'Oh, I thought I recognised her – Bella Brown.'

Murdoch raised his eyebrows. 'I wouldn't have put you down for following gym bunnies.'

'She's not just a gym bunny. She promotes health foods, fitness, health drinks. I think she calls it wellness.'

Murdoch turned his dark brown eyes to the woman. 'Well, she does look well.'

Sophie laughed. 'How observant of you.'

'Are you following her because you're unwell?' he asked hurriedly, making the connection and studying Sophie.

'How nice of you to be concerned, Muddy,' she teased and saw him grimace at the use of her nickname for him. 'No, I'm very well, maybe not as well as her,' Sophie said, sizing up the woman. 'She has great juice recipes and I was trying to drink healthier.'

'Sounds boring,' Murdoch said. 'Anyway, to business. Bella Brown is her name, as you pointed out, and she claims to be stalked. She's blaming a competitive influencer who is out to unhinge her, allegedly. I personally think she's doing this to increase her profile, they do that these influencers, or so I have heard. So, can you tell if her claim is for real?'

'I'll give it a shot. If you agree to be my protector,' she said, with a chin-up movement and a smile.

'Oh no you don't,' Murdoch said, 'I'm not playing that game. And no. I'm not going to be your protector, but thanks for offering me the job.'

'Why?' she whined in a soft voice. 'I'll behave.'

He smiled at that and gave her a small shake of his head. 'That I doubt. But later for this discussion. The boys are finishing up,' he said with a nod to the uniformed police who had taken an inventory and were departing. 'Will you help me?'

Sophie sighed. 'Sure.'

'Thanks.' Touching her arm briefly, he moved past Sophie to Bella Brown to start questioning her. 'Ask a question if you want to,' he said back over his shoulder. 'Ms Brown, let's begin. This is Sophie Carell, a consultant we work with.'

'So lovely to meet you,' Bella said, offering Sophie her hand to shake. She seemed genuine which Sophie appreciated. Bella indicated the couches and sat. 'Fire away, Detective.'

Murdoch and Sophie sat opposite, and Sophie dropped her glasses down to view Bella.

'I know you've filed a few police reports, but let's start at the beginning,' Murdoch said. 'How many times do you think you've been followed and is this the first time someone has been in your apartment?'

Bella took a deep breath and began. 'No, yes, well, yes and no. I think I've been followed about three times, but it is the first time someone has broken in.' She looked around, frowning. 'Nothing appears to have been taken but things have been touched and moved. It's creepy.'

'Sure is,' Sophie agreed, and Murdoch looked at her. She straightened, aiming to be more professional. She forgot that Murdoch liked that, whereas his partner was more casual.

'I was scared before, but now, I'm terrified,' Bella said and gave a little shudder. 'I wish I had a boyfriend; I'd insist he stayed over with me or I could go to his place.' She glanced at Murdoch who didn't take the bait. Sophie hid a smile; it wasn't the first time a damsel in distress had batted their eyelashes at the detective so he could act the hero. But Sophie noted Murdoch was either oblivious or disinterested or both. In fairness, he did lose the woman he loved less than a year ago, not that they had ever been together – she was his fiancée's best friend. Ex-fiancée's best friend. It was complicated and it was Sophie's first case with the detective, and about the only time she had ever seen him vulnerable.

'Please tell us about the stalking experience,' Sophie said, refocussing. 'When did you first notice someone stalking you?'

Bella nodded. 'I hire a small studio space at South Bank where I make my wellness videos three times a week. They have a fully equipped kitchen and gym there, it's very cool. The other days I just do off-the-cuff stuff for my followers here, or in the park.'

Sophie smiled encouraging her, and she heard Murdoch draw in a laboured breath beside her. Patience wasn't one of his strengths.

'It's not that far to the studio, 15-minutes max, so I usually walk there and home, but someone has been following me on my way home. You know, you get the feeling?' she said, looking at Sophie with her perfect face, big brown eyes and pouty lips. Sophie couldn't imagine how Murdoch was staying attentive to Bella's story, she couldn't focus on anything but the influencer's beautiful animated face.

Picking up her cue to say something, Sophie nodded, she knew the feeling. 'I think every girl has experienced that,' she agreed. 'Hearing noises behind you, someone walking too close, a glimpse of a man walking the same way as you at night, or that guy on public transport staring at you inappropriately and for too long.'

'Exactly,' Bella continued. 'The first time, I was coming home just at dusk, and I heard footsteps behind me. I wasn't too phased because it was still early enough in the evening. But then the footsteps got faster. I whirled around and saw someone in black ducking into a laneway – a cyclist was coming up behind him. I think the cyclist saved me.'

Images were appearing around Bella's head as she spoke. They were the usual images Sophie saw when she put the glasses on, bringing to life the topic her subject was relating. Bella was telling the truth. Sophie saw that someone was following behind her and she felt Bella's fear. Sophie saw the next time it happened before Bella told them, and the next time. She let Bella keep talking, hearing Murdoch respond to her, as she watched the images appear like film frames. Sophie was trying to see the man's face and then she felt a blow and reeled back. He was over the top of her, grinning, pressing down on her, pressing into her.

Sophie gasped for air, the weight on her chest and the hand around her throat restricting her. Murdoch grabbed her arm. 'Sophie! Are you okay? What's happening?'

Sophie pulled the glasses off and sat forward, breathing fast. 'I'm sorry, silly of me,' she said, embarrassed. 'A panic attack of sorts. Your story, Bella, just reminded me of a similar incident I had – a flashback,' she said haltingly, breathing fast and trying to explain her actions.

Bella reached across and took Sophie's hand. 'I'm so sorry, but thank you for understanding my fear.'

Sophie gave her a shaky smile. She tried to control her staggered breathing.

'I'll just get some fresh air and leave the detective to finish getting your statement,' she said apologetically. Bella nodded; her expression sympathetic.

Sophie jumped to her feet, keen to depart, and Murdoch rose beside her.

'No, you stay,' she told him and hurried to the door before he had a chance to follow or detain her. But he did follow and

Sophie heard him saying to Bella that he would be back in a minute.

Sophie raced outside the apartment, down the couple of stairs, and hurried to her car, breathing heavily.

'Wait, wait,' Murdoch said, reaching for her arm, and spinning her around before she had the car door opened. 'What's happened? Are you alright?'

Sophie shook her head. 'She's dead, Murdoch. She's dead.'

CHAPTER 5

MURDOCH WATCHED SOPHIE DRIVE off and stood frustrated, hands on his hips hoping she would turn and come back. She did not.

'What the hell am I supposed to do with that?' he muttered, and turned around, before turning back one more time to look at the way she departed in hope. He exhaled in frustration. He ran a hand over his mouth and thought for a moment.

Can Bella be saved? Are Sophie's visions changeable?

If she were dead, could Bella be revived?

When is this all going to happen?

What the hell!

He turned and strode back into the apartment complex and found Bella Brown where he left her, still sitting on the couch in anticipation of his return.

'Sorry about that,' he said, schooling his features to look calm and in control.

'Is she okay?' Bella asked.

'Who? Oh, Sophie, sure, she'll be fine.' He sat opposite and cleared his throat before speaking. 'I believe we need to take this very seriously.'

'She saw something?' Bella said, leaning forward, her eyes huge. 'She saw him, didn't she?'

Murdoch stopped and cocked his head to the side. 'You know who Sophie is?'

'Of course, everyone does,' Bella said. 'She saved that little girl who was kidnapped and outed the bomber at the psychic fare. She's amazing.'

Then the truth hit her.

'Oh my God, it's worse than you are saying, isn't it? He's going to get me.' Bella rose and paced to the window; she pulled the curtain slightly in front of her to hide behind it. 'Why? Who would be doing this?' Bella whirled around to face Murdoch, 'Am I going to die?'

'Woah, slow down.' Murdoch rose and went to her. 'We can't rely on Sophie's predictions, that would be crazy,' he said to calm her but not believing the words coming out of his mouth. He had long believed that Daphne Shelby's predictions, and now her niece, Sophie's visions, were superior to the many clairvoyants and charlatans that had crossed his path during his years in the police force. Daphne and Sophie had never been wrong, not once.

'However,' Murdoch continued, 'you have had several stalking experiences, and now this break-in. I'll get any CCTV footage we can get and see if we can identify who is following you. Can you give me the exact date and times of your movements so I can narrow down the footage?'

'Yes, sure,' she said, moving to a desk in the corner of the room that overlooked the river and grabbing a pen and pad from it. She returned to the kitchen counter and wrote down all she could remember, pausing now and then to think and adjust her times or dates.

'I want you to stay with someone. A friend? Family member? Someone. Find a flatmate, right this minute,' Murdoch said with authority.

Bella read through the list and then handed it to him.

'Can you pack a bag now and I'll take you to wherever you want to go,' he continued to instruct Bella.

She shook her head. 'Not yet. I don't want to be driven out of my home and I don't want to stay with family and friends. I like my space, I need it.'

'I understand that, but we're talking about your safety here,' Murdoch said, frustrated.

'I could stay with someone and then be attacked on my way to work; it doesn't mean I'll be much safer. I'll get extra security,' she said.

'Someone has already broken in, and this is supposedly a secure building. I'll talk to your neighbour and make sure they don't buzz anyone in that they don't know,' Murdoch said.

'Don't tell them about me being stalked!' she said, alarmed. 'We don't know each other that well and I like my privacy.'

'Okay.' Murdoch began to wonder why an influencer who made her living putting herself out there, was so over-the-top about her space and privacy. 'I'll just tell them there have been break-ins in the area. But no walking back at dusk or at night, no going into alleys or lanes as a shortcut. Understood?'

She nodded. Murdoch stood and headed to the door; she followed behind. He handed her his card with his personal number on it and insisted she locked the door behind him.

He needed to speak with Sophie, now.

Nikolas Saggers hit the glass wall and grunted with pain. Fortunately, he did not go through it. He stood up, dusted himself off and cursed Orli for her protection spells. The back door of the *Optical Illusion* store opened and Orli appeared, her white hair framing her small face, her pale blue eyes wide with surprise. She bit her lip with concern and tried not to laugh.

'I thought you only put the protection spell on the front of the store,' he grumbled and followed her inside, closing the door behind him.

'Sorry, Nik,' she said sweetly, 'but Lukas has been so off-kilter of late, that I thought it best to protect all the glass, even the back windows. Had I known you were coming the unconventional way...'

'Forget it, I'll ride my bike over next time.'

She smiled and he rolled his eyes and leaned in to kiss her on the cheek. 'Where's everyone?'

'Uncle Alfred is closing the shop for the night and Lukas is locking away his timepieces.'

'Has he settled down?' Nikolas asked.

'I heard that,' Lukas called out. 'And no, I haven't, so watch out.'

Nikolas laughed and followed Orli through to the shop that was now empty of customers.

'Hello, Nik.' Alfred smiled at him and the men shook hands.

'Alfred, good to see you again,' Nikolas said, and turning to Lukas added, 'and you hothead.'

'Yeah, yeah, what did you expect? The Raven brings out the worst in me and your performance didn't help,' Lukas said, finishing locking up the watches and rising to full height.

'No!' Orli declared. 'We are not starting on who is to blame and who is the better protector again, are we Uncle Alfred?'

'I agree with Orli, let's move on. I shall make tea and if you want something stronger—'

'Definitely,' Nikolas cut off Alfred and looked at Lukas.

'Scotch?' Neat?' Lukas asked.

'I'll take some water in it, thanks,' Nikolas said and followed the family into the back room. 'So, what do we do now about Sophie?'

'I was hoping Grandpa might have a talk with her and bring her round,' Lukas said with a glance to Alfred.

'That's exactly what I shouldn't do, lad,' Alfred said, preparing the tea for himself and Orli. 'She's a strong-willed, intelligent and independent woman. She'll know I've been selected to convince her to go the traditional route.'

'What do you suggest, Alfred? Is there any precedence to this, anything similar in our history?' Nikolas asked taking a seat at the table in the backroom office.

'No, the Raven and the doves have always run parallel, but from my readings, I believe Murdoch in this era has been the calmest. It is quite unprecedented his befriending of Daphne,' Alfred said and looked to Orli. 'Would you agree, my dear?'

'Definitely Uncle Alfred. I suspect that is a sign of the times as well as his personality, but that's not to say I don't think he is capable of violence if provoked.' Nikolas saw the glance she gave to her cousin, Lukas, as a warning. Lukas made a scoffing sound.

'We don't know how strong he is, but you, Lukas, need a hell of a lot of training. He's bound to be stronger than you.' Nikolas stirred him as he accepted the scotch.

'Want to wear that?' Lukas asked as he passed it to Nikolas who laughed at his words.

Lukas sighed. 'You are right though and I need to get up to speed.'

Nikolas bristled.

'I'm not saying I'm going to go back to being Sophie's protector,' he added before Nikolas started being territorial. 'I think Grandpa and Orli are right that I can have the best of both worlds by being with Lucy and remaining Sophie's friend. But I need to get up to speed in case all of this drama starts a war.'

'Will you train him, Alfred?' Nikolas asked.

'We haven't discussed it yet,' Alfred said looking at his grandson. 'But we started when Lukas was Sophie's protector.'

'Why can't we continue?' Lukas asked, sitting down beside Nikolas as Alfred and Orli joined them with their cups of tea.

'Perhaps you could ask nicely,' Orli suggested. 'I'm sure Uncle Alfred has better things to do than throw fireballs at you all day.'

Nikolas laughed and Lukas grimaced at both of them.

He turned to his grandfather. 'Do you think we could continue training please, Grandpa?' he asked dutifully which got another round of laughs.

'For your safety, I think we'd better, young man,' Alfred said.

'Somebody should give Nik flying lessons too,' Lukas suggested.

'Oh ha-de-ha,' Nikolas smirked. 'It's a very efficient way of getting around if Orli could just leave a few windows unprotected. Or better yet, I might talk with that new flatmate of Sophie's, Melino. See if she has a brew that cuts through Orli's spells.'

Orli took the teasing in good faith. She was the master of spells and they all knew it.

'Does she have skills?' Orli asked out of curiosity.

'I've only met her a few times,' Nikolas said, 'but she has something. There's black magic there and healing powers. Time will tell.'

'It might be a good thing for Sophie to have her in the house,' Orli said.

'So, if Murdoch rejects Sophie's request, you are definitely backing off the protector role now?' Nikolas turned to ask Lukas seeking a guarantee.

'Yes. Unless Sophie asks for me. Then I'll deal with it.'

'Are you sure you're in love with Lucy and not Sophie?' Nikolas stirred him and then grinned seeing the look of anger flash on Lukas's face. 'You're quick to anger these days. Better start those lessons sooner than later,' he joked.

'I'll do better than that,' Lukas retorted. 'I'll envisage you when I return fireballs.'

Nikolas laughed. He turned his attention to Alfred. 'In the books, the history of the families, has anyone ever tried to end the curse?' He continued without waiting for an answer, 'I was thinking, if Murdoch representing Harley's line and that of the Raven, did not want to be the beholder of the Raven's powers, and this family—yourself Alfred, Orli and Lukas— descending from Hadley's line and the dove, also gave it up, what would happen?'

'It can't be done, can it?' Lukas asked. 'Because there's Sophie's line, the cursed line and they're powerful witches in their own right. Would they just give up that power of visions now that it is not so much a curse as a destiny?'

'I don't know if it could be ceased,' Alfred said. 'There is no record in the history books of anyone wishing to, but it is a bigger picture than Murdoch.'

'How so?' Nikolas asked.

'There's always a succession plan, like there is with us. I have stepped down, and there is yourself Nik, as well as Lukas and Orli to step up. Murdoch will have the same should he wish to give it up, or he can transcend into the next generation.

Whoever his successors may be, might not be as laid back or open-minded about the curse and about Sophie as he is.'

'So, Uncle Alfred, you're saying it is better the devil we know and we should be happy that Murdoch is the Raven for this generation?' Orli summed up her uncle's thoughts.

'Exactly, my dear. The Raven is ours to manage for Sophie's sake. She has him nearby, but at the moment, we are the ones not managing him well and we need a plan.'

CHAPTER 6

SOPHIE TURNED HER ATTENTION from the garden view as she sat at the table near the window and accepted the cup of tea from Miss Sharpe; she wanted something a lot stronger.

'I'm sorry dear, what a shock,' Miss Sharpe said, her face a picture of concern. 'Are you sure the young lady died?' She whispered as if saying it out loud made it official.

Sophie shook her head in the negative. 'I can't be completely sure, Miss Sharpe.' She placed her hand on her chest. 'I just felt him on her, I felt her struggle for air, and I felt her slipping away and he was pushing—'

'I understand,' Miss Sharpe cut her off, not wishing to distress Sophie further.

'What a terrible thing to experience,' Mel said, sitting with the two ladies. 'That's why it is called a curse even though there's plenty of good that comes from the glasses as well.'

'That's so true, Mel. So, what are you going to inflict on me?' Sophie asked and smiled, seeing the small vile of pink potion that Mel had departed to fetch earlier when Sophie returned shocked and distressed.

Mel studied the concoction—it was her favourite colour—and she smiled with delight.

'It's a calming balm. One of my grandma's potions that she used to dispense for hysteria. Not saying you are hysterical of course,' Mel added quickly, 'but it should help. Drink it all in one gulp.'

Sophie accepted the vial, unplugged it and with a quick sip, did as instructed. She put the plug back in and handed the small tube back to Mel.

'Thank you, that tasted like fairy floss,' she said surprised. 'I'm sure I'll feel better in a moment or so.'

'That was powerful company here today,' Mel said. 'I could sense the warring in the air.'

'That is a very good word for it, Mel,' Miss Sharpe said. 'It was tense for a moment there, but Blaine and your arrival could not have come at a better time. It was a relief to see you at the door.'

Sophie gave a small smile. 'I think I am feeling better already, Mel, thank you. I feel like I am lightly buzzing and quite relaxed.'

Mel smiled with relief. She took her work seriously. 'Would you like a vial, Miss Sharpe?'

'Thank you, dear, but I'm off to choir now. That should do the trick.' Miss Sharpe looked to the driveway. 'Detective Ashcroft is here.'

Sophie frowned and looked outside but could not see him. Moments later he drove through the gate. 'I've been expecting him since I left him hanging,' Sophie said with a sigh. 'Best get it over with.'

'I shall head off to choir then and leave you to speak with Murdoch. You have no appointments until 11am tomorrow, dear,' Miss Sharpe said, rising.

'Oh, Miss Sharpe, I have been meaning to ask... did I really calm that storm?' Sophie asked, hopeful she had that power developing.

'Yes and no, dear,' Miss Sharpe said. 'You were able to do it because Lukas and now Nikolas were your protectors and the storm was generated by them as a result of your actions. You can always put a stop to anything your protector does in regard to your own behaviour. It protects you from them should that ever be needed.'

'Right,' Sophie said frowning. 'I think that raises more questions than it answers, but thank you, Miss Sharpe.'

Miss Sharpe gave a small laugh. 'It's a lifetime of learning,' she agreed and Mel rose to leave as well.

'I don't need to return to the office, so I am going to play in my lab and work on my spells. Very exciting,' she said and beamed. 'If you need me...'

'Thank you,' Sophie said and watched them both go. She looked down at her dress and bare feet—her shoes lay nearby—and decided she was respectable enough. Moments later, Sophie heard Murdoch and Miss Sharpe exchanging a greeting on the front steps and soon after he entered.

'Just in time to pour me a drink,' she said, pushing her tea cup away. She could see the relief on his face. He must have expected to be rejected. 'There's red wine top shelf, help yourself.'

She watched as Murdoch poured them both a glass and joined her, offering her the glass, placing his on the table in front of them, and shucking off his suit jacket. He dropped down onto the chair opposite her and they sipped before speaking.

Sophie was drawn to him, and not just professionally. He was strikingly handsome, his features more masculine than Lukas but not as rugged as Nikolas. He rocked a suit, and she always had a soft spot for a man of few words. There was something mysterious about Murdoch Ashcroft, something untouchable. And there was that night, that dream after he told her they had been together in a past life and romanced her. Sophie dreamed they were in Aunt Daphne's home, now her home—she wasn't used to thinking that way yet—in Victorian times. She was dressed in her finery and he in a morning suit with his top hat. He had scandalously made love to her. It wasn't a dream she could easily forget, in all honesty, she hoped to have it again. Sophie took another sip of her wine, a rather large one, and returned her mind to the now, hoping she wasn't flushed at the thought of her dream.

Clearing her throat, Sophie said, 'I'm sorry I ran off.'

Murdoch shook his head. 'You have nothing to be sorry about. I, on the other hand, am sorry I put you in that position.' She felt him studying her. 'Are you okay?'

Sophie nodded. 'Is Bella?'

'She won't move out, but she's locked in for the night. Can we talk about it?'

'We'd better,' Sophie agreed. 'I don't know if she can be saved. I know I said she was dead, I felt her disappear, for want of a better word, but she might be revived or... I don't know.'

Murdoch nodded. 'Do you have any idea of timing? Like when this attack might take place?'

Sophie shook her head in the negative.

'Did you see anyone?'

'Yes, fleetingly, I saw his face. I didn't at first. I saw him following Bella as she described the first time, and I saw him the second and third time before she spoke of it. And then I saw him on top of her; I felt her fear and panic. He was very

45

heavy on her and he began to choke her. He was... pushing into her.' She looked away. 'He was raping her.'

'You experienced that?' he asked, disturbed.

'I cut off the image, that's why I had to leave.'

'Of course.' They both sipped again and then Murdoch asked, 'would you recognise him?'

'Yes. But I don't know him. If I study Bella again and maybe go to the gym and her office space, I might see him.'

'Can you do that? I'll be with you.'

'Yes.'

Murdoch exhaled. 'Thank you. She recognised you, so she knows she is in danger, given your reaction.'

'Oh.' Sophie thought for a moment. 'Well, that's good and bad. She'll be warier, hopefully.'

'When do you want to do this?' he asked.

'I'm guessing you want to go now?'

'No. I've organised extra surveillance and police patrols around her building tonight. It can wait. Tomorrow if that's okay?' he pushed, hopeful.

'First up in the morning,' she said, and he agreed.

'Thanks. I appreciate it.' Murdoch moved forward, leaning over the small table between them and in an intimate gesture, he held out his hand and Sophie put hers in his.

'If I was your protector, I would have failed today,' he said, studying her small hand.

'That's a catch-22, isn't it?' she agreed and smiled. 'Why won't you be my protector?'

Murdoch sighed, realising he couldn't avoid this conversation. He took his hand back to loosen his tie and turned to face her. 'For two reasons. The first is that I can't serve two masters. I'm on call with the police around the clock. Protecting you would require the same commitment. I'd end up letting one side down and the result could be fatal. I don't want to live like that.'

'I understand,' Sophie said. 'But you have some special powers, don't you? You can conjure up ravens after all. Can't you be in two places at once? What else have you got in your box of tricks, or are Lukas and Nikolas the only magical guys?'

He frowned at her, and Sophie smiled.

'Okay, sorry, another time to hear about your *powers*,' she said, saying the word in a hushed and mysterious voice and making Murdoch smile. 'Point number two then?'

He sobered. 'I don't know what the outcome of taking on your protector role would be to the curse. I could trigger something that none of us wants to deal with or could handle. It's not the safest course.'

Sophie read his expression for sincerity. 'Okay. But you won't harm me?'

'I won't harm you; I never harmed your aunt. But Sophie,' he made sure he had her attention, 'don't test that theory, okay? Because every person has their limits.'

Sophie nodded. There was a dark side to Murdoch Ashcroft after all.

That night, while sitting on her lounge chair with Bette Davis nearby, purring, Sophie wondered about her own powers. She stroked the beautiful white Persian as she thought about her inherited *magic* glasses and her skills, none of which seemed to have developed or changed that she was aware of since taking on Aunt Daphne's mantle. If she was the top of the tree, as Miss Sharpe had said, and supposedly going to be the greatest clairvoyant of her time as Aunt Daphne had told her, shouldn't she then feel something or be able to do something?

Sophie turned off the television, rose, and grabbed a file of papers that Lukas had given her – copies of several chapters of the family history so she could read at home when it suited her without having to come into *Optical Illusion*. With a glance at the clock, it was nearing 10pm, she sat back down near Bette Davis and flicked through each page. She scanned for mention of her ancestor, Issbelle and her spirit daughter, Elsopeth, who went by the nickname of Sophie. Surely that might provide some clue to the powers in her family line.

After five minutes, she closed the folder and sighed. There was nothing amongst that lot of pages, but that was only a small section of the many hundreds of volumes held in safekeeping for descendants and protectors. She made a note to ask Alfred specifically next time she went to the store. She was due to meet with the family later in the week to update them on Murdoch's decision and choose a protector, if he was not going to take the role, and apparently, he was not. She would ask Alfred about her powers then, he was the most generous of all the family when it came to sharing knowledge, the most informed as well.

'In the interim, Bette, it looks like I'll need to experiment,' Sophie pronounced, which had no effect on Bette Davis at all. 'I know, I'm excited too.'

She crossed her legs in front of her, sat upright, closed her eyes and thought about Murdoch in her mind. Then she said the words, 'If you can hear me, Murdoch, give me a sign.' She waited. Sophie opened one eye tentatively and then the other. *Nothing.*

'Right then, that experiment was a dud,' Sophie informed Bette Davis. She tapped her fingers on her knees deciding what else to try, and then her phone pinged with a message. She grabbed for it and cried out with glee – a text from Murdoch.

'Pick you up at your office at 8.30am to go to Bella's place if that suits you?'

'Sure.' She tapped back. 'Did you just get my mind message?'

'Your what?'

'Did you just feel me trying to connect with you?' she tried again.

'No.'

'Night then.'

'Tomorrow,' he replied.

'Great, probably thinks I'm nuts, more so than usual,' she muttered. 'Right, sit back, resume the pose and try for another strategy.'

Sophie didn't want to try to message Lukas or Nikolas in case they showed up in her lounge room, which they had the power to do, especially if they still had protector rights and could sense her if there was such a thing. And she was in her pyjamas, after all. Sophie had an idea and grabbed her phone again, thumbing to Bella's videos.

'Can I read anything from you, Bella, by watching you host your videos?'

The thought made her search with urgency. Sophie had never tried this. She couldn't read people from photos, always needing to see them and to get them thinking on a subject to see their past and future, but what if it was a video and the person was live, so to speak, talking to a camera? She wouldn't be able to ask questions, but could she read anything from them?

Sophie flicked past the videos of Bella doing exercise routines, food preparation and creating juices and went to an interview. She grabbed her second set of the special glasses off the coffee table and as Bella spoke to the camera about her life and what she hoped to achieve, Sophie put them on, waiting and hoping for the inevitable images to appear. They didn't. She sighed, closed the site and removed the glasses. Sophie sat back thinking, pressing the phone to her chest.

'I must have a superpower, something I can do besides wear a pair of glasses and see visions, Bette Davis, but what?'

Taking a deep breath, Sophie forced herself to think about her vision this afternoon, for beautiful Bella's sake. How might the stalker have broken in? Why did he only move Bella's stuff around? Clearly, that was meant to freak Bella out. She thought of Bella telling the constables what had moved and how they looked sceptical given nothing was stolen. Sophie braced and thought about the man again, searching in her mind for his face.

'Oh my God!' She sat bolt upright, startling Bette Davis. 'Sorry Bette,' she said jumping up. She ran to her room, pulled off her pyjama bottoms and pulled on her jeans and runners. Grabbing her keys, Sophie assured Bette Davis that all was okay, then raced down the huge sweeping staircase of her new home, out the front door and straight to the garage, calling Murdoch as she ran to her car.

'What is it?' he asked, alarmed. It was not like Sophie to call after hours. In fact, she never had.

'She knows him, she trusts him, he could be there now,' she said, jumping into her car and starting it. 'I'm on my way.'

'Don't go in without me,' Murdoch said.

'Don't call the police for backup!'

'What? Why?' he demanded.

'Don't!' Sophie hung up and tore down the long driveway to Bella's complex.

CHAPTER 7

BELLA BROWN HESITATED AT the front door, not opening it to the stranger. She glanced at the large wall clock in her lounge, a very modern piece she had brought from the James Street Markets, that told her it was nearing 11 o'clock.

'Sorry, who did you say you were?' she asked only able to see half of the man's face on the video security screen.

'Constable Hewitt, Zach Hewitt. Detective Ashcroft asked us to add some extra drive-bys to your place. We met this afternoon,' he clarified. 'I was taking your inventory.'

'Oh, yes, of course,' she said but didn't buzz him in.

'I saw your lights were still on and it was late, just checking all is okay. Can I come in and check your locks and have a quick look around?' he asked.

'Thank you, that's very kind,' Bella said relenting with relief. She buzzed him in and opened her door to him, admitting the young uniformed officer to her home. 'That was good of the detective to organise extra security for me, I really appreciate you taking this seriously.'

'No problem,' he said, removing his hat. 'So, you've noticed nothing out of the usual tonight?'

'No, it's been quiet, thank goodness.'

Bella watched as the police officer tested her windows and checked they were all secured. She had done it herself, but it made her feel better knowing that he was double-checking. Besides, if the stalker was staking out her place, seeing a police officer present was probably a good deterrent.

She noticed he kept looking at her and smiling shyly. He was handsome with a boyish face but his physique was very much that of a man. He obviously worked out given his solid build.

'You need a man around to look out for you, or a partner, if you bat for the other side,' he said with a smile.

'I know, it would be a good time to have a boyfriend,' she agreed. 'It must be hard on your partner when you get the night shift or do you meet up and go out afterwards?' Bella asked turning the conversation back to him.

'I'm a single man. I'm not saying I don't want a girlfriend; I just don't get much time to meet anyone in this job.' He pointed down the hallway. 'Okay to check down there.'

'Sure, thanks,' she said and watched him walk down the hallway. He wore his uniform well; she imagined how safe she'd feel if she was dating a cop.

Minutes went by. Long minutes. 'Is everything okay?' she called out hesitantly. There was no response. She waited, wringing her hands, not sure what to do. Bella grabbed for her phone and the card with Detective Murdoch Ashcroft's phone number on it. Then she heard his voice, it was strained.

'Something's not right in here, Miss Brown. Can you check this out?'

Relief swept through her that at least he answered and was okay. He must be looking thoroughly and not have heard her call out.

'On my way,' she said, putting down the phone and heading down the hallway. She glanced in the bathroom and he wasn't there, then to her small second room cum study, not there either. She entered the main bedroom and couldn't spot him either.

'Where are you?'

Bella moved into the room, and the bedroom door slammed behind her.

Sophie pulled into a visitors' carpark space to the side of Bella's apartment, relieved she could get a parking spot. She was out of the car in moments. A glance around told her Murdoch had not yet arrived, but she couldn't wait for him. She didn't have any great plan to overpower Bella's assailant, but someone demanding to be let in might just save Bella's life if the young cop took off, and she knew now, that it was the police officer she saw taking the inventory that was stalking Bella. The connection came to her sharply as she recalled her vision and his face earlier that day on the job.

Sophie buzzed at the glass door, hoping to have gotten there before the police constable, hoping that Bella would let her in and she could explain what she saw. No one answered. Sophie pressed again and pressed the neighbour's buzzer. There were only two large townhouses in the apartment complex, and a man's voice answered. Sophie explained hurriedly, and he told her he'd come out. She sighed with frustration, but he appeared quickly and let her in.

'Sorry, just had to check you didn't have a guy with you or weren't coerced to buzz me and someone was lingering behind you,' he said with a shrug.

'Good thinking, thanks,' Sophie said and ran to Bella's door. She tried the door handle while banging against the door, knowing it would be locked and it was.

'Want me to call the cops?' he asked.

'They are on the way,' she said and relieved, nodded to the door where Murdoch appeared. The neighbour raced to let him in. Murdoch ran past him and then Sophie saw firsthand one of his powers. He hit the door open with his hand and it flew back, hitting the inside wall with a force that put holes in the plaster wall.

Murdoch was in the apartment in seconds, racing through each room until he came to the main bedroom; Sophie was close on his tail. He threw the door open and Sophie raced in with him, her vision was being played out.

Murdoch made a sound that was more wild animal than man, and pulled the constable off Bella. She was half naked, not moving, her eyes closed. Sophie covered her and shook her.

'Get an ambulance,' Murdoch yelled to the neighbour who followed them in and stood in shock at the door. He scurried off to do so.

'Bella! She's not breathing.' Sophie couldn't feel, see or hear her breaths but knew she was gone, she had felt it in her earlier vision. She began to press on Bella's chest to resuscitate her.

Murdoch held the thrashing officer down. Despite the constable's stocky physique, he was no threat to an enraged Murdoch Ashcroft. He restrained the stalker with the officer's own handcuffs and raced to Sophie's side.

'They're coming, I'll wait out front and let them in,' the neighbour said, appearing momentarily in the door and disappearing again.

'Tell them they'll need a defibrillator,' Murdoch called after him.

'Come on, Bella, come on,' Sophie hissed between pushes, the exertion quickly wearing her out.

'Take a break,' Murdoch said, taking over. They heard the wails of the ambulance as Sophie stood back, out of reach of the trussed-up stalker. She slipped her glasses on and breathed a sigh of relief as pictures of Bella sitting up in a hospital bed appeared, followed by television interviews and magazine covers. She turned to the offender. He appeared in his prison cell and she removed the glasses. She had seen enough drama for one day.

CHAPTER 8

LUKAS HIT THE GROUND before he had time to react. He appreciated his grandfather's training, but it was pissing him off to no end. Alfred's reflexes were annoyingly fast for an old man, and Lukas was not always hyper-alert or trained to think like that. He pushed himself up from the back office floor, took a deep breath and looked around for his offending grandfather who was nowhere in sight.

Orli hid a smile, but not very well. 'Oh, that must have hurt.'

He gave her a smirk.

'I did warn you,' Alfred said from the other room.

Lukas grunted. 'My reflexes aren't as fast as yours. Yet.' Lukas walked through to the front of the store where his grandfather stood behind one of the glass counters.

'Well done, lad,' Alfred said beaming.

Lukas sat opposite on a chair in front of his timepieces and gave his grandfather a confused look.

'What have I done well?' He cricked his neck from the latest fall.

'You read my mind. I didn't say "I warned you" out loud, nor did I send the thought to you.'

Lukas's expression changed to surprise and satisfaction. 'Two steps forward, one step back. Well, that's something.'

'You'll get better at the reflexes,' Alfred assured him, speaking the words out loud this time. 'My father was a very good teacher, but I can't bring myself to be as tough on you as he was on me. I was always wary of him, even as an adult. He took his responsibility of training myself and my brothers very seriously, to the limit.'

'So, you don't want me to take off when I see you coming?' Lukas asked with a grin.

'Preferably not,' Alfred said with a chuckle. He subtly studied his fair-head grandson, often amazed at the resemblance he bore to Alfred's son, Mendel – Lukas's father. 'Is that timepiece giving you trouble? It's held your attention for some days now.'

'It's magnificent,' Lukas said looking at it with admiration. 'An early 19th-century French quarter watch. I've only seen one before.' Holding it and admiring its gold open face and roman numerals.

'And it was a young lady who brought it in for servicing. I wonder how she obtained it or if it is sentimental to her,' Alfred pondered.

Lukas turned it over in his palm. 'It's key wound, and has a small engraving "*For M, My Love for all Time, V*", just beautiful.' Lukas remembered the question and looked up at this grandfather. 'No, it hasn't beaten me, I've just been admiring it. It is ready for collection.'

'I shall let the young lady know,' Alfred said. 'They don't make timepieces like that anymore, sadly.'

'Don't I know it,' Lukas said gently putting the gold engraved watch back into its case, and moving on to a more modern watch requiring repair. Suddenly Alfred stood, catching Lukas's attention in his peripheral vision.

'Goodness, he's here,' Alfred said in a startled voice which was most unusual for his usually unflappable grandfather.

Lukas looked at each of the external glass windows, scanning the area. 'Who?'

'The Raven. I mean Detective Ashcroft, he's coming.'

Lukas stood and saw the detective across the road coming their way. His eyes narrowed.

'Stand down, lad, let's not give offence when none may be due,' Alfred said. 'I suggest you return to your work, or at least sit back down, it will create a calmer atmosphere.'

Lukas made a guttural sound and did as his grandfather bid, not taking his eyes from the approaching detective who stopped outside the shop door but did not enter. They watched as the Raven hesitated, reached for the door handle and drew his hand back as if burned.

Alfred hurried to the door to greet him.

'Detective Ashcroft, welcome. Won't you come in?' Alfred asked, cordially standing aside.

'Mr Lens, thank you. I came to advise you in person of my decision regarding Sophie.'

'Most kind of you,' Alfred said. Lukas refrained from snorting behind him, although he understood grudgingly that Murdoch was showing remarkable good manners in observing the protocol of respect to the senior power, even if it was a rival line.

'It appears I can't enter,' Murdoch said, drily.

'My apologies. One moment please,' Alfred said and called to his niece, Orli.

Orli appeared from the back room where she had been preparing optical lenses for her customers.

'Why didn't you tell me he was here?' she said to Lukas in passing.

'Why couldn't you sense him?' Lukas asked.

'None of us can while Sophie is in limbo, except for Uncle obviously,' she said in a hushed voice and joined Alfred at the front door.

'Forgive me, Detective,' Orli said, making sure peace prevailed. 'I put the protective charm on because of Lukas's unpredictable temper at the moment, not to ward off guests, I assure you.' With a wave of her hand, she removed it.

Lukas glared at her in alarm. They were vulnerable now.

Murdoch smiled and entered the store of glass as invited. 'You are in an unfortunate business for one with a temper,' he said and gave Lukas a smirk which Lukas did his best to reciprocate.

'Can we offer you a cup of tea or if you are off duty, something stronger?' Alfred asked.

'No, thank you. I won't stay. I just wanted to let you know that I have declined Sophie's offer. Not because I intend to be her enemy,' Murdoch clarified with a glance to Lukas, 'but as I told her, my work requires me around the clock and I cannot be sure of giving Sophie the attention needed.' He paused before continuing, 'And...'

'You are concerned about what we might unleash should we challenge the status quo?' Alfred asked.

'Exactly,' Murdoch said with a firm nod.

'I agree with you, completely. And thank you for letting me know in person, very kind of you,' Alfred said with a smile and walked behind the detective as he turned to go.

Murdoch stopped suddenly and turned to Lukas. The three fair descendants of Hadley's all froze as the Harley descendant stood dark and powerful amongst them.

'What is it?' Orli asked.

Murdoch looked around the room, and Lukas braced. His instincts told him that they should not have left themselves unguarded and he sent the message in his mind to his grandfather. He saw Alfred give a barely discernible shake of his head and he received the message back loud and clear. '*Wait, do nothing.*'

'There is something in here calling to me, that's odd,' Murdoch said.

'Why?' Orli asked. 'Don't you receive signs?'

Murdoch did not reply.

Lukas waited, tense. He knew Murdoch would not want to give away the source or depth of his powers. But then the Raven strode to Lukas's counter and Lukas arced up, standing to take him on.

But Murdoch stopped short and looked at an antique jewellery case in front of Lukas. He said in a low voice, '"*My Love for all Time*".'

Lukas reached for the case and opened it. The watch bearing the inscription was displayed.

Murdoch took a hasty step backward, making a stifled sound from his throat, and turned, heading rather quickly to the door.

'Thank you, Mr Lens, Orli,' he said and gave a swift nod in Lukas's direction. He swung the door open and departed with haste.

Alfred locked it after him and turned the sign to closed. 'What was that about, lad?' he asked Lukas.

'This timepiece.' Lukas held it up. 'The 1810 timepiece, he sensed it and knew the exact inscription on the back without evening seeing it.'

Orli looked over her uncle's shoulder. 'It's inscribed to "M". Could the *M* stand for Murdoch? But it's 1810.'

'It's his watch, somehow, this is linked to the Raven,' Lukas said returning it to its box as if it were cursed.

Orli waved her hand and put the protection spells back in place. 'Just in case,' she said.

Lukas's mind was racing with the implications.

I need to get up to speed.

Grandpa is not a young man and if anything should happen to him, I'm not ready or strong enough to defend this family.

I need to get Nikolas and Orli to train me as well.

I must have the strength of the three of them.

'I couldn't agree more, lad,' Alfred said out loud. 'The sooner, the better. Tomorrow, Sophie will be telling us whom she is choosing as her protector and I'm guessing you are still in the mix.'

Lukas gave a small nod. But he sensed he had blown it with Sophie, that she would choose Nikolas and he would be able to keep Lucy happy. He was not happy with the thought of writing himself out of the history books.

It was declared cocktail hour at Sophie's office. She sat with Blaine, Mel, and even Miss Sharpe had stayed on for a quiet drink as she put it, and to discuss moving the business forward given Sophie's explosion of fame.

Blaine sat back in one of the large winged-back chairs near the window, holding court over the three ladies around him. His glass of red wine between his fingers. He was groomed to within an inch of his life, his hair stylish—as one would expect of a hairdresser—and his clothes fashionable. It was an unspoken agreement that he would never mention Lucy, and whether he continued to see her or not, Sophie did not know or enquire.

Beside him sat Mel in her bright colours, energy bouncing off her, and her hair a statement of self-expression, the pink stripe particularly notable. Miss Sharpe sat next to Mel, in her navy suit and crisp white shirt. The leather of her navy court shoes gleamed from polish and her jewellery was tasteful. Their hostess, Sophie joined them sitting opposite Blaine, after filling everyone's glass and reaching for a handful of pretzels from the bowl in the middle of the table. She was a mix between casual and business in jeans, boots, a white t-shirt and a black dress jack.

'You need to give the house a name now,' Blaine said, surveying the large room where Sophie did her business.

'You should,' Mel agreed. 'So, you can say dramatically, "*I'm returning home to Ravenswood*" or something like that.' She spoke in a plummy accent and then laughed.

Sophie grinned. 'That's a great idea! But we will definitely not be calling it Ravenswood!' She looked to Miss Sharpe who gave a smile and nod of agreement.

'You do get your share of blackbirds around here though,' Blaine said.

'Did Aunt Daphne ever name the house, Miss Sharpe?' Sophie asked.

'No, but she did consider it. She was going to name it after one of her ancestors, your ancestors, Sophie. Perhaps that's a good place to start,' Miss Sharpe suggested.

'Excellent idea. Perhaps I should name it after my namesake—the daughter of Samuel Rayne and his witch wife, Issbelle—and call it Elsopeth House.'

'Ooh, that's pretty,' Mel agreed.

'It's hard to pronounce quickly though and I've only had one drink,' Blaine said, trying the name a few times on his tongue. 'I like Ravenswood better.'

Sophie rolled her eyes. 'Miss Sharpe and I cannot work in a house called Ravenswood. The Raven has implications in our family history.'

'Spooky, righto then,' Blaine conceded. 'Something nicer.' He stopped hearing a voice in the other room.

'It's the answering machine message bank. We've been inundated with bookings. Miss Sharpe and I were just finalising what we'd do when you two crashed our business meeting and forced cocktail hour upon us.' Sophie scolded them playfully.

Blaine laughed. 'From memory, you beat me to the bar.'

'It's been one of those days,' Sophie said with a grin. 'We are inundated, are we not, Miss Sharpe since saving Bella Brown? We need a new plan.'

'Indeed we do, Sophie,' Miss Sharpe said delicately pausing to sip her sparkling wine from a beautiful flute glass.

'I'm not surprised,' Mel said. 'Once Bella Brown's story hit the media and she posted how you saved her, I knew your bookings would go nutso.'

'What are you going to do? There's only one you, so you can't hire help to read your visions,' Blaine stated the obvious.

'Well, we have made a couple of big decisions,' Sophie said. 'Miss Sharpe wants to remain part-time and I don't want to take on more clients and get burnt out. We're both content as is. So, I've decided to narrow down my client base and just do the things I really enjoy.'

'Why wouldn't you?' Mel agreed. 'I hope to work full-time with my potions one day soon.' She sighed. 'That would be so good.'

'With your own label and everything,' Sophie added enthusiastically.

'I suspect it will be pink?' Miss Sharpe asked.

Mel laughed. 'How did you know?' She turned the spotlight back to Sophie. 'Go on then, who are you going to have as your clients since you get to be selective?'

'Well, we are going to continue to see Aunt Daphne's clients at the same rate she quoted, just out of loyalty to them and Aunt Daphne,' Sophie said.

'There's not too many these days,' Miss Sharpe added. 'Most of them came just to have an outing and gossip with Daphne, and several have, well, dropped off,' she said delicately, with a glance above to indicate they had joined Daphne in the hereafter.

Sophie nodded her agreement and continued, 'I'm going to keep working with the police, but at this stage, only Murdoch and his partner, Gerard, because that's enough police work, and the cash rewards when paid, allow Miss Sharpe and me not to have to take on a lot of clients and will pay for another staff member.'

'Oh wow, you're building an empire!' Blaine said dramatically and Sophie laughed.

'Hardly,' she said, but saw the interest from Blaine and Mel in this development.

'And then as to being selective and picking the people or readings I want to do, the new assistant will filter the information and then the decision will be easier,' Sophie said. 'So, we are looking for a full-time assistant who will work under the guidance of Miss Sharpe.'

'Someone who can maintain social media pages and the web page,' Miss Sharpe said with a look that said all that was far too foreign. 'Plus, make a spreadsheet of clients and meet with Sophie every few days to discuss and select which ones to book for appointments, and then he or she will politely decline the others. So... a young person with those skills.'

Mel leaned forward as if she was going to whisper a secret. 'Will they have to come from... you know... the *family*, like Lukas and Nikolas do?'

Sophie looked to Miss Sharpe, who answered, 'It would be best if they have a connection of sorts.'

'Miss Sharpe and Alfred will know best,' Sophie said.

'To your expansion,' Blaine said, holding up his glass to toast.

'How exciting,' Mel added, clinking her glass against the others.

Sophie glanced at Miss Sharpe and saw Miss Sharpe subtly raise an eyebrow. *Exciting indeed. Let's see who else is out there in the magic pool*, Sophie thought.

CHAPTER 9

IT WAS NEARING 7.30PM and Sophie was home alone with Bette Davis in her huge mansion. The small offices had closed and the tenant staff gone, Blaine and Miss Sharpe had left, and Mel was out for the evening with a girlfriend. Sophie felt surprisingly safe while alone in her home and was getting used to the creaks and noises in the night. She wondered if Orli had put a protective charm around the large estate. It was then she saw the headlights coming up the drive and a car that was larger than Mel's so it was not her housemate returning early. She knew the vehicle.

Murdoch. The Raven.

Sophie felt a small rush of delight at his arrival. They hadn't spoken since he saw Bella into the ambulance and the handcuffed constable was taken away. Sophie had left before then and Murdoch never invited her in for closure, like his partner, Gerard, did with their one case—a cold case—of a murdered beauty queen that they had solved together.

Sophie went to the front door to let Murdoch in and watched as he took the stairs to the front entrance two at a time. He looked up at seeing her.

'Sorry to come unannounced. Is now an okay time?' he asked.

'It depends. Is it business or pleasure this time?' she asked with a smile.

'Pleasure.'

'Well, then it is a very good time, I'm home alone and was going to order takeaway.'

'Do you ever cook?'

'Yes. But your arrival provides the perfect excuse not to. Have you eaten?' she asked moving aside to let him enter. She noticed he braced before coming through the door.

'What's that about?'

'What?'

'You looked like you were expecting to be zapped,' Sophie said, leading the way into the living area that was nicely lit with Daphne's high-hanging chandeliers, through to the kitchen where she grabbed a menu.

'No, just checking you hadn't repelled me since the last visit.'

Sophie laughed. 'Wish that I had that skill,' she teased and earned his smirk. She also noticed he was checking her out; he hurriedly lifted his eyes when caught. Clearly, Murdoch had normal male tendencies after all, and she knew from her dream that the Raven was a good lover if dreams reflected true life.

'Where's the cat?' Murdoch asked.

'Bette Davis is upstairs, asleep on my bed I imagine,' Sophie said watching him for a reaction. If he wanted to bed Sophie, Bette Davis was never going to be happy about it. 'She can probably sense a large, unfriendly bird in the house and is lying low.'

'Probably best,' he agreed, but seeing Sophie's worried look added, 'don't worry, I would never hurt your precious furball.'

'If you're staying, relax,' she said with a nod to his jacket.

Murdoch removed it, placing it over the back of a chair in the kitchen. He took off his tie, pocketing it in his suit jacket and undid the top buttons around his neck. Sophie tried not to watch him undress, but she could not help but approve of the casual look and how it changed his persona. She thought this would be what it was like if he came home to her every night.

'So, you're still not going to cook for me, after all I've done for you?'

'Yeah, thanks for everything,' she said seriously, and he laughed. A deep, sexy laugh that she also loved having the power to draw from him, so different from his normal countenance.

'I brought wine but left it in the car; I thought it might be presumptuous to arrive at the door with it,' Murdoch said. 'I'll grab it.'

'I've already had cocktail hour with Blaine and Mel, but I'll join you in a glass,' she said, easily persuaded. She nodded to a small collection of wine bottles on a rack. 'Use mine. Last time we got Thai. That okay?'

'Will they deliver up that long driveway? It's almost two trips,' he joked.

'They've done it before,' she assured him.

'I bet they have, domestic goddess,' he teased her and while Sophie got his preferences and called to order, Murdoch wandered out to the living room taking a bottle of wine and two glasses with him.

Imagining himself living in the grand mansion—and the thought had appeal—Murdoch poured them both a glass of red wine. He moved away and stood at the window, hands in his pocket, looking outside and seeing little but the lights in the garden. His brow was furrowed with concern. He rounded his shoulders and straightened them again attempting to loosen his stance, feeling the weight of the world there.

It had begun. He noticed his breathing increased at the thought, and he calmed himself to relax, to stay steady. Murdoch wondered if Alfred Lens knew or suspected what was going on. When he said to the old man that he wasn't sure what Sophie might unleash by asking him, the Raven, to be her protector, that wasn't quite true, he had a fair idea.

Murdoch hoped by playing down Sophie's request, by not thinking about it, not talking about it, and refusing the offer, then nothing would come of it. He was wrong. That timepiece. It took all of Murdoch's self-control not to react on seeing it, on feeling it.

Sophie had stirred the pot, woken past jealousies, and Venetia was nothing if not the jealous type. Lukas would not have the strength to protect Sophie from her. Nikolas Saggers might, Murdoch conceded, cocking his head characteristically on the side as he thought. He thought of the engraving on the watch – *For M, My Love for all Time, V* and his mind went straight to the last words she had spoken to him. Words from the poet, Robert Browning, an acquaintance whom Venetia had befriended sometime in history. Browning had written the words with love for his betrothed, but Venetia had not said them to Murdoch with the same affection. The words escaped his lips in a low hiss:

'Escape me?
Never—
Beloved!
While I am I, and you are you,
So long as the world contains us both.

Did it still contain them both? Murdoch feared the truth of it. His head jerked up, realising he had said the words out loud and catching Sophie's reflection behind him in the glass, he wheeled around and smiled, trying to look relaxed.

'I've ordered,' she said, studying him, as he lifted the two glasses of wine and offered her one. They clinked glasses and sat. 'What were you saying?'

'Nothing,' he said lightly, trying to distract her and sitting back in a relaxed manner. 'I was just going over work stuff, sorting cases in my head.' He kept his voice as casual as possible. 'That's why I'm here, to thank you for your help with Bella Brown's case. I know that wasn't easy for you.'

'It was a better result than I thought, thank God,' Sophie said. 'I'm sorry that I told you she was dead and panicked you.'

'It might have been a good thing that you did, we all took it more seriously.'

Sophie agreed.

'I'm congratulating myself too,' he said with a smile.

'Oh, for what?' She smiled. 'Driving there fast.'

He laughed and then sobered. 'For involving you – she would have lost her life otherwise.'

'A daunting thought.' Sophie shuddered.

Murdoch changed the subject. 'I dropped in on the Lens family this afternoon at *Optical Illusion*.'

'Oh?' she said, looking at him with renewed interest. 'That must have been cosy.'

He chuckled.

'Ah, that's when you got zapped,' she said, putting it together.

'Yes. Orli assured me it was to protect the windows from Lukas's latest glass-breaking feats, but I suspect the spell had several purposes,' he said drily. 'Anyway, I officially let Mr Lens know I would not be your protector for the reasons I told you.'

'That was nice of you,' she said, impressed.

'That's expected,' he corrected her. 'You have a lot to learn.' He regretted the words when she rolled her eyes and her look of affection for him quickly changed.

'Yes, so everyone keeps telling me. I started late, and yes, I know that's my own fault before you throw that back at me.'

'Wouldn't dream of it,' he said and gave her a teasing smile to try and relax the mood again. 'I suspect you've been kept in the dark a bit too.'

'Yes, don't even start me on that,' she said, her clipped voice showing annoyance.

He gave a small casual shrug. 'It's a lot to take in and nothing is ever static.'

They let that hang in the air while they thought about it.

'I saw one of your superpowers... your strength,' Sophie announced and Murdoch could feel her eyes boring into him waiting for an explanation.

'Yes.'

Sophie laughed. 'That's it?'

He shrugged. 'I'm strong.'

'I see.'

They sat for a few moments, relatively comfortable in silence, given the time they had spent in the car together. Then Sophie told him of their changes in the office, their decision on the client base, and the new staff member they intended to hire.

'Thanks for keeping Gerard and me on your books,' he said, pleased.

'You're welcome,' Sophie said in a sing-song voice and smiled at him. He shook his head at her antics. 'I enjoy the police work and when we score a reward it can be quite lucrative too. It lets Miss Sharpe and I pick and choose clients, and stay off the breadline.'

'You could just charge huge amounts, you're credible enough for that. But then you would only be reading and helping the rich or some poor sop who gives you their last dollar to get relief.'

'I agree, I wouldn't do that, and thanks for making it sound so mercenary,' she said.

'You're prickly this evening,' Murdoch said.

'Am I?'

He could feel her studying him. He was equally as prickly and evasive, and he knew it. He glanced outside and was conscious that he had done that several times now as each time he saw only their reflections in the glass and the lights in the garden. There was nothing out there.

'It is not me. You are not yourself,' Sophie declared. 'You need an answer to something, don't you? Do you want me to get my glasses and read you?'

'No. Never,' he snapped without hesitation.

'Are you sure about that?' she joked, and he had the good grace to smile.

'Thank you, no. That I am sure about.'

'Will I see things that might shock me?' She feigned innocence, and he laughed.

'I hope there would be a few shocking things there,' he said playfully and wondered if she thought of his nocturnal visit—her dream—often. The slightly flushed look she gave him aroused his suspicions and his desire, and her next comment confirmed it.

Sophie cleared her throat. 'You said to me on that very staircase,' she nodded towards the large ornate timber staircase leading to the upstairs living area, 'that we had known each other in a past life.'

'I was just stirring you,' he said and glanced outside again.

'No. You weren't. You said to me that we had met in many past lives, that you and I go way back.'

'Did I?' He frowned, wishing the takeaway would arrive and he would have an excuse to divert the subject.

'What is going on, Muddy?' she asked, using the nickname he hated. 'And don't tell me it is nothing. I heard you... who is trying to escape you or who are you escaping from?'

CHAPTER 10

Nikolas Saggers agreed to meet Lukas Lens but chose the venue – his local pub. If he had to contend with Lukas challenging him for Sophie's protector role or any more of Lukas's anger, he reasoned at least he'd get a meal and a pint of beer. Nikolas pulled up outside the *Bell and Gate*—an old English Pub he had chosen because they did hearty meals and he was no small man—and locking his bike helmet in the seat, he stripped off his leather jacket and headed inside. Spotting Lukas's car on the way in, his eyes searched the clientele on entering – he recognised several of the regulars. Lukas signalled to him from a corner where they could talk in a booth without being overhead; Nikolas gave a wave to the owners who worked the bar and knew him as a customer.

'Thanks for meeting me,' Lukas said, pushing a beer towards Nikolas.

'No problem. What's this about?' Nikolas dropped into the booth seat opposite, laying his jacket on the seat beside him.

'You don't want to make some small talk first?' Lukas joked. 'The weather, the footy score, the number of windows I've broken this week, or doors you've run into?'

'Bloody protection charms,' Nikolas said with a grin and raised the glass. He took a sip. 'Thanks for that. Actually, I haven't met a charm I couldn't break through except for Orli's.'

Lukas laughed at his double meaning. 'Yes, that famous charm of yours,' he said drily. 'How come you've never asked Orli out? I thought when we were teenagers that there was something between you two.'

Nikolas gave a casual shrug. 'Sometimes it is good to date people outside our sphere,' he said, referring to the magic. 'Safer that way, too. Like you and Lucy. How's that going?'

'Yeah, good,' Lukas said equally as casually. Neither man could be accused of being expressive when it came to romance.

'Think you'll marry her?'

'Probably. She's keen to get married, wants kids soon and all that.'

'Will you invite Sophie to the wedding?'

Lukas exhaled. 'I would but Lucy's weird about it. For a woman who is so beautiful and has people telling her that all day and every day at her shoots, she's insanely jealous.'

Nikolas thought on this for a moment. 'She and Sophie don't see each other anymore, do they? Sophie told me when we were at the fair that they'd fallen out.'

'More like Lucy fell out with Sophie. I don't know why; she wouldn't tell me.' He lowered his voice. 'I just hope Lucy doesn't do anything stupid.'

'Like what?' Nikolas asked, surprised.

Lukas shrugged. 'I'm probably overthinking it. But every time she sees Sophie's name mentioned, like when that influencer recently raved about Sophie, Lucy was pissed off.'

'Really? So, she's jealous of Sophie's success, not just you two hanging out together,' Nikolas said and shook his head in disbelief. 'Maybe because Lucy is normally in the media and now Sophie is being called "The Sexiest Clairvoyant" out there.' Nikolas chuckled.

'I'd be surprised if Sophie's bookings from men haven't gone through the roof,' Lukas agreed.

'I thought you might have been keen on Sophie,' Nikolas said, their relationship familiar enough to put it out there, but he didn't expect a response. 'Is that what this meeting is about? Are you putting your hand up again to be her protector?'

Lukas ignored the protection question and instead answered, 'I need you to train me. Will you?'

'You didn't answer the question.'

'I don't know, truthfully. I want to hear what Sophie wants,' he said and finished off his beer. 'Will you train me?'

Nikolas studied him. 'Why do you need me? Isn't Alfred doing that?'

'He is and he knows I'm asking you. I'm going to ask Orli too.'

'What's happened?' Nikolas bristled.

'Nothing yet, relax,' Lukas assured him. 'This is nothing to do with protecting Sophie, well not directly, it's about my skills.'

'What do you need them for, if not that? Planning on adopting another witch?' he joked.

'Know any?'

'Sure. Not here in our city, but if you're prepared to travel,' Nikolas said with a chuckle. 'So, what's going on then? Why are you upskilling?'

'It's not upskilling, my skills aren't that good yet to be upgraded.'

They stopped talking as the waitress approached them with several menus tucked under her arm. She was young and attractive, dressed in a short black skirt and white shirt with a black apron over the top. Her blonde hair was swept high in a ponytail and she was clearly a favourite amongst the customers, notably the men.

'Hi Gabby,' Nikolas said, greeting her with familiarity.

'Hello Nik,' she said, giving him a special smile that he often received from women given his face and stature. 'I always thought you were our most handsome customer, but you've got a run for your money tonight.' Assessing the fairer Lukas sitting opposite.

'Gabby, meet Lukas.'

'Good to meet you, Gabby,' Lukas said with a smile that said polite but not encouraging.

'And you, Lukas,' she said and turned to Nikolas. 'So, the usual, Nik, or would you both like menus?'

'What's the usual?' Lukas asked before Nikolas could respond.

Gabby answered, 'Slow-cooked lamb shank with mashed potato and vegetables.'

'That sounds bloody good,' Lukas said. 'That'll do me, thanks.'

'Make that two then, thanks, Gabby,' Nikolas said and sent her on her way. He returned his attention to Lukas and nodded at him to continue.

'I'm feeling my mortality,' Lukas said.

'Is Alfred ill?'

'No, but he's not getting any younger, and it hit me that while Orli is powerful,' he said, lowering his voice, 'I am the next male in line. It's my responsibility to protect the family, including any future family.'

'Why? Tell me what's really going on?' Nikolas asked, narrowing his eyes.

Lukas gave Nikolas a less than happy look.

'Tell me, Lukas,' Nikolas pushed again.

Lukas grimaced and cleared his throat. 'Because of what happened in the store today. The Raven visited to say he wouldn't be taking the role of Sophie's protector.'

'No surprise there. Did he get repelled by Orli's protection charm?'

'Burnt his hand when he touched the doorhandle.'

'Good.' Nikolas smiled. 'I'm glad I'm not the only one it bounces.' He took a large mouthful of his beer and thought for a moment. 'So now, Sophie will make her choice again.'

'Tomorrow, I believe she's going to drop in on us at the store, and I'm guessing you'll be up for a visit after that.'

Nikolas nodded. 'So why do you suddenly feel inspired to get your powers up to scratch after one visit from the Raven?'

'There was this timepiece...' Lukas started and told how the Raven reacted to it. 'The inscription read "*For M, My Love for all Time, V*" and he sensed it before he saw it, and got out of the store in a hurry.'

Nikolas swore under his breath, ran a hand over his mouth and looked away, distracted.

'You know something about this?' Lukas quizzed him.

'Didn't Alfred tell you?'

'He said he would tell me and Orli before the owner came to collect it next week and that we needed to be on guard. He wanted to refresh himself on its history first, allegedly,' Lukas said carefully, knowing his grandfather could read his thoughts and might do so if he heard his name mentioned.

'I doubt he needs a refresher,' Nikolas mumbled. 'More likely he wants to talk with Miss Sharpe and plan a strategy.'

'I bloody hate being out of the loop,' Lukas said frustrated. 'Why do you know about this?'

'Because I'm older than you,' he saw Lukas's confused expression and added, 'by several centuries. You and to some degree, Sophie—because she isn't aware of her history or followed it—are new to this scene. The Raven, Alfred, Orli and I go way back. So does this watch.'

'What's it mean? Why would the Raven freak out about it?'

'The V stands for Venetia. Ring any bells?' Nikolas asked.

Lukas shook his head. 'Can't say I've come across her name yet. Not that I have the Raven's chronicles, only our own but she hasn't come up in anything I've read of those either.'

'Venetia was, is, the Raven's lover for centuries, and then he threw her aside for someone he claimed to love more. Venetia didn't take it well. Still doesn't by the sounds of it.'

'Hell,' Lukas muttered. 'I'm servicing her watch and she's a powerful, angry, scorned woman. Great.'

'As long as you did a good job on the watch and don't overcharge her, you should be fine,' Nikolas said, breaking the mood, and both men chuckled.

'So, who did the Raven throw her aside for?' Lukas asked. 'Will she come in for a timepiece service as well?'

Nikolas grinned and then sobered. 'She has already.' He laughed at Lukas's shocked expression and explained, 'a few centuries ago, the Raven left Venetia for Elsopeth.'

Lukas froze. 'But Elsopeth was a child spirit, wasn't she?'

Nikolas leant forward and said quietly, 'Elsopeth, like her witch mother, Issbelle, was whatever she wanted to be.'

CHAPTER 11

SOPHIE BID MURDOCH GOODNIGHT and leant against a beam on the verandah as she watched him drive away. It was a lovely balmy night and quiet – the benefit of having so much land around protecting her from the traffic noises from the street. She was frustrated; he was such a closed book when he wanted to be, and tonight he gave away nothing. But Sophie had distinctly heard his words when she had entered the room, *Escape me? Never— Beloved!* She couldn't remember the other few lines, but she wouldn't forget those words or the manner in which he hissed them as if angry.

Who was he speaking about? Me? She mused. No, surely not? He can escape me anytime and besides, he's the one asking for my skills and hanging around.

Did he mean I couldn't escape him? But then he said "Beloved" as if he didn't want the person to leave because he loved them. Would that be so bad if he wasn't a vengeful Raven?

She frowned, thinking back on the words. Was it someone he loved? Maybe he had started seeing someone, but he never mentioned her. Sophie grew annoyed at the thought. If that was the case, why was he wasting his time visiting her then? She had better things to do than get to know and like him if she was just a fill-in.

In the garden to her right, Sophie heard a sound as if someone was walking toward her. She snapped to look there. Nothing. She huffed at her own reaction. Probably a night creature – a possum or mouse, or something crawly. Nevertheless, she suddenly felt uneasy and turned to go back in and lock the door like she promised Murdoch she would on his departure.

Entering and securing the door behind her, Sophie called out, 'Bette, he's gone,' and was relieved to see her lovely cat was already downstairs, drinking from her water bowl. 'I know, I'm sorry, but he is a friend. Perhaps you two can come to some arrangement.'

She went to the kitchen bench and flicked on the kettle, pulling a white mug down and throwing in a tea bag. There was something on Murdoch's mind tonight; he was edgy and alert but wouldn't share it. Perhaps he never would. His reaction to her reading him was certainly extreme.

Tomorrow, she had to let Alfred, Lukas, and Nikolas know her choice of protector. There was no choice, it would be

Nikolas. Lukas had made his bed and he would have to lie in it, with Lucy, as it turned out.

Sophie smiled at the thought of Nikolas. He would be fun, and Lord knows he was strong. She wouldn't mind doing a bit more of that vanishing and travelling stuff with him again. The first time was rushed and she had no idea what was coming except the need to get out of the psychic fair fast. She wouldn't mind a ride on the back of that motorbike either.

'You'll like him much better than the Raven, I imagine, Bette,' she said. 'But then again... if he can shapeshift to a wolf.' She waved her hand dismissing the thought for now. But thinking about Nikolas's skills made Sophie consider her own.

'What are my strengths?' she said, frustrated as she tipped boiling water into the mug and topped it up with milk. 'I have to have some, surely, Bette Davis.' She thought of the Lens family, each with their own magical traits. 'I wouldn't want to take on Alfred... the way everyone reveres him, he must be powerful behind that calm and gentlemanly exterior.'

She removed the tea bag and binned it, sipping her tea as she thought. 'What magical skills did my ancestors have, Betty? The Lens family has all my family's history written in the journals but none of my ancestors seemed to show any great magic skills, well none that I've read. They just lived normal lives using the glasses as they saw fit, with the protector being the source of the magic. So why did Daphne say I'd be the most powerful clairvoyant ever and Miss Sharpe agree? Where is my power coming from and when is it coming? Soon would be good!

'Where's the Raven's history? Has he got it logged somewhere?' She continued to mutter aloud as if Bette Davis might answer if she talked on long enough. 'The diaries that the Lens family manage are from Samuel's side of the family—my cursed lot—but what about my other side, Issbelle's side and her daughter, Elsopeth? The witch I half-descended from and my namesake. Did they ever take quill to paper?'

She leaned back on the counter, drinking from her mug of tea. 'If I'm supposed to be powerful, then I should be able to do more than wear a pair of glasses and see visions. I must have powers from Issbelle's genes. I must.'

She watched Bette Davis rise, walk out of the kitchen, glance back at Sophie as if inviting her to follow, and head to the library as Aunt Daphne used to call it – the large room with one wall of books, a desk and some comfy large, wing-backed chairs and a couch. Sophie followed. Could there be something in the library besides Aunt Daphne's favourite classic novels and a few romance books? Bette Davis entered and took to the couch near the window, rolling up in a ball and making herself comfortable.

'Thank you, Bette, that's a very good thought. I shall check out the bookshelves,' Sophie said and stood in front of the wall-to-floor bookcase. She walked along the row at eye level and read some of the book spines – everything from Dickens to a selection of world atlases.

'My glasses,' she said with enthusiasm and left the room to grab them, returning moments later. Putting down her cup, Sophie stood in front of the bookcase.

Should I ask questions and see if the books answer? She gave a small shrug, although she thought the idea was probably useless. *I've got nothing to lose.*

Sophie put on the glasses and the books rushed at her, volumes tumbling towards her from all shelves, hard and fast. Sophie yelped, covered herself with her arms and jumped back. She pulled the glasses off. The books were all still on the shelf, nothing had moved.

'What the hell? That was super weird,' she muttered, her breathing still quickened from the experience. She calmed herself and vowed to try again. This time, Sophie decided to only call for one book by one name.

She stood ready and positioned the glasses, then lowered them and called out at the same time, 'Elsopeth's journal'. Sophie screamed as a book from the top shelf hurtled at her and she covered her face, hurriedly stepping out of the way.

She pulled the glasses off and turned to look for the book, but it wasn't there. Nothing had fallen.

'Gotcha,' she said, smiling and addressing the top shelf of books. 'You're up there still, but at least I know your whereabouts! But of course, you would be on the top shelf.' She grimaced, studying the half a dozen volumes in the middle of the highest shelf, not quite sure which one flew at her, but at least she had a row and a direction. Spotting Aunt Daphne's small step ladder on wheels, Sophie pulled it from the corner, ignoring its squeaky protest. It had clearly been a while since anything on the top shelf was reached for.

She wheeled the steps into place and climbed up, looking at the book spines. There was nothing obvious that called to her. In fact, all the books on that shelf were titled and by authors and none appeared to be a personal journal. There was *A Victorian Lady's Guide to Being the Best Wife* by Elspeth Marr. 'I bet that's a hoot,' Sophie said. Next to it was the Charles Dickens classic *Nicholas Nickleby*, and beside it, *The Poetry of Edgar Allan Poe*. 'I'm guessing that's by Edgar Allan Poe,' Sophie mused. She grabbed Elspeth Marr's book and opened it.

Sophie gasped. Inside was not a printed book or any tips for Victorian ladies. It was a handwritten journal and the first entry started in 1584. On the left of the page, written in beautiful handwriting was: *Personal diary of Miss Elsopeth Rayne*.

'Oh Elsopeth, I have found you,' she whispered. She grabbed for the book by Dickens, *Nicholas Nickleby* and opened it to find it was not the expected Dickens novel. It was a handwritten volume as well and it appeared to be about the Saggers family... Nikolas's story. Sophie closed it and with a huge sense of relief that battled her rising levels of excitement, she looked to Betty, who was watching her.

'Thank you for the tip-off, Betty, this is just what I need.'

She returned her attention to the books and grabbed the poetry book of Edgar Allan Poe – he was, after all, the poet of the famous poem, *The Raven*.

'Soon again I heard a tapping,' she said aloud, reciting the only line she could remember of the poem having been forced to study it at school with a bunch of other dead poets' work that seemed totally boring to a then fifteen-year-old girl. Now, Sophie wished she had paid more attention.

'Oh my,' she said and smiled. As she hoped, it was a volume of handwritten notes. A volume exclusively about the Raven by her descendants. Observations, attacks, cautions, but nothing by Elsopeth in there as she was never the cursed. Sophie held the book to her chest for a moment, binding and bonding with her fellow cursed, before setting it down and checking the other volumes around it; they were what their spines said they were. Sophie ducked down a step on the ladder to a shelf lower and grabbed a few random books. But they too were true to their covers and the actual book they were meant to be.

'Right then, I shall work through the top shelf,' she said reluctantly returning the books she had left lying on their side to the upright position on the shelf, except for Elsopeth's journal. She wanted to read them all immediately but knew she would have to pace herself. She wondered if Miss Sharpe knew of these books and why Aunt Daphne had not told her of their existence in her letter of instruction. Sophie glanced at Bette. Maybe Bette was meant to reveal the secret when the time was right.

'Did you and Aunt Daphne have an agreement, Bette?' she asked the cat as she climbed down from the step ladder and pushed it back to the corner. Not expecting a response, she returned and sat beside her fluffy white cat, who slept on. Sophie was too impatient to start at the first page, she was on a mission, and making a promise to Elsopeth to come back and read it from the beginning, she scanned the beautifully handwritten pages, one after another, until she found the name, Raven.

Sophie couldn't believe her eyes. She expected to see references to the Raven, but there was his name, *Murdoch*. Had every Raven in history been named Murdoch or just select ones throughout the generations like herself, christened a version of the classic name Elsopeth? She saw he was only mentioned fleetingly in that entry, so Sophie turned more pages, and then she came across an entry that Elsopeth had titled 'My heart' – she was obviously a theatrical young lady, like herself. Murdoch featured predominantly in this entry. Sophie smiled at the two things she and Elsopeth had in common—a flair for the dramatic and a "Murdoch" in their lives—and she settled back to read the entry.

My heart

April 2, 1744

Today my heart nearly burst from my chest, first with fear and then with something I am hesitant to relegate to the romantic term of passion, but there, I have said it. I know of the Raven, of course – the first Raven. He was the troubled young man, Harley. Unlike his sister, the fair Hadley, Harley could not forgive my father for declaring Harley's mother a witch and seeing her hanged. She had not deserved it for saving my father when, unbeknown to her, he did not want to be saved. He was mourning me and filled with anger at what he claimed was the treachery of deceit by my witch mother. In the end, he deplored all that was magic, except for me, his half-witch daughter.

My poor darling mother did nothing more than present her original self to Papa. That was how she once looked before she was cursed. Why should she not display her best self to the man she loved? But his anger and pride, his humiliation, would not allow him to understand her reasoning, or accept me in the spirit form that comes from my half of their joined bloodline. I am, after all, half mortal, half witch. I love you, Papa. I am so sorry that life did not turn out as you wished.

But is the Raven of whom I speak when I talk of my heart. I have seen Harley's descendants come of age and carry forth their anger, but the one named Murdoch is the Raven of this era. I have watched him, unseen, or perhaps he sensed me, but he caused me no harm. Nor should he... I am not my father's mortal descendant who carries the curse and wears the optical lenses with the visions, the one that needs a protector. I am the witch's daughter first and foremost.

After moving into each other's world without introduction or happenstance, today I encountered him flesh to flesh. I was walking through the gardens at dusk, with my dearest friend, Charlotte. We often take exercise together, leaving the carriage with the other vehicles to collect us afterwards. Charlotte and I share a love of music and met while taking lessons; we both love to stroll at dusk and enjoy the beauty of the approaching evening. I find the soft glow settles me more than the dawn. As I came around a copse of trees, walking our usual path to the lake, I saw him. He was walking towards me, also strolling but with another man of his own age. They looked enough alike to be siblings, but I too looked similar to my friend, Charlotte, but we are not related.

He did not see me at first and I confess I panicked, quickly glancing around to see if we could take another path, or turn back and remove ourselves from his direct onward route. I was sure if we were to pass and acknowledge each other, our true selves would be revealed.

'What is it, Sophie?' Charlotte asked, sensing my distress, but I could not form words to tell her. How do I explain the curse that threatens my Papa's mortal family because of his actions and my spirited origins?

Then, to my mortification, while hurriedly looking for an escape, I stumbled in fear and the gentlemen hurried forward. The Raven caught me so effortlessly before I fell to the earth and with his strong hands around my waist; he steadied me and then, realising he still grasped my waist, hurriedly stepped back.

'Forgive me, Madam,' he said, 'are you hurt?'

'Thank you Sir, I believe I am unhurt due to your quick action.'

I am sure he knew who I was as his stare penetrated through to my soul, but it was not unkind. I gave a quick curtsy, wished them both a good day and, clutching Charlotte's arm, I hurried forward, not waiting to accept his bow or turning back to see if he followed me or watched me. I was too disarmed.

But oh, how his touch burned me in a way I have never experienced before. I am sure he lit a fire within me, and the look in his eyes, on his face, was not that of hatred.

What shall I do? Now that he has seen me in this world, and I have felt his touch, I fear something has been set in motion that should not ever have been.

Sophie turned the page, but that was the end of that entry. She lowered the book, nestled down in her comfortable seat, and sighed.

'Oh Murdoch, you heartbreaker,' she said and smiling, closed her eyes and thought of the encounter and the two of them in all their finery.

Elsopeth knew he had arrived, as she always did. Not because she had any special powers to sense the Raven, but in her early throes of fervidness, it was as if she felt the change in the air. Her heart began to beat faster, her eyes searched for him in the dusk light, and there he was, strikingly handsome in the fine cut of his dark suit, his waistcoat threaded with gold and his shoulders so broad to carry the weight of both of their worlds. She watched him as he entered her grounds, walking with a confident gait and taking to the stairs two at a time, as if he could not get to her quickly enough. He stopped momentarily to look up at the window where he knew she dressed, slept, and waited for him, and seeing her, he gave her the smallest of smiles that sent her heart racing.

Murdoch broke their gaze and entered her large mansion, disappearing from sight. She heard the timbre of his voice, speaking with the butler, no doubt unburdening himself of his hat and coat, and then she heard the Raven's steady footfall on the long staircase that led to her private room where she remained waiting by the window for him. He tapped, but did not wait to be admitted, swinging open the large timber door with gusto. He did not meet Elsopeth's eyes but immediately dismissed Elsopeth's maid with instructions that they were not to be interrupted, closing the door and locking it behind the departing maid.

In three large strides, Murdoch arrived in front of her, lifted and spun Elsopeth toward the large bed. She laughed with surprise and delight.

'You have missed me,' she said, touching his face as he lowered her onto the bed.

'Only every minute of the day, Sophie my darling girl,' he said, pressing his lips to hers and sighing as if all in the world was well again. He pulled back slightly. 'Have you been pining for me?'

'I have been very busy, but—' she started, and he laughed at her playfulness.

'Where is that dainty, shy young girl that fell at my feet in the gardens but a few months ago?' he said with a frown.

'You are sadly mistaken, Sir,' she teased him, her hand touching his handsome jaw and feeling the rough of his stubbled cheek. Her fingers trailed through his hair, which made him groan with the discipline of having to converse before he could ravage her. He leant into her hand to feel her touch.

'I was never shy nor dainty,' she assured him. 'I merely tripped in my hurriedness to avoid you, but apparently, that did not go as planned.'

'Apparently not.' He chuckled, and then cleared his throat as if emotion restricted him, his mannerisms tightened. 'Last time we...' Murdoch thought on his words, not one for eloquent statements, 'we came together for the first time. Did you enjoy it?'

'Yes.' Looking from his eyes to his lips and back again. 'Immensely.' In all truthfulness, it had dominated her thoughts every waking and sleeping moment since. 'Did you not?' she asked hurriedly, concerned.

'More than I can say. So much so that I fear I must have you again, immediately.'

Elsopeth gave a delighted laugh. 'I believe I feel the same. Please do not let me detain you.'

With a rush of power, Murdoch quickly moved off her, rising from the bed and Elsopeth's heart dropped with disappointment. But he did not leave or delay her gratification. Instead, his large hands grabbed for her and with deft movements, he pulled his lover to her feet, spun her around against the end of the bed frame and enjoying her laughter, he began to undo the multitude of ties, ribbons and corsets that would allow him to have his prize.

Elsopeth glanced over her shoulder at him, enjoying the determined look on his face.

'Could you not change into your bathrobe when you see me coming?' he muttered.

'But isn't the pleasure found first in the anticipation?'

'Trust me, I'll have my pleasure, but I would like to have it sooner,' he said, succeeding in unhooking one of her undergarments.

'If I was to wait naked for you beneath my bathrobe, then you wouldn't get to appreciate me in my finery.'

He succeeded with his mission, her gown falling to the floor as he stripped Elsopeth of her corset, then the chemise, and undergarments from her body until she stood completely naked before him. Turning her, Murdoch said with his own obvious physical appreciation, 'this is your finery.'

She flushed with the embarrassment of being so wholly exposed to him, and could not hide that, as sophisticated as she may want to be, in matters of love, she was like that girl who fell in front of him. He was the only man who had ever laid hands upon her.

Murdoch lifted her once more and returned her to the bed where righting himself, he stripped off his waistcoat, shirt, pants, and all that remained between himself and Elsopeth.

'Oh my, it is a fine view, Sir,' she said, wide-eyed and watching him. 'Aside from your good self, I have never seen the skin of a man before that was not of his hands or face.'

He smiled at her. 'I certainly hope not, and thank you for the compliment; I aim to please, Madam.'

As strong and as disciplined a man as he was—and he had perfected that over many, many decades—Murdoch could not mask the tremble of anticipation as he returned to lay beside her, and Elsopeth felt a strange pleasure in having that effect on him. Her body welcomed him, but her inexperience in matters of love and physical intimacy was displayed in her nervousness around him, her desire and yes, even fear. It came off her in waves and Murdoch strived for gentleness despite the effort of harnessing his arousal.

It was love. Pure, simple, life-changing love and Elsopeth only hoped that Murdoch felt as she did.

Sophie woke up with a start and looked around for the journal, relieved to see it on the bedstand next to her bed. She didn't want to leave it where Miss Sharpe or Mel might see it – the books were her discovery and she felt sometimes as if she had so little power, but now these books and their whereabouts would remain her secret until she was ready to share if she did indeed share at all except in notes to her descendants.

It was thinking of a descendant that suddenly jolted Sophie to a sitting position. Dressed only in a thin white slip, she looked about, pulling the bed covers around her. She had no memory of coming to bed or bringing the journal with her.

'Murdoch,' she whispered his name, remembering her dream. But was it a dream?

Was the scene she recalled in the bedroom with Elsopeth and Murdoch part of the diary and the last thing she read before sleeping?

No!

The last entry she read was of Elsopeth tripping when she encountered the Raven in the flesh. It certainly had nothing to do with the Raven seducing Elsopeth! Sophie closed her eyes to bring the dream to mind. In it, she or rather Elsopeth, had encouraged Murdoch, welcomed him to make love to her and they did, long and languishing love. Sophie opened her eyes.

'And now, here I am,' she said, 'but my last memory of being awake was sitting with Bette Davis on the couch.'

Rising, she looked around, lifting her bed covers and seeking the telltale black crow's feather that she found on the sheet in her room the last time she dreamt of making love with Murdoch. But there was nothing there. Sophie grabbed a dressing gown, unsure whether she felt relieved or disappointed at not finding some evidence of the Raven's attendance. She rifled through her clothing of yesterday which lay over a chair, but no, there was no feather. She had to confess, though, she felt strangely sated.

CHAPTER 12

VENETIA CAWTHORNE KNEW OF the Lens men from *Optical Illusion* —well, Alfred Lens at least—long before she dropped in her timepiece for the younger Lens man to service. He was quite a surprise – handsome, refined and charming. If she did not prefer the tall, dark, moody type, Venetia might have considered Lukas Lens as a potential lover.

She was not surprised they did not recognise her. Alfred Lens had probably only seen her a couple of times, and that must be over fifty years ago or more. But she thought her name and the watch might have stirred some memories. After all, the Raven's great loves were legendary and truth be known, she was a little insulted this generation had not taken the time to learn more of the Raven's history and not just their own. She was considered one of the greatest beauties of her time over the many generations she had lived. And nothing had changed.

Having just spent years on the Continent, she never competed for the love of a man. Her feline-like narrow green eyes, light olive skin, dark tresses and hourglass figure made her stand out from the crowd, and there was a time when the Raven could not resist her. Until he met that other witch. For well over a century, the Raven had been hers and then she had lost him, to her. Losing did not sit well with Venetia.

It was late afternoon and not long before *Optical Illusion's* closing time; she hastened her step. Waiting to cross the road, she saw through the small glass panes that both men were in attendance and a woman was talking with Alfred. A fair-haired woman and for a moment her breath caught. No, it wasn't Elsopeth, although this woman did look familiar, but Venetia could not recall her name. Relieved, she crossed and made her way to the store to retrieve her timepiece, which she intended to return and regift to the Raven. Lukas Lens had been recommended to her as a master in antique timepieces so he had best not disappoint, she thought with a smile upon her lips.

Lukas grinned in good humour as Orli ran through the protection charms she could offer him before he began training with Nikolas. The small bell above the door tinkled as a customer entered – Lukas sobered and Orli disappeared into the back room to finish up for the day.

Lukas did not recognise the customer; he had not been in when Alfred accepted the work on his behalf, but his grandfather rarely forgot a face and was prepared.

'Miss Cawthorne, lovely to see you again. You have come to collect the vintage timepiece?' Alfred said warmly greeting her and while not recognising her name, Lukas could sense his grandfather's wariness. Alfred had given Lukas and Orli the abridged version of Venetia Cawthorne's influence in the life of the Raven. Thanks to Nikolas, Lukas was as informed as could be. It was a powerful and sentimental timepiece that he had been given the responsibility to work on.

'Mr Lens, hello! And yes, I hope your talented grandson that you spoke so highly of, was able to work with it,' she said with a glance to Lukas.

Lukas grimaced at the flattery, knowing his grandfather did tend to wax lyrical about his talents. He stood and introduced himself, putting the watch on the counter between them. He was taken by her beauty; the woman was stunning, there was no other word for it. It was a heady mix of beauty, confidence and something else... aloofness, no, he couldn't quite place it, but it was hard not to look at her with her striking features – the dark hair, tanned skin and bright green eyes. He cleared his throat and got to the matter at hand. This was an area in which he was, after all, supremely confident of his skills.

'It is the most beautiful timepiece I have ever worked on and in excellent working order,' he told her in all honesty. 'Did you inherit it?'

'It's been in my family for generations,' she said in a soft and sophisticated voice with the hint of an accent he could not place. Maybe French, maybe Italian. 'Were you able to fine-tune and service it?'

'Fortunately, yes. It is working to the second,' he assured her, and she smiled delighted, picking it up and caressing its gold casing in her hands.

Lukas watched her studying it for what seemed a long time before he realised his grandfather was staring straight ahead at the door, in the same manner in which Venetia Cawthorne was gazing at the watch. They were talking, his grandfather and Miss Cawthorne, and yet again, his skills—this time for mind reading—were not up to scratch to allow him entry to their discussion. He glanced to the backroom but could not see Orli. Was Alfred in danger? Were they all?

'Miss Cawthorne, I thought you looked familiar—you have a beauty that is not easily forgotten—but I did not recognise the name,' Alfred said in his mind and she answered immediately without turning to face him.

'It was my mother's maiden name, I took it out of loyalty to her, and thank you, Mr Lens, for your kind words. It must be well over half a century. I believe I was better acquainted with your son. Forgive me, I cannot recall his name.'

'Mendel, he has since passed.'

'I am sorry,' she returned the thought to him with sincerity.

'Thank you. I assume you are looking for the Raven?' Alfred asked directly.

'Always.'

'And you thought to look here?'

'No. I wanted to re-gift the timepiece to him. It was a gift on our engagement, but he gave it back when he broke it off. As you know,' she said, her words trailing off as he received them in his mind.

'I am sorry that still pains you. But why now?'

'You are much more direct than I remember you to be,' she said frankly.

'It is a different time, different era, I suspect I have adapted,' he said, softening his tone. 'Forgive me if I sounded abrupt.'

Neither said anything for a few moments and Alfred glanced towards her back. His grandson had risen to collect a box to put the watch in but she stood holding the timepiece in her hand.

'She's unprotected, isn't she?' Venetia asked without saying the words aloud.

'Only for a brief period.'

'It's enough. She opened the door.'

'Grandpa!' Lukas exclaimed out loud breaking them both from their reverie. 'What's going on, are you okay?'

'Fine lad, fine,' Alfred assured him, and now Venetia did turn to him as he moved from behind the counter to open the door for her to depart. He hoped it was not obvious that he was keen for her to depart and that she might just attribute it to closing time. She gave him a smile that was cool at best, sly at worst. Settling her account with Lukas, Venetia then accepted the boxed watch.

'Thank you, Lukas,' she said, saying his name in a purring manner.

'It was a pleasure to work on it,' Lukas said with a nod. 'I hope it keeps good time.'

'Sixty beats per minute, just like a heart,' she said, and turning to the door, she bid Alfred good day and departed.

Alfred hurriedly closed the door, mumbling that he hoped Sophie was delayed. He glanced outside anxiously, watching Venetia cross the road, and breathed again when she was out of sight and Sophie not yet in sight. He did not want them to encounter each other.

'Sophie will be here any minute, but the coast is clear now,' Alfred said, his stance relaxing somewhat, but he looked at his grandson with some intensity. 'Lukas, you need to accept Sophie's decision without challenge. We don't need any more drama. Agreed?'

Lukas grimaced. 'Yes, agreed. But before Sophie gets here, tell me what's going on. What were you and Venetia saying to each other?' he demanded, joining his grandfather at the store entrance and crossing his hands over his chest.

Behind him, Orli answered, 'The Raven's great love. Is she back for him?'

'Yes,' Alfred confirmed. 'She's back for him because the accursed was unprotected… it allowed Venetia to find us. Next, she will find Sophie if Sophie remains unprotected. That ends tonight with either you or Nik in the role of protector.'

CHAPTER 13

THE NEXT MORNING, SOPHIE lay in bed musing over last night and how Lukas and Nikolas accepted her decision with good grace. There was no need to rise early as her morning travel time to the office took all of one minute since she moved into the residence in the wing next to the offices in Daphne's mansion. She had no more excuses for being late but that didn't mean she arrived early.

She heard Mel leave about thirty minutes earlier to go to her employer's workplace – one of the tenanted spaces in another wing of the sprawling mansion. Just before 9am, Sophie entered the office knowing Miss Sharpe would already be in attendance. She gave out a yelp of alarm and almost dropped her phone and handbag. An enormous man with a light beard, wavy hair to his shoulders, arms wider than her head, tattoos visible on his neckline and peeking through the cuffs of his long sleeve white shirt, stood and held his hands out in front of him to pacify her. Miss Sharpe ran into the room.

'Oh, Sophie dear, I was held up on the phone, I'm sorry,' she said smiling and looking from Sophie and the large man and back to Sophie. 'I see you have met Jack.'

Jack extended his sizeable hand, which Sophie accepted and felt her own small hand engulfed in it. She guessed he was about her age, nearing thirty, but it was a little hard to tell with all the facial hair.

'Jack is our new assistant,' Miss Sharpe announced, having sourced him with Alfred's help after Sophie happily removed herself from the process.

'He is? You are?' she said looking up at him. He was a giant – tall, solid and all of it appeared to be muscle.

'I am,' he agreed with a grin. 'The name is Jack Eabe, pleased to meet you, Sophie. Don't worry, I know what you're thinking.' He spoke with an Australian accent blended with what sounded like a touch of Scottish.

'What's that?' Sophie said offering him a smile now that she realised she was safe in her office once again.

'You're thinking Jack and the Beanstalk, a big giant, I get it.' He chuckled.

'No, but now that you mention it, I see why that might draw comparisons.' She placed her bag and phone on her desk. 'So, you've been an assistant before?' She couldn't imagine his large hands on the keyboard but noticed a pair of thin wire-framed glasses on his desk.

'Lots of experience,' he informed her. 'I was raised by a single mum who ran a massage business. Therapeutic, not the sort you're thinking of.'

'I hadn't got to that thought yet,' Sophie said surprised and laughing.

'Most people do. As a young lad, I made all her appointments, took the money, kept the books, paid myself and handled complaints. I was big enough to ensure no one took advantage of her.'

'I bet you were,' Sophie said still looking up at him. 'Well, welcome, Jack. I'm sure we'll all work really well together.'

'Let's have a "*Welcome Jack*" cup of tea and then I'll get Jack up to speed,' Miss Sharpe said, and turning to Jack in a conspiratorial voice added, 'Sophie is not much of a morning person.'

Sophie laughed.

'Best time of the day!' Jack declared and Sophie groaned.

'We're very lucky to get Jack,' Miss Sharpe continued, 'he just came out of a contract and was keen for a change.'

'I'm lucky,' he said again, or rather boomed. 'Your work schedule suits my training schedule perfectly.'

'Oh, what are you training for?' Sophie asked as Miss Sharpe went to make a pot of tea for the three of them.

'I'm in the state chess team. It's a mind sport,' he said tapping his skull. 'The strategy involved challenges my brain.'

He grinned and then said, 'I know what you were thinking. That I'm training for a weightlifting competition? Nah, I just go to the gym to let off steam.'

'Lots of it, by the looks of it,' she joked and indicated they should sit at the table for a chat. She hurriedly cleared away some papers and threw them on her desk.

He laughed and wagged his finger at her. 'Can't say I'm much good at reading you though since you weren't thinking half the things I thought you were.'

'Don't beat yourself up,' Sophie teased him, 'I'm not quite awake yet or I probably would have got there faster.'

'Well best you tell me specifically if you need anything or I'll guess wrong.'

Miss Sharpe re-entered with the tea tray and Sophie reached out to help.

'So, if you are part of our wider family connection, what's your witching pedigree? Got any special powers?' Sophie asked and Jack huffed in surprise. He turned to Miss Sharpe.

'You're right Miss Sharpe, she's direct.'

Sophie grinned and enjoyed seeing him take the dainty tea cup from Miss Sharpe. She served them all a slice of cake. 'Lemon cake for breakfast, the day is looking up,' she said enjoying Miss Sharpe's scolding expression for skipping breakfast. 'So, Jack...'

'I'm a grifter. Met any of them yet?'

Sophie looked to Miss Sharpe. 'I don't think so, have I?'

'I don't believe so, all in good time,' Miss Sharpe said serenely. 'Isn't this nice?'

'Yes,' Sophie agreed with good humour looking at her two odd tea dates, but she wasn't letting the subject go that easily. 'So, what does a grifter do, dare I ask?'

Jack sat back and smiled as if he were about to tell a fairy tale. 'Well, we're very ancient, not me personally, but the grifter line. And we're only really known to magical and spiritual folk and that's the way we like it.'

'I understand, my lips are sealed. So, what do you do?' Sophie pushed.

'We accept a gift, provide a protection spell or blessing and return it,' he said, with a small shrug. 'Hence the name grifter, so it's gifter with an "r" in there because the gift gets returned.'

'Right.' Sophie studied him. 'Mel, my housemate makes potions and remedies... is your field similar in that it's peace of mind then?'

He thought on that for a moment before responding.

'Perhaps give an example,' Miss Sharpe suggested.

'Excellent idea,' Jack said with a nod. 'My friend recently came to see me with a suitcase full of hazel twigs—that he'd gathered from the ground, of course, not cut off the tree—and presented them to me.'

Sophie laughed. 'That's a nice gift. What are you supposed to do with that?'

Jack smiled. 'Fires were raging through his area and my friend and his lovely wife had just built their first home, she's expecting. He wanted me to protect their home. So, I accepted the hazel twigs, placed a protection spell on them and re-gifted them to him. He went home, put them around on his window sills to protect against the fire storms and it did.'

'Seriously?' Sophie said, wide-eyed with surprise. 'Couldn't it just have been good luck?'

'No. Every other house burned around them, except for his and one other. My friend subtly put some of the hazel twigs on that house too, just so it didn't look suspicious,' Jack said. 'Besides, his neighbour was elderly and very kind to them, so he was keen to help her.'

'Wow,' Sophie said and nodded, thinking about what Jack had said. 'Grifters,' she repeated the term.

'Oh, I best get another cup, Nikolas is here,' Miss Sharpe said, rising and heading back to the kitchen.

Sophie looked out to the carpark and couldn't see anyone arriving. A few moments later, Nikolas appeared riding his motorbike.

'How does she do that?' Sophie asked, and Jack chuckled.

'She's got an inbuilt radar for it, I suspect. That's what makes her so good as an office manager, she knows what's needed.'

Miss Sharpe reappeared with another cup and the sugar bowl. 'You need more sugar in your tea, Jack?' she said, and he raised an eyebrow in Sophie's direction.

'You read my mind, Miss Sharpe,' he said, and gratefully took it.

They saw Nikolas coming up the stairs, his leather jacket under his arm, and he appeared at the doorway moments later.

'Just in time for tea,' Sophie greeted him.

'Perfect. Good morning, Miss Sharpe,' he said, and then saw the new addition to Sophie's office team. 'Jack!' Nikolas exclaimed.

Jack laughed and rose; the two men hugged, patting each other on the back. Jack even made Nikolas look small and Nikolas was a good-sized man.

'So, you know each other?' Sophie said drily. She was hoping Nikolas would get the same shock that she did on entry.

'We go back forever,' Jack said, making room as Nikolas sat beside him and accepted the cup of tea from Miss Sharpe with thanks.

Sophie dished Nikolas a piece of cake. 'Apparently, everyone goes way back except for me.'

'No, I can remember you in the—ow!' Jack shut up.

'Ah ha!' she proclaimed. 'I do go back, too. And Jack was about to tell me and one of you shut him up with a kick under the table.' Pointing her spoon from Nikolas to Miss Sharpe with a suspicious look on her face and earning their laughter. 'Tell me, Jack, where do you remember me from?'

'I think I was mistaken,' he said, narrowing his eyes at her. 'Yeah, I'm sure I was.'

Sophie grimaced at them all and then remembered she was keeping her own secrets – the journals she had found. She decided not to push the issue just yet but warned them, 'None of you has heard the last of this.'

'No doubt,' Nikolas said under his breath. He turned to Jack. 'So, Sophie informed me last night that I am her new protector.'

Sophie looked surprised but Miss Sharpe patted her hand and said, 'Jack knows all about the Raven and protectors, and the Lens men.'

'And Orli,' added Jack. 'Such a beauty.'

'Isn't she?' Miss Sharpe agreed. 'Inside and out. Like our Sophie.'

Sophie laughed. 'Thank you, Miss Sharpe, too kind. But I think Orli is an ethereal beauty beyond compare.'

'How did Lukas take it?' Jack asked, looking from Nikolas to Sophie and showing he was very much up on the family news.

Sophie gave a small shrug. 'Hard to say. I think he agrees it is best for his relationship if he steps away. So now it is Nik and me, watch out!'

Nikolas laughed. 'C'mon, how much trouble can we get into?'

No one said anything for a few moments and then Miss Sharpe smiled and the four began to laugh.

For a moment, Sophie sat back and watched the conversation flow around her. She was lucky, she knew it. Surrounded by people who barely knew her but genuinely cared for her or wanted to do their best for her. And now Jack, this interesting new giant who had stepped into their midst. She was expecting a small, officious woman similar to Miss Sharpe to take up the assistant role, but Jack was certainly an interesting addition. She was looking forward to Murdoch's reaction to him more than she cared to admit. No sooner had she thought of him, than her protector, Nikolas, snapped to look towards the carpark. Miss Sharpe began to reach for the cups and hurriedly packed the tray, rising to leave, and Jack sat up sharply. He inhaled as if smelling the air.

'He's here,' Nikolas said. 'The Raven.'

Sophie quickly glanced to Miss Sharpe and then back to Nikolas and Jack, who bristled beside her.

'This is going to be okay, isn't it?' she asked hurriedly. 'Jack, Nik? There's not going to be any issues?'

'Of course not, dear,' Miss Sharpe assured her and used a tone that reminded Nikolas and Jack that the Raven—for now—was no threat. 'It's business as usual and I suspect Detective Ashcroft is here on police business.'

Nikolas gave a less than convinced sniff.

'Jack?' Sophie asked again in a low voice, rising and regarding him suspiciously. There was no point in him taking the role if he could not control himself around Murdoch, as Sophie had every intention of keeping the friendship and working with him.

'It's all good,' he said in his deep voice and rose beside her, giving her a tight smile. 'Best I get to work then.'

'Yes, let's go to my office and I'll start the handover,' Miss Sharpe agreed, lifting the tray. 'Although an introduction is in order, given you will be here for the detective's visits,' she said to Jack and hesitantly placed the tray back on the table.

Sophie looked at Nikolas. 'Did you come to see me about something in particular? I can tell Murdoch we're meeting and catch up with him later?'

'No. Yes, it's not important.' He stopped as he watched the Raven walking up the stairs. 'Actually, it relates to the Raven, so it might be good if he is here.'

Sophie issued a soft groan and quickly looked around. 'Everyone, promise me there will be no warring today, and Jack, no warring in the future.'

Both men nodded just as Murdoch arrived at the door and knocked. Sophie saw the look of surprise on Murdoch's face and his glance to the carpark as if he could not escape back there now, having been seen.

'Detective Ashcroft, lovely to see you as always,' Miss Sharpe said cordially, trying to make him feel welcome.

'And you, Miss Sharpe, Sophie.' He gave a brief nod of his head to the ladies, and then Sophie saw his eyes narrow as he took in the other two men.

'Nikolas,' he said.

'Murdoch. I'm glad you're here, I've something to discuss and it involves you,' Nikolas said.

'No doubt.' Murdoch sighed as if he had heard it all before. He sized up the giant in the room. 'Jack.'

'You know each other?' Sophie asked and threw up her hands in exasperation. 'Of course you do. Everyone goes way back.'

'I wouldn't say way back,' Murdoch said, cocking his head on the side like a Raven.

'But far enough,' Jack agreed. 'You're looking better than the last time I saw you at—'

'Best we start that training then,' Miss Sharpe cut in and, with a nod to the door, encouraged Jack to walk through before her. 'I'm sure you'll see each other regularly when the detective calls in for Sophie's help.' As the two left the room,

Miss Sharpe called back over her shoulder, 'you have two hours free before your first appointment, Sophie.'

Sophie thanked her and gave a small smile. Jack was going to be too honest for his own good, and that indiscretion would serve her well for fact gathering. She turned back to find the two men staring at each other. They were similar enough to be mistaken for brothers, except that Nikolas was larger in frame.

'Shall we take a seat?' Sophie asked.

'No,' they both answered in unison.

'Fine.' She sighed.

'I came to see if you could help with a case that Gerard and I don't want,' Murdoch said, tearing his eyes away from Nikolas long enough to ask the question.

'And you think I want it if you don't?' she mused.

'No, but I'm hoping you can see through it, so to speak, and we can put it to bed right away.' He gave a small shrug. 'It's got us stumped. Gerard's on site now, but no drama if you can't help.' He returned his gaze to Nikolas, eyeing him as if Nikolas would be responsible for holding up the law, and detaining Sophie.

'It sounds intriguing,' Sophie said.

'And I'm leaving in a minute,' Nikolas added. 'I just came to warn Sophie about something, but it's related to you and it's probably good you are here.'

Sophie saw Murdoch bristle.

'Don't say it aloud. Not here,' Murdoch said, his voice icy cold, his dark eyes glanced to the windows and the outside view then back to Nikolas.

Nikolas glared at him. Sophie, confused, looked from one man to the other.

'You know then?' Nikolas asked.

'I guessed. Shouldn't have opened the door,' Murdoch said.

'I can't argue with that.'

Sophie crossed her arms over her chest. 'Hello? What's going on or should I just leave you two alone and go do my own thing?'

Both men looked sheepish.

'She has to know,' Nikolas said.

Murdoch thought for a moment and then nodded. 'I'll tell Sophie on the drive, but not here. Safer that way.' He turned to look at her. 'That's if you have time to accompany me now? Won't take long, hopefully.'

'Why not?' she said and sighed. 'It might be the only way I find out what is going on.' She looked at Nikolas. 'Anything more, or am I dismissed now?'

He smiled. 'Can I have one minute?'

Sophie nodded and Murdoch, taking his cue, said, 'I'll just catch Miss Sharpe, check she got the last reward payment and I'll be back here in a minute.'

Nikolas waited until he departed before speaking.

Sophie sat heavily on the lounge chair and exhaled. She rubbed her temples.

'Are you okay?' Nikolas dropped down in the chair opposite and leaned over to touch her arm.

'I am, thank you,' she said and looked up at him. 'I'm just tired.'

He frowned. 'No, you're more than that. That's what I wanted to talk about. I'm your protector, I can sense you now that the role has come to me.'

'Can you read my thoughts?'

'No. Only Alfred has mastered that. But, if you call for me—call me by name loud and clear—even in your mind, or call out the Raven's name, I will hear you.'

Sophie nodded, satisfied.

'You're drained and—'

She cut him off with a wave of her hand. 'It's nothing, I just haven't slept well, that's all. Last night, I was awake with wild dreams.'

Wild sex dreams about Murdoch more like it! She was grateful he couldn't read her thoughts.

'It's more than that. When you've been tired in the past, um, in other times, you crash, for want of a better word...'

'I'm not the fainting type,' she assured him. *Nor the swooning type according to my dreams, but I've been known to fall at the feet of men!*

He frowned at her. 'Your energy is being sapped. I have to warn you—'

'Ready?' Murdoch asked from the doorway and Nikolas rolled his eyes.

Sophie saw his hand was still on her arm and noticed Murdoch watching Nikolas with more intensity than usual.

'I'm fine, but thank you, Nik,' Sophie said and showed a softer, more vulnerable side than she normally did. In truth, he was right – she felt drained, as if she could climb into bed and sleep for hours. She made a mental note to talk with Mel and see if she had something that might help boost her energy supply. But for now, Sophie rose, ready for work. 'Let's go, Muddy.'

'You know I hate that nickname,' he grumbled.

'I know,' she said with a small smile and grabbing her bag and phone, followed the Raven out the door, her protector close behind her.

Before they had reached the end of the steps, Nikolas halted. 'Sophie, I just need to talk with Murdoch. I'll be quick.'

She stopped and looked at him suspiciously. Turning and seeing Murdoch was willing to talk, Sophie nodded and accepted Murdoch's keys to let herself into his car. When she was far enough away, Nicholas said, 'She's weakening.'

'I know, but I don't think it's because of *her*,' the Raven said.

'Maybe. We always knew this day would come, but why now then if not for *her*?' Nikolas said, thinking aloud.

'Sophie's overloaded with information. You've all kept her wrapped in cotton wool so she wouldn't get to this point, and now she's built up no resistance,' Murdoch said with a glance to Sophie in his car. He then admitted, 'She's found Elsopeth's diary.'

Nikolas swore under his breath. 'That'll do it.' He studied the Raven suspiciously. 'How do you know?'

'I saw it by her... never mind, I know.'

'I'll be watching you, Raven.'

'I expect nothing less,' Murdoch said casually, as if the threat was of no concern to him. He turned and departed.

CHAPTER 14

ARRIVING AT THE SITE of Murdoch's alleged crime scene, Sophie noticed a scattering of people around the house and the yard as Murdoch pulled to the curb and parked the car. She put her glasses on, wearing them on top of her head for now, and followed Murdoch into the large, split-level brick home. It looked like something built in the seventies, and with a glance around, Sophie thought nothing had been done to it since then either by the looks of it. They entered the living area and Sophie heard a familiar voice.

'Well, if it isn't the lady herself,' Detective Gerard Oakley said with a small bow towards Sophie and got the laugh he expected. Sophie knew the cantankerous senior detective had long been cynical of Murdoch working with her Aunt Daphne and then with Sophie, but after Gerard enlisted Sophie's help on a cold case he wanted to solve before his retirement, he had to withdraw his objection. They not only solved the case, but Gerard had enjoyed her company and admitted it. Murdoch told her—with a roll of his eyes—that his grouchy partner thought her sassy and not bad on the eye.

'Detective Oakley,' Sophie grinned in delight at seeing him again, 'I've been waiting for the day when you grace my doorstep again and we work on another case together.'

'Sure you have.' He eyed her suspiciously, and they both laughed again in good humour. He fished inside his jacket pocket and pulled out an invitation. 'I was going to give it to Murdoch, but now I can deliver it in person. My retirement party, I hope you can come?'

'Murder and mayhem would not keep me away,' she declared, and he looked pleased. Sophie raised an eyebrow in Murdoch's direction. They had made a bet when Gerard had first grumbled about using her services, that she would turn him around. Sophie bet Gerard would invite her to his farewell party and mention her in his speech. At the time, Murdoch laughed at the impossibility, but she was halfway there with the invitation. The latter was yet to prove true, but Sophie intended to win the bet and enjoy Murdoch taking her to the restaurant of her choice; she would not go easy on him.

Murdoch leaned closer to her as a constable interrupted Gerard. 'Being there does not guarantee you will get a mention in the speech. Besides, I've selected the restaurant you're taking me to,' he said with a wry look.

'Don't make the booking just yet,' she joked.

'Rest assured, the pleasure is found first in the anticipation.'

Before Sophie realised what Murdoch had said, he had turned away and was no longer looking at her. But he had quoted her... the words Sophie—or rather Elsopeth—had teased him with in their sexual dream.

'Right, do you want to explain, or will I?' Detective Oakley asked Murdoch as he re-joined them. Sophie turned to face the older detective, confused, clearing her thoughts and trying to be in the moment. She would need to think about what Murdoch said. Think long and hard, but later.

Murdoch did his best not to look at her, although he knew he must look like the cat that got the cream, an unfortunate analogy for a Raven. On the ride over, Sophie had pushed him to know what he wanted to tell her – what Murdoch and Nikolas agreed she could be told on the drive away from the house. Given her weakened state, Murdoch delayed giving her the warning he intended to deliver. Instead, he told Sophie that Nikolas wanted to set the perimeters for what he would be doing as her protector and to warn the Raven he was on the job. That much was true at least, and she seemed to accept that answer, for now. Besides, Murdoch consoled himself that it wasn't his job to make sure Sophie didn't take on too much, he was the enemy after all. But he did have a vested interest in her.

He didn't want to say Venetia's name out loud or think of her. If there had not been that window of time when Sophie was unprotected, this would not have happened. Venetia would not have been able to sense the cursed, and in doing so, track the cursed to find her lover, the Raven. She wouldn't have cared who the cursed was—Venetia had no interest in harming them—but she knew if she found the cursed, the Raven had to be nearby.

He knew it was more sinister than that. Once she found him, she would be searching to determine if Elsopeth and the Raven's love had transcended into the current era. She would be looking for Elsopeth with no idea that for the first time in history, the cursed was different. The cursed was expected and powerful and futures were unwritten. Because, for the first time in history, the curse was not just a descendant of Samuel Rayne. This time, the cursed was half Samuel Rayne and half Issbelle, his witch wife. The cursed was Elsopeth herself reborn in a new era. Reborn as Sophie Carell.

And the Raven never stopped loving her. Nothing came between their love. For the first time in history, even though he feared admitting it, a Raven was in love with an accursed.

'Detective Ashcroft?' Gerard addressed his partner formerly in front of the owner of the house.

Murdoch started. He snapped to look at Gerard. The house owner had entered the room and Sophie was now wearing the glasses. Whatever had been said, he had missed it. 'Sorry, I was thinking about the case,' he muttered.

Gerard gave him a weary look. 'Keep up,' he said with a sigh, which made Sophie laugh. 'Do you recall the murder that happened here twenty years ago?'

'No,' Murdoch answered. 'I'll need to read up on it.'

'Forensics wasn't as good then as it is now,' Gerard said. 'Might be good to revisit it.'

Gerard nodded for the woman to continue as they all stood around the kitchen island, the woman reaching for a stool as the others remained standing. Murdoch recalled her name from their earlier introduction—Abigail Middleton—and put her in her mid-forties. She had a rough edge about her; dyed black hair, her eye make-up was overdone with a dark pencil, and he could smell the cigarette smoke that lingered on her.

'Yeah, so, as I was saying, Dad was murdered here, in this very room 20 years ago to this day and the cops have never found the killer, but they thought it was one of his bikie friends,' she said.

No doubt, Murdoch bit his tongue from retorting. He glanced at Sophie, keen to know what she was seeing.

'My husband, Steve, and I are moving out. We've put the house on the market, but some smart arse is trying to make sure everyone knows it's a murder house. Someone who has a grudge against us so we won't make good money on the sale.' She looked around. 'You saw the broken front windows this morning, and my husband's den has everything thrown off the shelf.'

'The anniversary date must be significant,' Murdoch pointed out the obvious.

'Yeah, I guess the anniversary date is a weird coincidence, but why now? Hasn't happened any other year,' she said.

'Maybe because you're selling up,' Gerard suggested. 'Is there anything in the house or anything buried in the grounds that someone might be worried about if the new owner rebuilt or put in a pool?'

Abigail gave a dry laugh. 'My relatives have lived here for decades, it's my family home. I inherited it when Dad died. Dad's body was cremated and Mum skipped out years ago, no idea where that bitch is but hopefully dead, so I don't think there's any surprises or secret treasure.'

Gerard gave Sophie an apologetic glance for the swearing, which surprised Murdoch. The grumpy old bastard really did respect Sophie.

'But if you think we've buried bodies here, go for your life and dig them up,' she said and added another dry laugh at the end.

Sophie spoke up, 'Forgive my ignorance, but just wondering why the detectives are called in and not the police. Has something else happened?'

'Sure has,' she said, 'come and see this.' Murdoch motioned it was okay for Sophie to follow Abigail and they went downstairs to a huge room that was obviously the husband's den. It was obvious that Steve—the husband—spent more time and money on his den than the rest of the house. The room was decorated like a club trophy room, painted in dark burgundy, with lush carpets, a big billiards table and shelves of trophies and collectibles. Abigail was right; it was ransacked. Across one wall, the word 'Murderer' was scrawled.

'Is that written in blood?' Sophie asked.

'We don't know yet,' Gerard said, it's off being analysed.

They could hear a knock at the door upstairs and Gerard and Abigail took the stairs back up to the living areas leaving Murdoch and Sophie behind.

'What do you think?' Murdoch asked.

'I can see why you've been assigned it, but Abigail has nothing to do with her father's murder, from what I could see.'

'Waste of time,' Murdoch said with a frustrated shake of his head.

Sophie turned sharply to look to her right and gasped in fright. Murdoch snapped to look in the same direction. There was no one there.

And then Sophie faded from sight.

CHAPTER 15

SOPHIE SAW THE MAN beside her and then, as quickly as he appeared, he dispersed into the air.

What the hell was that? A ghost?

She turned to ask Murdoch if he had seen it but his reaction was weird too. Murdoch had stepped back, he was looking around as if he saw the man disappear but then he did the weirdest thing; he called for her.

'Sophie!' he hissed. 'Are you still here?'

'Murdoch!'

He couldn't hear her or see her. Sophie felt the panic rising inside her. Was she dead? But she wasn't lying on the floor. In fact, her body wasn't anywhere to be seen except—she observed—still attached to her head and neck and in its palest form.

'If you are here, try to touch me,' he said. 'No! Wait up.'

Sophie heard footsteps on the stairs and Gerard appeared at the top, looking over the stair rail but not coming all the way down.

'Finished down there?' he asked and then looked around. 'Where's Sophie?'

Sophie saw the uncomfortable look on Murdoch's face.

'She saw something and raced off, out the back way.' He shrugged. 'I suspect she'll be in touch.'

'Let's hope it is something to close this case down. Bloody waste of time,' he grumbled under his breath. 'C'mon let's get out of here.'

'I'll be up in a minute,' he answered and Sophie waited while Murdoch watched his partner retreat. He looked to the area where Sophie was last standing but she moved beside him.

'If you are still here, touch me or give me a sign,' he said in a low voice.

Sophie reached out to touch him, hoping he could feel it. If she had been in a sexier, playful mood, she might have tried kissing him, but she was freaking out.

I'm dead! I don't want to be dead.

She ran a hand over his hair and stepped back.

'Okay, you are here,' he said and looked in the right direction, facing her now. 'Listen to me, Sophie, don't panic. You are okay, you are not gone for good, not dead. I'm here with you.'

She sagged with relief, although this was a nuisance situation. But then again... a jumbled mass of thoughts ran through her head... maybe it was a good thing, maybe it could be useful.

'This used to happen to Elsopeth too,' Murdoch was saying, 'and I know you realise now you are Elsopeth, a descendant, whatever,' he waved his hand with the description, 'we can talk about that later. It happens when you become overwhelmed or overtired. She would fade from sight – half mortal, half spirit.'

'I know,' Sophie said. 'She died as a child and her mother, Issbelle, couldn't live without her so brought her back to life in the two half forms. What am I saying? You can't hear me,' she said with frustration and stopped talking since Murdoch started talking over her.

'You need to get out of here. Call for Nikolas, as loud as you can, he'll come and get you, take you home. I won't leave until he comes,' he promised her. 'Give me a sign when you have done that so I know he's on his way.'

'Nikolas!' she yelled loudly and was surprised Murdoch could not hear her. But nope, she was truly a spirit, she marvelled. She saw a pen on the table nearby and moved it so Murdoch knew she had called for Nikolas. He nodded that he understood.

Nikolas appeared moments later. 'What is it?' he asked, panicked looking at her, then at Murdoch.

'You can see her?' Murdoch asked at the same time as Sophie spoke.

Nikolas held up his hands. 'One at a time. Sophie?'

'Apparently, I'm a ghost but you can see me at least.' She put her hand to her heart and breathed out.

'So you are,' he agreed. 'It's okay, it's temporary. You'll be just fine.'

'I told her that,' the Raven snapped behind him.

Sophie gave Murdoch a smile of thanks but remembered he couldn't see her.

'I'm okay,' she said sounding less than convinced, and followed her comment with a casual shrug.

'I'm pleased you're not panicking,' Nikolas said. He continued to hold up his hand for Murdoch to wait.

'I was, but Murdoch explained what was happening, even though he couldn't see me. Can you tell him, thanks, he was really supportive,' Sophie said.

'You can tell him later.'

'Tell me what?' Murdoch asked frustrated that he was unable to communicate with or see Sophie but Nikolas could.

'We're out of here,' Nikolas said reaching for her arm. He turned to Murdoch. 'She'll be fine.'

He nodded. 'Thanks,' he said, with as much gratitude as he could muster and headed for the stairs.

'Ready?' Nikolas asked and Sophie nodded. Within seconds she was in her bedroom, still a ghost. With Nikolas.

'Wow, that was a trip,' Sophie said swaying slightly and Nicholas helped her to the bed, sitting her firmly down. 'Thanks for coming so fast.'

'That's what I do,' he said and squatted down in front of her. 'This was expected, don't worry, you'll be back to your usual self in a moment.'

'Will I? That's a relief.' She liked it when Nikolas squatted in front of her, making her feel safe and small beside his bulk presence. 'Why was it expected?' she asked realising what he just said.

He brushed the question off. 'I'll just get Miss Sharpe, be back in a minute.'

'Why do we need to—' she stopped as Nikolas vanished, '—get Miss Sharpe,' she finished. Sophie looked at her arms and hands. She stood and moved to her dresser to see if she could see herself in the mirror, and she could. 'Bizarre.'

'You should sit to get your strength back,' Nikolas said reappearing behind her and startling Sophie.

Sophie uncharacteristically did what she was told and returned to the bed to sit down.

'This is most inconvenient.' She sighed and Nikolas chuckled. Shortly after, they could hear Miss Sharpe coming up the stairs.

'She wanted to come the conventional way,' Nikolas explained.

Miss Sharpe hurried in and to Sophie's side. 'Well, we were expecting this,' she said in a calm voice and took Sophie's hand.

'So I hear. You can see me too, Miss Sharpe?'

'Oh yes, dear, I wouldn't be much of an assistant if I couldn't find you, would I?' she answered as if that was obvious.

Within a minute of Miss Sharpe holding Sophie's hand, Sophie was fully visible again.

'How did you do that?' Sophie asked.

'It's my job, dear, to ensure you are relaxed and energised,' she said releasing Sophie's hand and standing back.

Sophie groaned and dropped back onto the bed; Nikolas chuckled. 'Someone explain, please,' she said dramatically and sat up again as Miss Sharpe and Nikolas both took a seat. Nikolas next to her at the end of the bed taking up a good half of the large queen bed, and Miss Sharpe on a nearby winged-back chair. Sophie saw Miss Sharpe's eyes drift to the book on Sophie's dresser.

'You've found Elsopeth's journal,' she said and returning her attention to Sophie, explained, 'Well in a nutshell, we've always known to expect you, Sophie. Daphne's mother saw it decades ago, and we knew it would be the first time in history that Elsopeth and the holder of the curse would be one and the same.'

'Which means the Raven will be torn between his greatest love and threatening an ancient enemy,' Nikolas said.

'Greatest love?' Sophie said, only hearing those words. She was still uncomfortable around Murdoch after the dreams which were all too real. Uncomfortable because she wanted him to come back to her room every night, she wanted him with a stirring of feelings that she wasn't sure she should admit to or was ready to surrender to, or even if it was safe to do so without bringing down their whole magical world on top of them.

'If you had worked with Daphne—and I'm not putting any blame on you, dear—but we would have prepared you for years so none of this was such a shock. But now, you've been thrown quite in the deep end,' Miss Sharpe said with a look of apology.

'I've only myself to blame, Miss Sharpe,' Sophie said.

But Nikolas disagreed. 'I've envied those without magic sometimes. Must be quite freeing.'

'I imagine there is good and bad for both lifestyles,' Miss Sharpe agreed. 'But Sophie, when you didn't want to know, we all tried to protect you from knowing because you were such a happy, ambitious, free spirit. It's why Daphne did not immediately leave her house to you, because without accepting the curse, it might have come at you just by the nature of being here. I hope that makes sense?'

Sophie nodded. 'Surprisingly, yes. I can imagine this house has its own sense of spirit.'

'Your spirit now,' Miss Sharpe said. 'At times, you'll become overwhelmed, frightened, or want to withdraw; you'll then assume your spirit form. I suspect that sounds terribly simplistic, but Elsopeth was half spirit, half human. I intended to let you know her journal was there when you learnt a little more about her and the connection to the Raven.'

'So they were lovers?' Sophie asked.

Nikolas huffed. 'The operative word being "*Were*". It doesn't mean they have to be forever just because Murdoch thinks he's entitled. Besides, Venetia is back on the scene.'

Sophie could swear Nikolas was jealous, and then she saw Miss Sharpe's alarmed look.

Nikolas swore under his breath. 'I was going to bring that up with a lot more diplomacy,' he said and gave Miss Sharpe an apologetic glance. 'I'd better get back to work, I've been gone long enough.'

'But—' Sophie stopped; Nikolas had disappeared. She turned to Miss Sharpe. 'It's a handy trick that.'

Miss Sharpe laughed. 'Indeed, it is. Come, you have appointments and I will tell you about Venetia when we break for lunch if you like. Best not to say her name too often though, let's call her V.'

'Okay,' Sophie said, rising to follow Miss Sharpe back to the office. 'I left the crime scene unsolved.'

'I am sure that won't be a problem, you can resolve it in good time. Why don't you call Murdoch and set up another time to revisit it?'

'On the phone?' Sophie said, surprised as they took the large staircase down to the front door. 'I never thought of that. It seems so ordinary now.'

'Yes, but it still works,' Miss Sharpe teased as she opened the door to the lovely day outside.

'Why couldn't Murdoch see me if he's a Raven? Aren't they carriers of the dead in mythology and if I'm part spirit, then doesn't that count?'

'Interesting thought,' Miss Sharpe mused. 'They've been associated with the dead and with lost souls. In Swedish folklore, ravens are thought to be the ghosts of murdered people.'

'Gross thought, is that why they call a group of ravens a murder of ravens?'

'Another good question,' Miss Sharpe said as they left the residence to walk around to the office wing. She continued without addressing the question. 'In German fantasy stories, ravens are believed to be damned souls, but that's just folklore and fantasy, dear.'

Sophie laughed. 'Unlike our weird world.'

Miss Sharpe laughed. 'I see your point, and they are intriguing creatures, ravens, or crows. They have a funeral for their dead, very interesting that.' She returned to the conversation at hand, 'But no, the Raven has never been able to see Elsopeth in spirit form, or any ghosts for that matter. Nor could you until you started to believe and accept this life, and now that vision is growing stronger in you. But Murdoch has chosen a career where he often works with the dead or attends death scenes. A lot of the past ravens have done the same.'

'Really?' Sophie said and waved to a couple of team members from the leased offices sitting having a coffee on a bench in the garden.

They headed inside out of the warmth of the day and Miss Sharpe added, 'Yes. Several in history were undertakers, a couple were surgeons on the battlefields or in hospitals...'

Sophie noted Jack looked pleased to see her. 'Thank goodness, you have a reading in 20 minutes and I'm expecting her any minute. Cup of tea?'

'Bring them both on,' Sophie said with a smile and sighed as she sat at her desk. *Never a dull day,* she thought, now excited and empowered by the discovery.

But who was that ghost at Murdoch's crime scene?

That evening, alone and in the comfort of her large bed amongst the clouds and sunflowers Nikolas had created for Sophie on the walls and ceiling from her vision, she opened Elsopeth's journal. The last entry she read described Elsopeth's face-to-face encounter with the Raven in the gardens and the burn of his touch when he gallantly hurried to assist her. The dream that followed of Sophie and Murdoch making love in past centuries was not in Elsopeth's journal, but Sophie would happily have it again. She read the last few lines of that entry:

'But oh, how his touch burned me in a way I have never experienced before. I am sure he lit a fire within me, and the look in his eyes, on his face, was not that of hatred.

'What shall I do? Now that he has seen me in this world, and I have felt his touch, I fear something has been set in motion that should not ever have been.'

What indeed, Sophie thought and turned the page to read on:

The bouquet

April 3, 1744

I do not know where the Raven made his enquiries, but today a most glorious bouquet arrived for me consisting of my favourite flowers—roses—in my favourite two colours. It was so large it took two footmen to display it in the drawing room and the colours were so striking – white and yellow roses, the longest of stems and beautiful waxy green leaves. Charlotte, who came to visit, was quite overcome by them and said white roses represent chastity and deep love, and yellow roses represent jealousy. But the Raven has no grounds for jealousy, nor deep love, but no doubt was merely providing what he discovered to be my most treasured and favourite rose colours. I am sure a man of his standing and responsibility has never given thought to roses having any symbolic colours attached to them.

I confess I have not left the drawing room since they arrived. I also have not stopped thinking of him since our encounter in the park and I can now assume that I, too, have crossed his mind. Or at least my health did as the card reads:

My Dear Madam, I sincerely hope this finds you in good health after your misstep yesterday. Your faithful servant, Murdoch Ashcroft.

Misstep is being kind as I literally tripped into the poor gentleman. I could not turn fast enough to avoid his presence and then it was too late and there I was, tumbling toward him. I can only imagine what a startling sight that must have been. Now, manners dictate I should respond at once and so on my best white stationary, lightly fragranced, I prepared a reply. But I trembled as I wrote, hoping I could cloak my delight at the gift and my fear of our encounter, in a restrained manner. Thus, I wrote:

My Dear Sir, I am in receipt of your most gracious gift which has brightened my day considerably. I assure you of my good health and I hope, despite my misstep and other maidens falling at your feet, that you similarly remain in good form. Your quick actions in rescuing this maiden from having to dust off her garments and pride does honour to your sex and your dexterity.

Yours most sincerely,

Elsopeth Rayne.

Goodness, I feel quite exhausted from the entire encounter and did not sleep at all last night. I have never had such a rush of feelings before. If I knew better, I might call this being enamoured, but I have nothing to compare it with. I must ask Charlotte has she ever been in love. Perhaps I just have a fever.

Sophie smiled at Elsopeth's innocence as she closed the journal.

'Oh dear, Elsopeth, no wonder he was smitten by you.' Sophie sighed. 'I imagine he took that innocence and a lot, lot more.'

CHAPTER 16

LUKAS LENS SPUN AROUND, dived as the fireball raced past his head, and stood just as quickly, destroying it with one quick hand movement.

'Ah ha!' he exclaimed with delight and looked at his grandfather who didn't look up from his work.

'What's that Lukas?' he asked looking up casually.

Lukas and Orli laughed.

'Good try, Grandpa.'

Alfred grinned. 'Good work, lad. You are definitely improving, and not a moment too soon.'

'Why? Have you heard more of Venetia?' Orli asked in a hushed voice, and Alfred shook his head in the negative. 'But we will.' He glanced to the world outside their glass-windowed store as if expecting to see her arrive, but instead Nikolas was pulling up on his motorbike.

'Brace yourself, Nik might test you as well,' Alfred teased Lukas, as Nikolas approached, removing his helmet and jacket as he walked, and opening the door to enter.

'You've decided to come the traditional way?' Orli teased him on entry.

'I was down this way to see a client so thought I would drop in. Definitely fewer bruises this way.' He chuckled. 'How are you all?' he asked looking first at Alfred then Orli then at Lukas.

'Very well, thank you, Nik,' Alfred answered. 'Lukas has just diffused a firebomb.'

'Impressive,' Nikolas said and grinned at his friend. 'Let's see how well you dodge my missiles. A session this evening? If you're free, come straight after work and we can grab dinner once I've pushed you around a bit.'

'Excellent, thanks,' Lukas agreed. 'I am pleased you are here, Nik, there's something I want to tell you all, two things actually.'

He had everyone's attention. Nikolas seated himself on a customer stool and looked at Lukas.

'Should I close the shop?' Alfred asked.

'No, that shouldn't be necessary,' Lukas said with a glance at the limited passing trade. The store was often at its quietest after the lunch break when customers return to their workplaces and the next wave of customers was en route having finished their lunch. 'It's about Lucy. She's keen to wed and I've proposed to her.'

Alfred clapped his hands in delight, and Orli sighed with pleasure.

'Congratulations, lad,' his grandfather said, coming over to shake Lukas's hand, while Nikolas hit him on the back and Orli embraced him.

Lukas accepted their congratulations and smiled although he was sure they could see right through him and his grandfather's comment confirmed that. Had he read his mind?

'I gather you want this too, but you may not have done it so soon?' he asked but did not wait for an answer. 'But still, it is best to keep the ladies happy and you would not wish to miss out on a diamond-like Lucy while you contemplated life.'

'She's a beauty, I'm sure you'll produce a beautiful brood,' Nikolas teased him and Lukas groaned.

'Oh, you would make a wonderful father, Lukas,' Orli agreed, and again Lukas brushed off their jests with a grimace and shake of his head.

'I heard that,' Alfred said with a raised eyebrow to his grandson and a teasing look in his eyes. 'Yes, a pay rise would definitely be on the cards if you have children to upkeep.'

Lukas laughed knowing his grandfather was joking. Alfred signed *Optical Illusion* over to himself and Orli some time ago and took no income, but continued to reside upstairs. Alfred was a wealthy man and through his accountant—Mr Saggers, Nikolas's uncle—had already bestowed large monetary gifts upon his loved ones so they did not have to wait until his death to be comfortable in life.

'Well, I'm glad you have it all worked out for me. I want to tell Sophie myself though before Lucy announces it. I'll drop over tonight after you attempt to disarm me,' he said to Nikolas.

'She faded today,' Nikolas said, and the group gasped. Nikolas resumed his seat on the stool and told of all that had happened. Then he recalled Lukas had two pieces of news. 'What was your second topic? Hurry, while the store is clear.'

Lukas lowered his voice. 'Venetia has been watching our shop. But you knew that didn't you?' he asked Nikolas.

Nikolas gave a brief nod of his head. 'That's why I am here – to tell you about Sophie vanishing and to warn you. I can sense all threats to Sophie. It comes with the job now.'

Lukas grimaced. He had lost the power since giving up his right to be Sophie's protector.

'How do *you* know?' Nikolas asked Lukas. 'Did you see her?'

Lukas shook his head and motioned for them to wait a moment. He returned to his work area behind the counter, closed his eyes for a moment, and stood motionless. Moments later he opened his eyes again.

'It's still there,' he said. 'I can hear the watch I serviced for her ticking.'

'Really? You can do that?' Nikolas asked impressed.

'Your father could too,' Alfred told Lukas and made him smile with the knowledge.

'It doesn't happen often,' Lukas told them, 'because most watches or clocks I repair or service leave the premises and don't come back. But she's close by.'

'Now?' Orli asked, and Lukas saw Alfred and Orli both trying to subtly scan the exterior of the shop.

'Right now,' Nikolas agreed with Lukas. 'Don't remove your protection spells, Orli.'

'I shall refine them even more.' She turned to Alfred, the strongest amongst them. 'What can we do?'

'At this stage nothing but be cautious, and warn the Raven,' Alfred said.

Nikolas and Lukas reacted as one.

'—hell will freeze over,' Lukas snapped.

'—I'm not warning him about anything,' Nikolas spat out the words.

Alfred sighed. 'She is waiting because she knows this is a safe place for the accursed—Sophie—and that Sophie may come here to read or contribute to the journals. Where the cursed is, the Raven may linger. If I warn Murdoch, he will either avoid the area or do the honourable thing and go to Venetia, and remove the threat from Sophie.'

'But it may not remove the threat,' Orli said.

'That is true. She may still come for Sophie if she thinks the Raven has feeling for Sophie as he had in past generations, or rather, Elsopeth,' Alfred said. 'But Venetia most likely does not know yet that the accursed and Sophie are one and the same, so let us not be the ones to show her that by hosting Sophie here, for now.'

'Then he must avoid Sophie until he declares his love for Venetia or releases her affections again in our current time,' Orli said.

'And I shall suggest that to him,' Alfred agreed, emphasising the word "suggest".

'How? Where will you meet him?' Lukas asked concerned. 'I'll come with you.' His eyes flared yellow.

'As will I,' Nikolas insisted.

'Absolutely not,' Alfred said, sending a private message to Lukas to calm himself. 'No. Two or more of us will only make him defensive and we don't want him to think we are threatening him.' Alfred frowned. 'Besides you two are too hot-headed.'

'You are right,' Nikolas begrudgingly acknowledged the truth of it. 'But you need to meet him somewhere neutral. Perhaps you should go to the police station.'

'As long as he doesn't come here,' Lukas agreed. 'And Nik, make sure Sophie knows not to come here too until all this is sorted out.'

Nikolas sighed. 'That will require me telling her about Venetia which I was hoping to avoid until she got a little more settled. But it seems unavoidable.'

They looked up as a couple of customers appeared at the door.

'Tonight then, my place?' Nikolas said to Lukas who gave a brief nod, and the party dispersed—Nicholas departing the conventional way, Orli moving to the back room—as the bell tinkled over the store entrance and the customers entered.

Detective Murdoch Ashcroft sat staring at the paperwork in front of him. He heard his partner, Detective Gerard Oakley droning on in the background, but his thoughts were with Sophie. The sheer torture of absence. Seeing her, watching her, waiting for her. All those years he partnered with Daphne—not that he didn't appreciate and want the eccentric clairvoyant's help—but it was all for the chance of a glimpse of Sophie, the niece, as she grew, and he waited for her to come back into his world. It had been almost a generation without Elsopeth and he would not lose her again.

'Murdoch!' Gerard snapped.

'What?' Murdoch responded startled back from his reverie.

Gerard frowned at his young partner. 'You haven't heard a word,' he said annoyed and slapped the case notes from the historic murder scene they had visited earlier that morning, on the desk in front of Murdoch. 'Read them in your own good time and you sort the case out with Sophie. You're clearly only half here today anyway.'

Murdoch looked apologetic. 'Sorry.' He reached for the papers.

'I'm going to lunch,' Gerard grumbled. 'I'd have a better audience from a sandwich than you.'

Murdoch grinned. 'Depends on the filling,' he retorted. 'I'll read these later, I'm going for a walk, clear my head.'

Gerard studied him. 'Lovers' tiff?'

Murdoch scoffed, rising and reaching for his jacket on the back of the seat. 'Given I haven't got a lover, it's hard to have a tiff with one.'

'I'm a detective, and an old one at that,' Gerard said, eyeing his younger partner's reaction. 'If you want to pretend you're not attracted to that lovely young lady then that's your undoing. But it's clearly mutual.'

Murdoch looked at Gerard with interest, giving himself away.

'Anyone can see that,' Gerard continued with a weathered smile, 'even someone with limited detective skills,' he stirred Murdoch and earned a grimace. 'Ask her out.'

'It's not that simple.'

'Why does everything have to be complicated with you young people? You just say "Can I take you out?" and she responds "yes" and then you get a haircut, have a shave, put on your best suit and off you go.'

Murdoch groaned as he followed Gerard out into the hallway. 'I never thought I'd see the day where I'd be getting dating advice from you.'

Gerard laughed and hit his partner on the back. 'I'll be back in an hour. Try and find your brains between now and then so we can get some work done this afternoon.'

Murdoch nodded. 'I'll go in search for them now.'

As he made his way down the hall to the front stairs, Murdoch froze – he sighted Alfred Lens approaching the reception desk. He was a distinguished man, erect in posture and dressed expensively – one of the few men Murdoch knew who still had a tailor make his suits perfectly cut to fit.

He has to be here to see me, Murdoch reasoned and then his blood stilled. Sophie, had she come to harm? He hurried his step to greet Alfred.

'Mr Lens?' he called nearing.

'Detective Ashcroft.' Alfred smiled instantly relaying Murdoch's fears. 'Forgive me for intruding on your workspace but would you have a moment?'

'Of course.' He looked around. 'Please this way. Is everything okay?'

'It is, don't be concerned. It is a matter we are hoping to prevent,' Alfred assured him and Murdoch started breathing normally again.

'We can use this interview room.' He opened the door and invited Alfred in, following after. He felt the shift in the air, a chilling energy from two powerful forces from enemy families. The lights in the building flickered.

'I have come in peace,' Alfred added also sensing the change.

'I receive you,' Murdoch added speaking the words of the past that were necessary to calm the warring families. The air stilled, and the lights surged back on brighter than before. He invited Alfred to sit and took the seat opposite.

'Venetia is watching our store, waiting for you, we assume,' Alfred cut to the chase.

'Damn,' Murdoch swore and rose from his seat. He webbed his hands behind his head and turned away for a moment to gather himself. He paced along the back wall of the interrogation room.

'The door was opened when—'

'Sophie was unprotected,' Murdoch finished and Alfred nodded.

'But you suspected as much, you sensed the watch Lukas was servicing,' Alfred continued.

'Yes.' He returned to sit opposite Alfred. 'I wasn't sure if she had brought it in or it had somehow come into Lukas's hands from a customer in possession of it.' He mumbled the words on the inscription, '*My Love for all Time, V.* So she is here,' he said accepting it.

'She is waiting and watching us knowing or assuming that eventually, you will stalk the accursed to the source of the journals, but I don't believe she knows that this time, the cursed and your soulmate are the same,' Alfred said.

Murdoch's eyes widened on hearing the term. 'Soul mate,' he repeated the word. Murdoch had always believed that, but he did not know that was how the other families had viewed their union.

'Would you not say so?' Alfred asked puzzled.

'With all my being.'

Alfred nodded. 'Permit me to make a suggestion?'

Murdoch nodded.

'Perhaps you should avoid coming near the store, not that you visit there except in duty.' He acknowledged Murdoch's recent visit. 'It would also be best to avoid Sophie for now.'

Murdoch snapped to look at Alfred. 'No.'

Alfred waitedand watched. The younger men—Nikolas and Lukas—would have challenged the Raven, but Alfred let Murdoch process his thoughts.

'You are right,' he eventually said under his breath. 'Until I sort this out with Venetia and send her on her way.'

'Can you stay away now that Sophie has realised she is Elsopeth?' Alfred asked sympathetically, a reaction the Raven was not used to from the enemy family.

Murdoch ran a hand over his mouth, and then through his hair. 'I don't know,' he answered in all honesty.

'None of this is written,' Alfred reminded him. 'It may be that Venetia accepts your decision for this generation, or—'

'It may be that she does Sophie harm,' Murdoch said in a lower voice and added, 'over my dead body.'

CHAPTER 17

As was the custom—a relatively new one—the office dwellers in Sophie's clairvoyance business, along with Mel when she was free, met for lunch at the large table near the kitchen.

Miss Sharpe had a healthy salad with the dressing on the side she had prepared beforehand and a cup of green tea; Mel and Sophie had a salad roll they purchased earlier when a lady in the tenant offices did her much-appreciated lunch run for all the tenants, and Jack had all the ingredients displayed before him to make his own sandwich fit for a giant. He rose to get a drink from the kitchen.

'Oh my, he is dreamy, isn't he?' Mel gushed, watching him depart.

'Is he?' Sophie asked confused and looked to the doorway where he exited.

'He is a very lovely man,' Miss Sharpe agreed. 'A real gentle giant and an excellent *grifter* from what I've heard.'

'He's more than that,' Mel sighed, 'he's gorgeous.'

'Really?' Sophie said again making Miss Sharpe laugh.

Mel rolled her eyes. 'I'm not surprised you haven't noticed given the parade of good-looking witches that come and go – Lukas, Nikolas and the detective.'

'Murdoch?' Sophie said, her heart speeding up. She had spent most of the morning trying not to think about Murdoch with very little success. The way he assured her she was safe, that he would stay with her when she was freaking out, and the way he had taken her to the edge and beyond in bed in her dreams, and they were just dreams... at least she thought they were. Sophie reached for her glass of water and was pleased that Miss Sharpe was speaking and she was not required to respond.

'Technically, Nikolas is more of a shapeshifter than a witch,' Miss Sharpe said, dabbing her mouth with a paper serviette.

Jack entered the room hearing her comment and resumed his seat, taking up the width of the end of the table and oblivious to Mel's enamoured gaze.

'I haven't seen Nik transform for a long time. I wonder if he's lost the knack,' Jack said, smiling at his play on words which he had to explain. 'Nik knack, you know the kid's rhyme, never mind.' Mel laughed at his play on words, earning an appreciative smile from him.

'What does he transform into?' Sophie asked keenly, 'I'd love to see that.'

'He's got a few party tricks,' Jack said with a chuckle. 'He can take several forms, but I think his most natural is the wolf. Pretty normal stuff.'

Mel scoffed. 'Like that's normal, maybe in your world.'

Jack acknowledged her words with a smile and a wink in her direction, which made her swoon even more to Sophie and Miss Sharpe's amusement.

Sophie sobered. 'I saw some interesting news today. Lukas and Lucy are engaged.'

'Oh,' Miss Sharpe said and placed a hand on her heart. 'I hope that hasn't hurt you, Sophie.'

'Why? Are you in love with Lukas?' Jack asked.

'Well, if I was, your diplomacy and sensitivity would be much appreciated,' Sophie said, playfully smacking him on the arm and earning a deep chuckle from Jack.

'Yeah, apologies for that. You're not then? I thought there was something between you and Nik?' he asked and took an enormous bite of his sandwich.

'Nik?' Sophie almost squealed.

'He's gorgeous,' Mel agreed.

Sophie rolled her eyes. 'You think everyone is gorgeous?'

'Including me?' Jack asked, swallowing, and Sophie saw Miss Sharpe's eyebrows raise with anticipation of Mel's response.

'Especially you,' Mel said, and he chuckled again, then looked a little puzzled, unsure if she was joking or flirting.

'I am sure Lukas intended to tell you in person, but perhaps he hasn't had a chance,' Miss Sharpe said.

'Maybe,' Sophie agreed. 'Lucy posted it online, but I don't follow her anymore. It came up in one of our mutual friend's feeds.' Sophie gave a small shrug. 'It was an initial stab of pain, to be honest, but now that I'm used to the idea, it's fine. I expected it.'

'Hmm,' Jack said, frowning. 'I knew Lukas's last girlfriend. She was lovely.'

'She was.' Miss Sharpe smiled.

'What happened to her then?' Mel asked, always keen on the gossip.

'Bit of a sensitive topic,' Jack said, scooping up a slice of tomato that had escaped his sandwich and eating it. 'She met Nik at her and Lukas's engagement party and fell in love with him.'

'No!' Sophie gasped.

'Sad but true. But Nik didn't feel the same way, and he wouldn't do that to Lukas anyway. That was the end of the relationship,' Jack said.

'Nik's too sexy for his own good, clearly,' Sophie joked, and they all laughed, acknowledging that indeed he was. 'Speaking of men, notably Murdoch,' Sophie turned to Miss Sharpe, 'you did promise to tell me about V over lunch.'

'Ah, yes, V,' Miss Sharpe said, finishing her salad and sitting back with her green tea.

Sophie turned to Mel and Jack. 'This is the Raven's girlfriend from previous generations I believe,' she said with a glance to Miss Sharpe, 'but we're not saying her name.' She then whispered 'Venetia' to Jack and Mel.

'Hmm, I remember Venetia,' Jack said.

'Oh wow, so does that mean Murdoch—or the Raven—automatically has a girlfriend in every reincarnation or generation, or whatever you all call it,' Mel said with a wave of her hand.

It was a question Sophie was keen to hear the answer to as well, and before Miss Sharpe could answer, Jack responded.

'It's not an automatic thing, but the Raven was with V for a long time, a really long time,' frowning while he recalled the details, 'maybe centuries. But then he met Elsopeth, and he was gone for her,' Jack said, making another sandwich for himself.

'So did he just drop V and go out with Elsopeth?' Mel asked.

Jack nodded to Miss Sharpe to continue the story, and all eyes turned to Miss Sharpe who lowered her voice. 'It was a very dangerous love triangle. V was not prepared to lose the Raven, but Elsopeth and the Raven were inseparable – it was a grand love affair,' she said, looking as melancholy as Sophie had ever recalled Miss Sharpe being. She wondered if Miss Sharpe was thinking of Alfred Lens, the love she denied herself for duty.

Miss Sharpe continued, 'Ironic when you think it was the Raven's ancestral mother's line that placed the curse, and Elsopeth's ancestral father's line that brought about the curse.'

'So is Murdoch expected to catch up with V then if she's back from wherever she's been?' Sophie asked and felt a pang of raw, green jealousy at the thought, the intensity of which surprised her.

Miss Sharpe glanced at the clock as lunchtime was coming to an end. 'It's a little more complex than that, Sophie dear. When you were unprotected for a short time there, when Lukas resigned his duty and the new protector had not been appointed, V could sense the accursed.'

Jack nodded, wrapping up his lunch items and wiping his hands on his serviette. 'Normally she couldn't sense the accursed because the protector radiates a charm field around them. Mind you, that doesn't stop the Raven from sensing the cursed, but it did protect the accursed from everyone else. You were just out there for a few days and she's sniffed you out for want of a better word.'

'Is she a wolf too then?' Mel asked.

'No, just a common variety witch,' Jack said as if they grew in the vegetable patch out the back.

'But what would she want with me anyway?' Sophie asked.

'She's not interested in you as such, but she thinks if she finds the cursed you'll lead her to her lover,' Jack said finishing as if it were a question and glancing at Miss Sharpe.

'Precisely so,' Miss Sharpe said. 'Now that she's located the city where the accursed lives, she knows that somewhere around you will be the Raven. She also knows the journals are with the Lens men and the accursed will read and write in them at the location of the Lens store. That's how it has always been.'

'Right,' Sophie said. 'So, she hasn't found me here yet, but is waiting there for me? And, if she sees me there, she thinks the Raven will be watching me, ready to attack and she can find her lost lover and have him back, or make sure he's not still hanging around with Elsopeth?'

'Yes, except...' Miss Sharpe hesitated.

Jack stepped in. 'It's the first time in history that the cursed and Elsopeth are one and the same, so if she wants the Raven back and recognises you, then she's not going to take it well.'

Sophie scoffed. 'What's the worst she could do?'

Miss Sharpe looked to Jack, and they both looked at Sophie.

'That's the problem, dear,' Miss Sharpe said, 'V is rather merciless and we have no precedence for what could happen, nothing was written, because, well we've never had this combination of you and the cursed before, ever.'

'So we don't know what you will do either,' Jack added, eyeing her suspiciously, which made Mel and Sophie laugh.

'It's complicated, isn't it?' Mel said.

Sophie looked to the windows and out to the gardens. 'Orli. I need Orli to place protection charms around the house.'

'She has already, dear,' Miss Sharpe said, 'but until further notice, can I suggest you avoid the *Optical Illusion* store?'

'Or I could bring it to a head and go there.'

Miss Sharpe and Jack responded at once.

'—No!'

'—Not a good idea.'

Sophie smiled. 'Scaredy cats.' *Cats.* The thought made her look at Bette Davis lying over near the far window on the couch in the sun, and the Raven's adversity to cats. And just like that, she was thinking about Murdoch again.

Murdoch pulled himself together, drilling down to do the job and making sure Gerard didn't suspect him of being off-the-boil again. But he had to see Sophie. The more he thought about not seeing Sophie, the more he had to see her, and the last thing he wanted was to out himself to Venetia.

But Alfred Lens was right. Murdoch never thought he'd say that, but he always had time for the stately gentleman who knew how to play the game, unlike his grandson and Nikolas. Like the head of the protector clan said, the honourable thing to do was to confront Venetia and send her on her way before she made trouble for all of them, especially Elsopeth – Sophie, he corrected himself.

As the day drew to an end, Gerard grabbed his coat to leave. They had several cases on the go at the moment, none of which Murdoch was applying himself to with any great attention.

'Tomorrow, first up, we'll catch up with the coroner and see if he has anything of value for us on that Torres Street murder, and then we'll have to go back to see Abigail Middleton again, otherwise, she'll be crying neglect on her case and taking it up the line,' Gerard said and sighed. 'Any news from Sophie on that one? Has she solved it?'

Murdoch shook his head in the negative. 'Nothing, yet.'

'Are you going to see her tonight?'

'No.'

'Call her then and ask her out. Why not?'

Murdoch gave him a look of disdain. 'Heading home, aren't you?'

'Simple question.'

'And being the seasoned detective that you are, you know better than to ask me a question you know I have no intention of answering.'

Gerard chuckled. 'Later,' he said, and departed.

Murdoch swore and leaned back in his chair, webbing his fingers behind his head and staring at the ceiling. He had to see Sophie, that was a given, but he wasn't prepared to start a war with her protector, Nikolas. Not that he feared that, he'd welcome a chance to release some aggression at the moment, but it wouldn't put him in good favour with Sophie or Miss Sharpe, and he loved one and liked the other.

The whole situation pissed him off to no end. Years he had waited, years and years, and now the protectors had dropped the ball and let Venetia find him. It made his blood boil at their incompetence and his angry surge made the lights flicker again. He closed his eyes to calm himself. A knock at the door had him bracing and the desk sergeant appeared around the corner.

'Ah, Detective, just letting you know we seem to be having a few power surges here today. I've called for the electricians, but they can't come until tomorrow.'

'Did you threaten to arrest them if they didn't get their butts down here?' Murdoch joked.

The sergeant laughed. 'How did you know? That's how I got the appointment tomorrow... they initially said next week,' he joked and gave Murdoch a nod as he headed down the hall to tell some of the other departments.

Murdoch knew the electrician wouldn't find anything; he had to control himself better. The timing of all of this was beyond frustrating. He needed Sophie's help on the case, but truthfully, he didn't give a toss about that. He wanted to kiss her, feel that merger of their powerful spirits come together and the grace of her human side welcoming him. He didn't have that with Venetia. She was all about sophistication, show and tell. Once that was a mix that enthralled and grabbed his attention. Now, well, he found Venetia sexy, she was beautiful, but she was not for him. Never would be again, even if Elsopeth was no longer in the world and that thought filled him with blind panic. He had rights in Sophie's past and he would have them again – her present would be his too.

For now, he would honour the agreement he made with Mr Lens and keep his word. He knew the only way to see Sophie was to go to her in her dreams.

Tonight.

After that, he would deal with Venetia.

CHAPTER 18

Venetia Cawthorn had been watching the store for several days now, using her skills to take on different disguises from the animal world to people. Neither the Raven nor the accursed had appeared. Not that she expected to recognise the accursed until she saw the Lens men pull out the journals for him or her to read or write in. It hadn't all been unpleasant or time-wasting though. The youngest Lens, Lukas, was a strikingly handsome and interesting man. She liked his stillness; he reminded her of Murdoch. She saw that he wasn't quick to speak or laugh, like Murdoch, but when she coaxed that from the Raven, it was as if his words and laughter were just for her. She wondered if Lukas was the same.

Was he as confident as Murdoch in bed, as sensual, she wondered, studying him through the windows. He moved comfortably in his body, and when she had collected her watch from him, he spoke with her as if they were the only two people in the room. He loved her timepiece, such good taste, classic taste; truth be told he appreciated it more than the Raven. Beautiful and the complete opposite to Murdoch in colourings; those crystal blue eyes were breathtaking.

Venetia pulled herself together; seducing Lukas Lens wasn't her mission. If she were being honest with herself, she was tired of seduction. The last decades with a lover in their coastal neighbourhood in Florence were pleasurable and the lifestyle easy, but Venetia wanted more. She wanted a great love again, commitment, and passion, that fit that set you apart from other couples. She wanted someone to need her so badly they would wait years, decades, centuries for that love to rekindle. Just like the Raven did for Elsopeth, and the thought made her seethe with anger. She wanted to see if the Raven looked at her in that way again, now. If he did not, well... they were moving in the store. Venetia focused on them as Alfred Lens came to the door and turned the sign to "Closed". The lights dimmed. Another day when the accursed did not make an appearance, and then she felt a rush of excitement. Lukas had unlocked a drawer and drawn out a large, worn-looking journal. She smiled.

Can they sense I am here and he is taking the journal to the accursed so he or she doesn't come to the store? Are they worried I'll bring the Raven here?

'Oh Lukas, you will have to try harder to deceive me,' she said in a low voice as if issuing a challenge. 'Let's see where you go then, we shall both go there.'

He disappeared into a backroom and not long after, reappeared in a T-shirt, jeans, and runners. Lukas exited the shop and made his way to a nearby car, Venetia transformed into a bird—neither a Raven nor a dove—but a black and white lark. A fitting bird, known for being territorial and mating for life. Venetia followed the black luxury sedan curious to see who the accursed was for this generation.

Lukas rang Lucy on his way to Nikolas's house – a large timber home situated on acreage surrounded by trees and backing onto a reserve. It was a thirty-minute drive outside the city's edge and a desirable location for a shapeshifter.

'I've put it out there,' Lucy said, excited.

'What's that?' Lukas asked, changing lanes to prepare for a turn-off.

'That we're engaged, silly!' she said as if she couldn't believe it wasn't dominating Lukas's thoughts all day.

Lukas's jaw tightened. He had wanted to tell Sophie before it became public knowledge, but he couldn't tell Lucy that.

'Great, how's the reaction been?' he asked casually.

'Good. I've had a couple of magazines and online news sites keen to get a picture of the two of us together with me wearing my ring. Are you around in the next few days if I set it up?' she said excitedly.

Lukas grimaced. 'How many are we talking about?' He could almost feel the chill come down the phone line. 'It's just that modelling is your thing, I'm bound to break the camera.'

She playfully hit him. 'As if! You're the most gorgeous guy I've ever seen.'

Phew, conflict avoided. For now. He relaxed but not at the thought of doing the photo shoots. Nothing interested him less; it was a private affair, and he hoped it would stay that way.

'I'll let you know,' she continued. 'I'm trying to negotiate a fee for an exclusive story and maybe exclusive wedding day photos, so you might only have to do one engagement shoot after all.'

'Right,' he said, less than impressed. 'Will we give the fee to charity?'

'What! No way, we need it for a house deposit. We can't live in your unit or mine... we need a house with a yard for the kids. I'm thinking of our future here,' she reminded him.

'Makes sense,' he said. 'I'm turning off to Nik's now so I'd best go.' They exchanged their farewells, and Lukas disconnected the phone, swore out loud and hit the steering wheel with his hand. He couldn't think of anything worse than having a magazine and engagement shoot in the false world that Lucy lived in. He took a deep breath.

'What price love,' he grumbled.

Lukas steered his car through the large entrance arch of Nikolas' estate and drove slowly up the driveway in case any animal crossed his path; Nikolas had half a dozen dogs or more, and a collection of random animals that wandered in and stayed at their own peril. The outside lights were on and Nikolas appeared in the doorway, dressed casually. He raised his hand in a wave. They'd have plenty of room to practice out here, away from prying eyes. Lukas parked and alighted from the car, patting every animal that presented itself before he joined Nikolas on the wrap-around verandah of the low-set house.

'Nice place you've got here,' Lukas said.

'You've been here before,' Nikolas said frowning at him.

'Yeah, but I forget how peaceful it is compared to living in an inner suburb unit.'

'I like it. Comes in handy,' he said with a nod to the surrounding reserve. 'Let's get to it. I'll blast you a few times and test you, then when we're done, we can drive to the tavern for a meal. Unless you need to get to Sophie's to tell her about your engagement?'

'Nope, just heard from Lucy and she's already promoting it. I suspect Sophie's heard,' Lukas said less than impressed. 'A workout and dinner would be great.' He followed Nikolas out into the yard and further to the back of the property behind the house.

'What's wrong?' Nikolas asked, as he stopped to prepare.

'Nothing.'

'You've got so much anger coming off you I could grab it and harness it,' he said and reached up into the air, Nikolas made a snatching motion and a crack of light like static electricity appeared and burnt out.

Lukas shook his head. 'Lucy is setting up some stupid photo shoot for our engagement.'

Nikolas stopped, then laughed. 'Yeah?' He laughed even louder, which brought a reluctant smile to Lukas's lips.

'Shut up,' he muttered.

'You always were the prettiest of us,' Nikolas continued and then, without warning, he ran, turning only enough to fire a flare towards Lukas.

Lukas's hands went up, and he dissolved it in seconds and found he did not have time to contemplate what just happened. Nikolas sent more angry bursts of fire his way and while Lukas deflected them, Nikolas raced for the forest, Lukas in pursuit.

'Great,' Lukas hissed. He'd not only have to contend with the fireballs and finding Nikolas, but doves were not known for being nocturnal birds and his night sight was not great at the best of times, let alone in a dark forest full of shadows.

Unbeknown to them, and far enough away not to be detected, Venetia watched from a high tree branch, amused by their training antics.

Lukas ran amongst the trees, alert, wary, ready for random acts from Nikolas, and wasn't disappointed. He was hit once, singed, pained.

'Fuck!' he swore out loud, bending over with the pain.

'You alright?' Nikolas yelled.

But Lukas didn't answer. Sensing where he heard the voice come from, he fired several good shots back, hearing Nikolas laughing at his retaliation and then swearing himself. Lukas looked up just in time to dodge Nikolas leaping towards him from a higher branch and took off, setting up his own wall which Nikolas didn't expect and hit, bouncing off with a loud grunt.

After thirty minutes, Nikolas called a truce. The men caught their breath as they walked back towards the house, brushing themselves off.

'That's a good workout,' Nikolas said, panting slightly. 'We should do that more often.'

'Appreciate it,' Lukas said. 'Not so much the pain, but the practice.'

Nikolas smiled and nodded. 'I want to show you a few tricks that might come in handy, Alfred might have shared them already...' He halted and put his hand up.

Lukas stopped next to him. 'What is it? Is this the trick?'

Nikolas turned around in a circle, looking skyward and then Lukas's hand went straight to his heart – sixty seconds to the minute, the same as a heartbeat, and his own heartbeat suddenly changed as if synchronising with a nearby timepiece. The altering of his heartbeat alarmed him initially, the irregular tug in his chest, as if he were having a heart attack, and then it steadied.

'Venetia!' Lukas said in a low voice for Nikolas's ears only. 'I can hear her timepiece ticking, she's nearby.'

'She's here,' Nikolas said, having the power as a protector to sense threats to Sophie and connections to the Raven. 'Show yourself, Venetia!'

From the branch of a tree nearby, a black and white bird landed in front of them and transformed into a beautiful woman.

Nikolas swore under his breath, and Lukas released a tight breath.

'Gentlemen,' she said with a smile, her beauty capturing them both, and then she turned to Lukas. 'We meet again.'

CHAPTER 19

Sophie and Miss Sharpe were expecting Alfred Lens, and he arrived promptly, apologising for detaining Sophie after hours.

'Your timing is perfect as always, Mr Lens,' Miss Sharpe said.

'Absolutely. You are always welcome, Alfred,' Sophie added, 'and I have nowhere to hurry off to. In fact, I've been ordered to stay out of the kitchen – Mel is cooking dinner for Blaine and me tonight.'

'Lucky you,' Alfred said with a smile, and then sobered. 'Can she cook?'

'Mm, remains to be seen,' Sophie joked. 'After dinner, I'm early to bed and journal reading. You are both most welcome to stay for dinner.'

'Thank you, dear,' Miss Sharpe said, 'but Mr Lens and I have theatre tickets this evening. I've wanted to see this Sherlock Mystery on stage for a long time.'

'Miss Sharpe will have worked out who did it before the curtain opens,' Alfred teased and Miss Sharpe laughed with delight.

Sophie loved how they still called each other by their formal names and wondered if they did it when alone, or only in mixed company. The small party sat and Alfred broached the subject of the Raven's predicament, and his need to stay away from Sophie.

Sophie's eyes narrowed. 'Ah, that makes sense now,' she said more to herself than the present company but did not elaborate. She returned her attention to Alfred.

'The separation may not be for long,' he was saying, 'just until he speaks with V, and determines if she will be a threat to you once she knows you are Elsopeth. I doubt she would be any threat to you if you were just the accursed, she has never taken an interest before,' he said, speaking in a low voice for fear of being overheard.

'It's really bad timing,' Sophie said. 'I'm working on a case with Murdoch.' Her despair was not related to the case alone.

'It might be one you have to let go, dear,' Miss Sharpe said, 'just this time. Unless you can visit the scene without him... maybe attend with Detective Oakley?'

'That's a good idea, Miss Sharpe,' Sophie agreed, but her disappointment was etched on her face.

Alfred cleared his throat lightly, as if to broach a delicate subject. 'I know you and the detective have become closer,' he said, choosing his words. 'I must tell you he was very resistant to the idea of not seeing you.'

'Was he?' Sophie brightened slightly.

'Yes, it took some convincing and I am not sure I succeeded, but he knows he has to deal with the issues from his past that have now arisen to ensure your safety.'

Sophie nodded. 'So, she is dangerous?'

'Love is dangerous,' Alfred said, 'where jealousy is involved.'

Sophie sighed. 'I seem to be the source of much jealousy at the moment, and yet I am single. Lucy won't let Lukas near me, and now Murdoch's girlfriend has come to claim him from me when we have just started to relax together outside of work.' She referred to Elsopeth without saying it aloud. 'At this rate, I will have to get Nikolas to make a list of suitable partners for me that won't cause the ladies any problems and audition the men,' she joked.

'Perhaps avoid Jack then,' Miss Sharpe said with a small smile, and Sophie laughed.

Miss Sharpe looked to Alfred to explain. 'I believe Mel has eyes for our lovely giant, Jack.'

Alfred looked pleased. 'Well, there is someone for everyone, is there not?' He studied Sophie and said sympathetically, 'It's very hard on the heart to be separated from true love... not that I'm saying you and the detective are on that course, but nevertheless, I wanted you to know why he might not be visiting for some time.'

'It was very kind of you, and thoughtful, thank you, Alfred,' Sophie said, 'and you are right, I would have wondered what I had done wrong and taken it personally.'

Suddenly, Alfred froze and put his hand to his temple.

'Manners my boy,' he said, and moments later, 'diplomacy then.' He would normally send the message without saying it aloud, but he was in safe company. Alfred dropped his hand and looked at the ladies. 'My apologies, a message from Lukas.'

'Is he alright?' Sophie asked, looking around as if expecting something to happen simultaneously in their surroundings.

And it did.

Nikolas appeared, saw Sophie with Alfred and Miss Sharpe, and disappeared just as quickly.

'What's going on?' Sophie stood, surprised.

'I think the boys have found Venetia,' Alfred said.

Lukas's eyes flared yellow. Beside him, Nikolas braced for the attack, but Venetia did not move. In his mind, Lukas said her name and location, sending the message to his grandfather to warn him.

'What are you doing here?' he demanded, surprised to see a look of hurt flash in Venetia's bright green eyes. He randomly thought about how feline she was.

'*Manners my boy,*' his grandfather's voice came through loud and clear and Lukas almost rolled his eyes in frustration. Did his grandfather think good manners were going to save the world? He obviously heard Lukas's thought and added, '*diplomacy then.*'

Lukas gave a brief nod, not that Nikolas or Venetia understood the discussion going on in his head.

'Forgive me,' he said with forced old-world politeness that he witnessed daily from his grandfather. 'You were looking for us?'

'Then you have found us,' Nikolas answered curtly, having ensured Sophie was safe and returning with no one aware of his momentary absence.

'You know I am looking for the Raven,' Venetia said, her voice almost purr-like.

'Why did you not ask me about his whereabouts when you visited the shop?' Lukas asked, not trusting her.

'In all honesty, I came to you to service my antique timepiece because you were highly recommended, and one of the few clocksmiths working with antiques. I didn't recognise you or Alfred at first. The Lens man I knew was not either of you.'

'My father, perhaps?' Lukas asked.

'He had an unusual name,' she mused, trying to think of it despite hearing it recently from Alfred's lips.

'Mendel?'

'Yes,' Venetia smiled, 'that is him. A lovely man and always kind to me and my family.'

Lukas softened towards her. He had so few years with his father, and he rarely met people whom he could discuss his father with, someone who knew him when he was alive.

'He's not here,' Nikolas cut in. 'The Raven... he's not here.'

'I didn't expect him to be, I just hoped you could tell me where to find him and in answer to your earlier question, I had hoped to find him without involving the Lens family. There was no need to involve anyone.'

'Yet here you are,' Nikolas said.

Venetia sighed at his continued aggression and, turning to face him, explained, 'I am not interested in the cursed you are protecting. I am just seeking the Raven and given she or he did not appear at the shop when I saw Lukas with the old volume, I thought he might be going to them directly and the Raven might be there.'

Nikolas begrudgingly accepted her logic with a small nod.

Lukas winced. 'Sorry, your watch is so loud.'

Nikolas frowned. 'It is? I can't hear a thing.'

'I am sorry,' Venetia said, placing her hand upon her chest, where her watch was settled on a chain around her neck. She touched it and it quietened. 'Better?'

'Yes, thanks.' Lukas looked impressed, and she smiled at him.

'I feel grounded hearing it,' she said.

'I am the same.' He understood her need for the heartbeat of a timepiece.

'My father's home was full of clocks, as is my home, the home I just left,' she said in a softer voice.

'Where are you staying then?' Lukas asked, conscious of Nikolas bristling beside him. He was impatient for Venetia to be gone and the threat removed.

'I am staying in the hotel near the lighthouse. It has a perfect timepiece that chimes on the hour,' Venetia said. 'Cambridge chimes.'

'I know it. It was once the largest public clock and most modern timekeeping piece in the country,' Lukas said, smiling. 'I service it.'

'Do you?' she said, pleased. 'You should come visit me then. We could ask for a tour of the clock tower.'

He nodded and smiled. Not sure where any of this was going.

Nikolas stepped forward and Venetia instantly stepped back, arching up like a cat. He held up his hands in a pacifying motion.

'I won't harm you. If I tell you where to find the Raven, will you promise to leave the cursed alone?' Nikolas asked, and Lukas snapped to look at him, unsure if that was the correct course to take. He heard nothing from his grandfather, who must be hearing his thoughts. He realised Nikolas had turned to him, waiting for his agreement to the plan, and Lukas consented with a small nod.

'I just want the Raven,' Venetia said again. 'You do not need to tell me anything of your cursed subject. Remember, it is not me you are protecting him or her from.'

Nikolas hesitated and then said, 'in this generation, he is a detective. You will find him at Roma Street police station.'

'A detective,' she said, fascinated. Venetia gave a small smile to Nikolas. 'Thank you.' She turned to Lukas. 'Again, it has been a pleasure.' With that, she turned in a full circle, raising her arms as she did and transforming into a bird. She flew from their sight.

'What's going on?' Nikolas asked, straight up.

'What do you mean?' Lukas said, confused, and still looking after her into the skies, he added in a low voice, 'I don't know.'

CHAPTER 20

Blaine sat back and moaned, placing his napkin on the table and declaring himself stuffed. 'That was delicious. Can we do this regularly?' he asked.

'Absolutely, I love to cook,' Mel said and glanced at Sophie's plate which was hardly touched.

'Me too. We should take turns whipping up a storm,' Blaine said.

'Good, because I hate to cook,' Sophie said. 'You two whip away all you like and I'll happily be the guest who eats. I'll clean up too, just to make the bargain sweeter,' she teased.

'Done!' Mel declared. 'But you haven't really done it justice.'

'Sorry,' Sophie said. 'I'm a little stressed with Nikolas appearing and disappearing earlier, some ex-girlfriend wanting to ensure I'm not on the scene, and now not being able to work with Murdoch.' She sighed and turned the conversation away from her. 'Next time, you should invite Jack.'

'That gorgeous giant of a man,' Blaine said and sighed.

'Really?' Sophie said again, confused.

'So gorgeous,' Mel agreed, and Sophie just shook her head, surprised. No accounting for each other's tastes, she thought.

'Any chance he might favour me?' Blaine asked, pulling his most handsome pose and making the ladies chuckle.

Mel shook her head firmly. 'I've already checked him out and you are out of luck. But he is definitely single. He might have a friend,' she teased Blaine.

'Next dinner party then,' Sophie declared. 'The more the merrier.'

As grateful as she was for the distraction of friends, an hour later, she was showered and in bed, keen to get to Elsopeth's journal. Sophie knew she should start from the beginning, but she didn't have the time or patience. She just wanted to go to the journal entries that might shed light on her current predicament. The last few entries she read were about the first encounter with Murdoch and the gift of flowers, but time dictated Sophie cut straight to the conflict – when Venetia meets Elsopeth.

She gently turned the old and delicate pages until she discovered the lady's name in Elsopeth's journal, and read:

The encounter

June 14, 1744

I have had the most fearful encounter today and now that I have composed myself, bathed and even indulge in a rather large glass of port, I can write of it. There are no words to describe the past three months with the Raven. I have never encountered a love of this kind and I know I never will again. Even my dear mother and spiritual advisers have told me it is a love for its time and that not everyone experiences such a coupling. Imagine if the world did, how would we ever get anything done? I digress.

Today, I was wandering and waiting for Murdoch in the gardens, expecting him after he concluded his business in town, when I turned and was struck to the ground by a woman. She was beautiful, of full figure with green eyes and dark hair, almost feline of nature. She had a familiarity about her; I think she may have been at a dance I attended, but we had never been introduced.

I screamed in fear; I didn't know why she chose to attack me and my cheek was stinging from her imprint. Then I heard the sound of running and Murdoch appeared. I have never seen the Raven angry, not once, but he was formidable. I understood he has, on occasion, harassed the cursed, but that is in his blood, a curse that cannot be changed. I am not the cursed and have done nothing to this woman. Or so I thought.

Murdoch raced to me, assisting me to my feet and with my assurances that I was able to stand unaided, he turned and seized her quite violently, calling her by the name 'Venetia'. To my shock and horror, she threw herself at him like a lover might, crying with the sweet relief of seeing him again. Did she think I had stolen him from her? Before this evening, I did not know she even existed in his world.

I did not stay to see their embrace. I have given my all to Murdoch and today, I find out that he was not mine to take. I fled inside, his voice calling after me, and I heard her threaten me to stay away from him. I no longer feel safe in my own home and will call on the powers to protect me.

I raced to my room and in the looking glass, I saw the angry mark on my face where she attacked me. Behind me, the door opened with gusto and Murdoch stood there, his face a mask of anguish and concern, but I could not look at him. He said my name and came toward me, but I disappeared, faded from sight, as I know I can choose to do or have done when worn with exhaustion or fear.

I was not gone from the room in spirit, only in body. I saw him searching for me, heard him calling my name, and read his heightened emotional state as he ran his hands through his hair as if despairing. I did not reappear, nor do I want to see him again. Eventually, he had no choice but to do the honourable thing and depart from my room. No doubt to return to her.

'Murdoch, you sly dog,' Sophie said aloud, closing the volume. 'So, V, you *are* the jealous type. Well, I'll be ready this time if you intend to come and slap me around a bit.' With that, Sophie put the book on the dresser, intending to read on but unable to keep her eyes open, and secretly hoping Murdoch may appear in her dreams tonight. She missed him, and she had no idea when she might see him again. But he was the Raven and she was the cursed, so he would always be nearby, somewhere, she accepted and oddly, the thought gave her comfort when it should not have.

CHAPTER 21

SOPHIE WOKE WITH A start. She could have sworn she heard her name called but no one was there. She raised herself on her elbows and stilled, looking for movement, listening for a noise, but nothing.

It was the Raven, she knew it.

'Murdoch?' she said his name softly so as not to alert Nikolas, and waited, she was alone.

'Ah, you can't come near me, I was told.' She fell back on the pillow and calmed herself after the jolt of waking. Sophie doubted she would fall back to sleep, but she drifted away sooner than she imagined.

He was here. Sophie saw him before he spoke and he gave her a gentle smile. How she had missed him, not that she wanted to admit that because... she frowned confused, he was Murdoch in the now. He was in his suit, with no tie, his collar open. It was not the Raven of her dreams in all his finery when he seduced Elsopeth. His voice interrupted her thoughts.

'It is the only way I can safely come to you at the moment and we need to talk,' he said.

'Am I dreaming?'

'I am in your dream but I am real. My message is real,' he clarified, hoping she would understand. 'I'm sorry.'

'For what?' she asked, rising from her bed. In this dream, she was wearing what she wore to bed—a pale pink singlet and short set—and not a glorious big ballgown as in her other dreams. She reached for her white satin wrap and slipped it on, feeling somewhat underdressed in his company.

'I am sorry for bringing this drama into your life.'

'Your girlfriend?'

'She's not... she was once, an ancient girlfriend. She slipped in when your protectors were drawing straws to determine who was going to look out for you,' he answered drily. There was no love lost between the Raven and the protectors.

Sophie studied him as he watched her intensely for her reactions. The dream seemed so real she could almost believe he was there in her room. Almost reach out and touch him and then she did. Touching his shoulder, running her hand down his arm and feeling his strength below the fabric. He felt very real. He caught her hand and held it for a moment. Then raised it to his lips. Sophie pulled it away quickly.

'You have a girlfriend.'

'Damn it,' he muttered and lowered his head. 'I don't have a girlfriend, but I have to deal with this.'

Sophie gave a casual shrug as if she were indifferent to it. 'Can't you just get her to slip out the way she slipped in?'

Murdoch's lips twitched into a small smile. 'Were it so simple.'

'Ah, she loves you,' Sophie said, moving to the window and opening the curtain to look out over the gardens which were lit with lamps. Like her garden of yesteryear. That's odd. She quickly looked around to see if Murdoch was still in his suit or wearing his waistcoat and jacket, and he was right behind her. He was still in his modern suit, but the garden... it was confusing.

'I don't believe you are in any danger,' he said. 'I won't allow you to be in any danger, but just give me some time to release her.'

'Break her heart again in this generation and send her away?' Sophie asked, and she saw Murdoch wince at the thought of the duty ahead.

'Do you love her?' Sophie asked.

'Are you asking me as Sophie or as Elsopeth?' He cocked his head to the side like a Raven waiting for her response.

'Does the answer vary?'

'It might.'

Sophie nodded. She and Murdoch had barely touched but to shake hands or share a few smiles when they have had victories on cases. He had overstepped the professional boundary raising her hand to his lips this time. She couldn't deny there had been an energy between them, but the romancing had been Elsopeth and the Raven in her dreams, and even if she was his ancient love, they had not started that journey in this generation. That reminded her of their shared work.

'I want to finish the case.'

'I want you too, as well. But I am sure your protector or Miss Sharpe explained that Venetia is not interested in you as the cursed, only as the Raven's former... partner,' he said, choosing his words carefully. 'If she knows you are one and the same, I don't know what might happen. So, it's not that I don't want to work with you or that I'm ignoring you...'

'You've just got to sort out your love life and professional life,' Sophie summed it up. 'Answer my question, do you still love her?'

'No. I haven't for a very long time, but I don't want to hurt her either,' he said with sincerity. 'We were something to each other once.'

'Of course,' Sophie said, annoyed and pained by Murdoch, the discussion, and Venetia. But she had to admit she liked that he felt respectful towards Venetia. She would want the same were the situation reversed. Then, to her mortification, she felt weepy. Why did she come up against obstructions that prevented her from forming attachments?

What was wrong with her that she couldn't be the one that men like Lukas were chasing and giving up everything for?

Why was she always pushed to the outside? An ex-girlfriend returns, a job beckons, secrets kept from her, safer to keep her wrapped in cotton wool, whatever!

No more.

Murdoch sensed her vulnerability and reached for her hand. Sophie pulled away.

'Best you get to it then. I'll see you sometime in the future on the job,' she said and shut down.

Murdoch stiffened, frowning at her sudden coolness, and his walls came down.

'Why are you angry all of a sudden?'

'I can't imagine. You have been here with me at night, making love to me, or do you deny that?'

He pulled back, frowning, considering his answer.

'Was I just dreaming, and you have no idea what I'm talking about?' she snapped.

Murdoch's lips thinned, his jaw locked, and he asked, 'Did you not enjoy it?'

'Irrelevant. Were you an active participant or was I dreaming?' she demanded.

'Were you forced into it?' he asked again, staying on topic.

'If you were there, you know I wasn't.'

'I have not touched you, Sophie. Not in the now, not in the flesh, not you. But mark my words,' he whispered, 'I have been tempted.'

Sophie's heartbeat quickened, and heat burned her neck. As Elsopeth had described, the desire for Murdoch was strong, incarnate, carnal. But now on hold. She felt as if she had been used, sport for a bit of nocturnal fun. Had he been laughing at her this whole time? Would he just take what he needed when he needed it? She straightened, a fierce and yet wounded look in her eyes.

'You have no obligation to me, Murdoch. As you said, you've never shown any interest in me in this life. Please, don't let me hold you up,' she said and crossed her arms across her body, staring at him in a determined manner.

'That's not what I said.'

'Go, I'm tired. With these interruptions to my sleep, I can't focus during the day. Just go!' she ordered, her voice raised, and feeling Murdoch's glare, she turned her back on him.

She had no idea of how her words pained him, the time he had waited for her, the measured approach he took to be near her. The yearning.

'You do not dismiss me!' he said through clenched teeth.

Sophie turned back to look at him.

'Have you never been rejected, Murdoch?' she asked, but not with kind teasing. Rather, her words were a statement, as if challenged to be the first to control him. 'Were you such a man of power and influence in the past that you could have anything or anyone you wanted? Well, not me.'

Sophie issued her demand again to be left alone, and she felt the rush of savage power that radiated from his body. Anger vibrated from him, his eyes darkened to almost black and for a moment she feared the wrath of the Raven. And then he was gone.

Sophie awoke and yelled out his name.

From nowhere, Nikolas appeared. 'Sophie!' He rushed to her bedside, taking her by the shoulders as she gasped for air, breathing hard and fast. Nikolas looked around.

'Where is he?'

Sophie shook her head, gasping. 'Not here. Dream. Sorry.'

Nikolas ignored her and went to the window, looking out on the grounds; it was calm and still. He went into her ensuite and walk-in robe; they were empty.

'I'm sorry, Nik, I didn't mean to disturb you,' she said, her breathing settling.

'You didn't,' he said and returned to her side. 'Are you sure he wasn't here?'

She nodded. 'It was a dream, but I saw him angry. I saw him as the Raven.'

Nikolas let out a low whistle between clenched teeth and sat again on the edge of her bed, taking her hand.

'Sophie, you need to understand something. The feelings Elsopeth and the Raven had in the past were unhindered except for the occasional disapproving family member and a jealous girlfriend. What I'm saying is that Elsopeth has never been accursed, so their love was never dangerous.' He hesitated.

'Go on,' Sophie said, leaning back on her pillows, allowing him to continue to hold her hand and feeling reassured by his strength and gentleness. He looked into her eyes, saying his words slowly and purposefully.

'This time, the Raven may love you with a timeless passion, but he is also torn by the curse. He is fighting against his instinct not to harm you the whole time he is with you.'

'But he wouldn't,' she said, shaking her head, but not quite as sure of that as she once was. 'He worked with Aunt Daphne for years and she was the cursed. He never harmed her once.'

'He never loved her and his work was only ever for a few hours, daylight hours now and then. They liked each other, but they were wary of each other, always,' Nikolas said. 'It's a case of keeping your friends close and your enemies closer.'

'Can't he suppress or ignore that part of him that makes him the enemy of the curse?' she asked.

'No more than any other being or creature in the animal kingdom can.' Nikolas winced and explained, 'Cats instinctively hunt birds, cats and dogs will hiss, fight and attack, always have, always will. The Raven will watch the accursed and, if provoked, must react.'

Sophie felt overwhelmed with weary despair, her body began to wane and fade.

'Woah, hold up, stay with me here.' He moved in closer. 'I'll leave you to sleep. There are no decisions to be made right now, but promise me you'll stay away from him, at least until we sort this out?'

She unwillingly agreed, and hovering between spirit and flesh, laid back on the bed, closing her eyes until a few minutes later she felt full bodied again. Nikolas was still there.

'I know it is not what you want to hear,' he said softly, 'but the sooner you start breaking away from Murdoch, the better for you, the better for all of us.'

CHAPTER 22

DETECTIVE GERARD OAKLEY PULLED his battered, old red sedan over to the edge of the driveway of Sophie's mansion and pushed open the door on the passenger side. Sophie skipped down the stairs lightly as if she had no problems in the world and slipped into the front passenger seat.

'Good morning to you, young lady,' Gerard said with a grin.

'Good morning, Detective Oakley,' she said teasing him with a formal address. 'Thanks for picking me up. Bet you've picked up quite a few ladies in your day.'

Gerard chuckled. 'When I was a wild young lad, maybe. But these days, I'm reduced to picking up that partner of mine, who may I say, is particularly grumpy at not being able to attend today. Has he asked you out yet?'

'Was he going to?' Sophie played along.

Gerard shook his head. 'You young people, so complex.'

Sophie grinned, and Gerard turned the car out of the drive and headed to Abigail Middleton's house, where they would meet with Abigail and this time her husband, Steve, would be in attendance.

'So, why isn't Muddy available?' Sophie asked, interested to hear the excuse Murdoch gave his partner to avoid her. 'Not that I'm not thrilled to be alone in your company.'

He chuckled again. 'Rightfully so. I'm much better company, yet people say I'm the grumpy one.' He shook his head. 'We've divided up the cases; Murdoch's got to interview a few witnesses that are only available this morning.'

'Good, as long as he's pulling his weight,' she teased. 'So, we've got the hubby along today?'

'Yep, Steve. They were newlywed when the father was murdered twenty years ago in the house the three of them shared. The case was never solved, thought to be bikie related, Murdoch might have mentioned that.'

Sophie nodded. 'Sorry about last time.'

'No apology necessary. You're doing us a favour coming along.'

'Yeah?' she said and eyed him suspiciously.

'Okay, I haven't always thought that way, but I'm coming around.'

Sophie laughed and regarded the detective whom she had come to like and admire as he ran a hand through his mop of grey flecked hair. They neared the familiar neighbourhood.

'I need to go back into that room I was in last time. Is that okay?' she asked feeling a little anxious at encountering the spirit man or whatever that was last time. She also silently prayed that she wasn't startled this time and wouldn't disappear. It would be hard to explain that to Gerard if he was there at the time.

'So back to Steve's den?'

'Yes, please, there was something there. Have they had any other strange things happen since the last visit?'

'Yeah, someone bought the house,' Gerard said and Sophie laughed.

'That is a surprise but there's a buyer for everything, or that's what my cousin always says – he's a real estate agent.'

'Guess so. But yeah, several more attacks – windows broken, messages scrawled about them being murderers. Abigail still thinks there's someone out to get them and stop the sale of the house or revenge them and ensure they don't get what it was worth, but she's got her sale now.'

'Hmm. Just a wild theory and I'm sure you've thought of it yourself, but do you think Steve knows more than he's letting on and doesn't want to sell the house? Could he be doing this without her knowing?' Sophie asked.

'Crossed our minds. But given we've got a body for the father-in-law, I don't know what Steve would be hiding other than a weapon or drug stash, and he could make short work of that.'

'I guess so,' Sophie said as Gerard pulled over to the curb and cut the ignition. She grabbed the clairvoyant-cursed glasses from her handbag and they approached the house, passing the sign with the SOLD sticker on it. Abigail opened the front door and a large man appeared behind her dressed in camouflage army pants with a black t-shirt that stretched across his muscled frame. He looked as if he spent considerable time in the gym and drank a lot of protein shakes. Abigail was wearing cut-off denim shorts and a crop top that showed a wiry frame. Her skin appeared leather-like from years of excess sun.

'Sold it, we did, and for a good price,' she said pointing at the sign in case they missed it. 'Whoever thought they'd scare off our buyers can get stuffed.' She gave a throaty laugh and looked to Steve who joined in, smirking behind her. He barred the entrance to the house.

'I know who you are and I'm not having any psychic nutter in my house,' he said to Sophie and crossed his arms across his chest.

'Nutter? That's harsh,' Sophie said and made Gerard laugh.

'We don't need your help now, we've sold the house,' Abigail said to Gerard and Sophie.

'We're not here by your appointment, Mrs Middleton,' Gerard said as if the police could be summoned on request.

'You advised the police a crime was being committed – it still is from what you told me yesterday, and there's a cold case murder here that might be connected. It's *our* decision when we wrap it up.'

Sophie had slipped the glasses on and was assailed by images around Steve. She was not surprised given his attitude that he'd led a life of thuggery and the images proved the same, but she needed images from 20 years ago when his father-in-law died, or of him doing destruction to the house, if she wanted to prove her own theory. She had to ask questions.

'So, you don't care or want to find out who was writing messages about you being murderers on the walls?' she asked.

'Nuh, we're out of here in a month's time, couldn't care less now,' he said and didn't budge from the doorway entrance. He also didn't let his mind wander and Sophie couldn't get any images of him doing the destruction. Perhaps he didn't.

'Could I see the wall again in your den where the message was written the first time?' she asked.

'I think we're done here,' Steve said.

'We need to see it to close our report,' Gerard told him not concerned by the size of the man. Sophie imagined he'd dealt with Steve's type a thousand times over the years. 'We can do that now, or I can get a warrant, which might delay the settlement of your house sale if that warrant takes a long time to get. Happens,' he warned them.

Sophie gave him a look as if he were a genius, Steve growled beside her and Abigail shrugged.

'Whatever, just let them go in, babe,' she said to Steve, 'then they can get lost.'

Steve narrowed his eyes and moved aside. Gerard nodded to Sophie to go ahead and he moved into the living area with Steve and Abigail. Taking out his notebook, he readied himself to jot down some final details. She heard Steve ask, 'What's she going to do down there?' as she took the stairs to his den, and Gerard replied drily, 'She's not stealing anything so don't worry. She's got her own trophies.'

Sophie chuckled as she entered the dark room, made her way to the window, and pushed open the curtains. Still wearing her glasses, her focus shifted to the nervous tension bubbling inside, her heartbeat loud as a drum. Sophie took a deep, calming breath and looked around, waiting for the apparition from last time to reappear, and then something bumped her from behind.

She fell forward and wheeled around. It was there. A ghost shape, a man. He was small in stature but with a solid build, and had an old-fashioned haircut, the part down the side. His colourings were washy so Sophie couldn't tell his eye or hair colour.

'Who are you, what do you want?' she said taking a step back and bumping into a desk with a large trophy on it. She steadied the trophy and looked up to find the man still there.

'Name's Mike, Abigail's father.'

'You're dead,' she said the obvious and felt stupid for it. 'I don't see dead people usually, maybe a shadow or spirit now and then.' She realised she was rambling and shut up.

'I've heard ghost hunters say I'm strong, got a strong presence, that may be why,' he said. 'Abigail got paid thousands to let them film down here.'

'Yeah?' Sophie said surprised, then remembering herself asked, 'are you strong enough to paint the word "murderer" on the wall and break a few windows?'

He nodded and gave a smile as if he was proud of his efforts. 'That was my work.'

'Why are you still here, Mike?' Sophie asked feeling a little more confident in his company.

'I died right here, 20 years ago,' he said and pointed to the rug. 'Her husband did it.'

'Abigail's husband? Steve?'

'Yeah, I never liked him, told her that too right from the start. He wanted the house and wanted me gone so he could set himself up for life and do what he does best – bloody nothing. He knew Abigail would inherit it.'

'Why now? You've had twenty years,' Sophie asked stating the obvious.

'I don't know to be honest,' he said, just as puzzled. 'Never been a ghost type before and I've been angry and sticking around here, but I think cause he's selling the house—I heard Abigail saying so—I got fired up that he'd never been found out. I had to do something before they moved out and I missed the chance.'

'I understand,' Sophie said.

'Can you help me? I'd appreciate it.' He smiled. 'You're a pretty little thing if you don't mind me saying?'

Sophie laughed. 'Thanks. You're the first ghost to compliment me.' She sobered and said, 'But, I can't get you justice with just your word, I can't prove anything from what a ghost says.' Sophie frowned and held a hand up to halt their conversation on hearing Gerard call from upstairs.

'All okay down there?' he yelled.

'All good. Won't be a moment,' she called back and turned to find Mike gone. 'Mike!' she called in a hushed voice.

'Here,' he said behind her and she wheeled around to see him nearby. Mike pointed to the wall. 'Behind that plaster, you'll find the knife he killed me with and his bloody clothes. I gave them half the house to live in until they could afford their own and he was turning this room into his den. I was helping even though I didn't like the bastard. So, he stuck the knife and clothes in the wall and plastered it that day, before Abigail came home and found me dead. He blamed my bikie friends.'

Sophie gave him a sympathetic look, but she was satisfied. 'That will do the trick,' she said.

He stood looking at her and did not fade. 'Was there something else, Mike? Something that will let you rest?'

He sighed. Sophie didn't know ghosts could sigh given they weren't breathing entities anymore. Truth be known she didn't know much about ghosts at all.

'Got a confession to make.'

Sophie saw his thoughts appear as visions above his head, just like they did with her living clients. 'You've murdered someone?' she whisperedand swallowed nervously.

'Ah, yeah. The wife didn't leave when Abigail was young, she's still here. I buried her in the backyard near the lemon tree and water meter. Guess you better dig her up and give her a decent burial while you're at it.' He gave a small shrug.

Sophie nodded. 'It's the right thing to do. Thanks for sharing. That it?'

'Yeah, haven't killed anybody else. And hey...' he started to fade, 'thanks.'

Sophie smiled at him and watched him completely disappear before raising the glasses and pushing them back on her head. She hoped Mike and his deceased wife would now both be at rest. A good day's work she thought smugly, keen to tell Gerard what she knew and put Steve in his place... in jail! Sophie climbed the stairs and saw all three faces turn to look at her as she re-entered the living area. For their safety, she decided not to tell Gerard anything until they got to the car.

'Thanks for that,' she said to Steve. 'I couldn't get any readings, so I think you're right, a new start will be good.'

He wasn't gracious enough to thank her, but smirked again and said, 'Told you it was a waste of time.'

'We'll close the file then if you don't want to make any more reports?' Gerard asked Abigail and Steve spoke up on her behalf.

'That's it, you can get lost.'

Gerard gave him a less than impressed look. 'Your wife called us, Mr Middleton. Remember that next time you call the police wanting action.'

They made their way to the car and safely once inside Sophie said, 'Don't be too quick to close that file. There's a knife and bloody clothes inside the wall belonging to Steve. He killed his father-in-law, and there's a body in the backyard near the lemon tree and water meter – Abigail's mother. Her father, Mike, admitted to killing her.'

Gerard stared at her for a moment and then swore. 'Screwed family.'

'You can say that again,' Sophie agreed, and Gerard wasted no time getting on the phone, calling for backup, a team to start digging and forensics.

He didn't even ask if she was sure or warn her she better not be wrong. Not this time.

The mood in Detective Murdoch Ashcroft's office was dark. Dangerously dark. The detective sat at his desk, preparing to go interview a few witnesses and he brooded. He couldn't remember the last time he was so angry. Or the last time he had been told to 'Just go' by a lady and then she turned her back on him!

Dismissed!

The nerve of her. Sure, he and Elsopeth had their passionate fights over time but they always ended in passion. His blood boiled and for just a moment, the police headquarters' lights flickered on, off, and on again.

'Damn,' he swore waiting for his laptop to reboot.

He wanted to be there on the case with Sophie this morning, he brought her to it, not bloody Gerard, it was his case. Murdoch wanted to return to her last night and almost did twice but he knew that was dangerous. He knew he wasn't in control, and despite every fibre of his being pulling him back to her, even just to put Sophie in her place, the Raven mastered the desire and stood resolute.

So, she thinks I've been using her.

Coming around for a nightly dalliance while waiting for Venetia to arrive back in my life.

For the love of all that is holy, that's where she's at with me after the trust we've been building?

He stood and walked around the room, stopping to look out his office window, hands buried in the pockets of his dark suit pants. Frustrated, Murdoch didn't focus on anything going on in the street outside his window; the city could have been crumbling at his feet and he would not have noticed.

He conceded he'd been planning and waiting for Sophie for a lot longer than she had known about him, or his significance in her life. He also conceded that her anger might be a good thing... she wouldn't be angry if she wasn't a bit jealous or invested in him. The thought made him smile a little.

What to do now? Wait. Storm the house. Visit her again in a dream.

He groaned. 'Damn, when did it all become so bloody complicated.'

'Something bothering you, Detective?' A soft voice purred behind him.

Murdoch wheeled around. His eyes widened and flared from dark brown to pitch black, and the police headquarters was thrust into complete darkness.

'I'm back,' she whispered, her voice floating across the room like she had reached out and touched him.

The lights kicked in again and the power came back on. The whir of machines re-starting could be heard and people complaining from down the hallway.

'Venetia!' Murdoch said, his voice as deep and dark as his eyes. His back straightened, and he braced, as she stood, cat-like and beautiful just inside his office; he had not heard her enter.

'You are a detective in this life, well done you,' she smiled. 'That's one you haven't been before.'

He read her relaxed state; no sense of attack, no danger and Murdoch exhaled and gave her a small smile. 'I've always been good at discovering things and putting matters to bed.'

'That you have,' she agreed with a raised eyebrow, and she gave a small laugh. 'Missed me?'

Loaded question. He hesitated.

'No? Not even a little bit?' she pouted.

'You are still as beautiful as ever,' he offered.

'Thank you, that's kind, and you look as handsome as I remembered,' she said accepting his compliment graciously.

Murdoch knew her wiles; she had years of practice at accepting flattery, and Venetia knew what men liked to hear.

The desk sergeant stuck his head into Murdoch's office.

'Ah sorry to interrupt, Detective, Miss, just letting you know the electricians are here now. You might want to save whatever you are working on,' he said with a nod to the laptop and a wave as he departed to tell the next office inhabitant.

'Power problems, how quaint,' Venetia teased. 'Been letting off steam again, Murdoch?'

'It hasn't been an easy few days,' he conceded.

Murdoch walked towards her and saw how Venetia's stance changed. She was not as confident as she appeared, he could sense her vulnerability as her eyes widened, her pulse in her neck quickened. He could read her desire for him. Still.

'You're nervous,' he said, taking charge.

She gave a small laugh as if the idea was ridiculous. He smiled in return but it was more of a grimace.

'So why are you back?' Murdoch asked standing close enough to touch her, trying to feel if his body reacted in the way it did with Sophie, but no, Venetia could no longer affect him, despite her beauty.

She raised her chin with defiance as if she would not beg to be taken into his arms.

'Why do you think I'm back?' she said, a hint of annoyance in her voice. 'I have come to see if we have a future in this generation. Perhaps you might want to make good on all those promises of love and protection you offered me in the past.'

Murdoch swallowed. 'Am I to feel guilty for not loving you for generation after generation? Forever is a long time and we had a grand love.'

'I know,' she said, her voice hitching.

'But Venetia,' Murdoch tried to be as gentle as he could be when delivering news that he knew would make her angry, 'our love has had its time. It had a long time ago.'

'If Elsopeth was not around? Is she around?' she asked.

'If she is or isn't, we have run our course. There was a woman a few years ago I might have wed, but she... died.' He offered this piece of himself in the hope it took her focus off Elsopeth.

Venetia looked surprised and then annoyed. 'I am sorry to hear that, but clearly timeless love means nothing to you anymore. Will you just take new lovers every generation?'

'If need be,' he said. 'Until I find—'

'The one,' she cut him off, 'the one you said that I was.'

'Then. Until I find the right one for me now.' He sighed. 'Let's not do this again.'

She stepped back, inhaled and studied him. Then Venetia gave a small shrug. 'It is of no consequence.'

Murdoch laughed. He had not meant to, but it was involuntary given her immediate dismissal.

'Oh good,' he retorted. 'Women are very good at dismissing me at the moment, so I'll do my best to get over it.'

'I've met someone,' she said, ignoring his attempt at feeling sorry for himself.

'Have you now?' Murdoch asked, raising an eyebrow. 'Well, I'm not surprised. You are beautiful and interesting, and any man would be lucky.'

She accepted his compliment with a small nod and smile and continued, 'Someone very much like me, who shares the same interests, who will appreciate the value of time, as I do.' Her hand went to the timepiece hanging around her neck which Murdoch immediately recognised. Venetia walked around his desk, trailing her fingers along it, as Murdoch watched her.

'Do I know him?'

'You do.'

Murdoch groaned. 'Is it mutual?'

She smiled. 'It will be.'

CHAPTER 23

THE ROOM THAT SOPHIE and Jack shared as their joint office was an enormous drawing room, as they would have been called in Elsopeth's day. The ceiling was so high it couldn't be reached with a conventional ladder, the front bay windows were glorious, running full length to the ground and with large deep red drapes on either side held back with gold cords. Cream and gold wallpaper ran down all the walls featuring stripes and roses, and Sophie and Jack's desks were placed so that Sophie was nearer the front and Jack nearer the door, but both could see out at the view of the garden and the steps up to the front of the mansion. Sophie got Jack's attention with a small laugh of surprise.

'Well, I don't know who this man is coming to see amongst the tenants, but not me, I imagine,' she said.

Jack looked out and grinned. 'I suspect it'll be for me.'

They watched as the small, middle-aged man approached carrying a round fishbowl that was three-quarters filled with water and two orange fish swam around inside.

'May I?' Sophie asked and waved her glasses at Jack.

'Sure, go ahead,' he invited her and Sophie put on her glasses to see the man's future as he neared. She could see several images, things that were top of mind to him or of concern. He was on a boat, a large boat with his family and the sea was hellishly rough. His children looked frightened, his wife was holding her stomach, and in the next image, they were all in life jackets. That was all she could see of his future without asking questions. The other images were a jumble of family images that flicked over one another. She removed the glasses as he moved inside the building out of sight and appeared moments later, knocking on the door with his elbow.

'Forgive the interruption,' he said with a friendly smile. 'I was looking for Jack if he's got a moment?'

'Come on in, I'm Jack,' the giant man said standing and offering his hand, then withdrawing it when he saw the man incapable of shaking it while holding the fishbowl. 'This is Sophie,' he said introducing them both.

'Hi, Sophie. Jack, thanks for seeing me.' He placed the fish tank in Jack's hands. 'I'm Ed, I'm taking a trip by sea and I'm hoping to gift this to you.'

'Of course, thank you, I accept your gift,' Jack said and invited him to sit.

Sophie watched with interest, a bemused look on her face. She'd never seen a grifter in action, never seen a grifter at all actually, and wondered if she should be watching.

'Do you need some privacy?' she asked. As the two men sat, the fish tank between them on the desk.

'Not at all, Sophie, but thank you,' Jack said. Besides, this is your office first and foremost, so if you don't mind me working here.'

'No, I'm fascinated,' she said and Ed nodded his head in agreement.

'I'd be lying if I didn't say I'm a little concerned about a water journey I have to make with my family. But I've heard you are the best,' Ed said.

Jack smiled and gave a modest shrug. 'Too kind. So, let's see what we can do for you. How many days are you at sea?'

'Six days. My wife won't fly and we have to take the journey by water to see an ill parent, her mum is not long for this world.'

'I understand,' Jack said. 'You will need to take some water from this fish tank with you. Just pour it into a sealed bottle, that will do the trick.'

Ed nodded. 'I will.'

Jack closed his eyes and placed his hands on the tank as if taking ownership of the gift. He started to say a small verse which Sophie sat forward, straining to hear:

> *'What ship is that upon the sea,*
> *In search of land, a family be,*
> *Let them rise from gentle beds,*
> *Promised safety for the days ahead.'*

'Ed, please accept this gift from me,' Jack the grifter said, and rising re-gifted the fish bowl and its contents to Ed.

'Thank you, I accept your generous gift,' Ed said, and with his sincere thanks, he bid Sophie and Jack farewell, promising not to forget to take the sample of water with him, as he carefully carried the fishbowl and departed.

Sophie hurriedly put her glasses back on and looked at him as he tread down the outside steps. The distressing sea images she had seen were gone and instead, were replaced by images of a family on the deck, the sea calm and the sun upon them. It was the picture of a pleasant journey.

'You've changed their future,' she said in awe, and turned back to face Jack, removing her glasses. 'And so effortlessly.'

'Ah, it might look simple, but there are generations of touch in that one encounter,' he said, pleased at her astonishment.

'Well Jack,' she said with a smile, 'you really are a marvel, in more ways than one.'

Jack laughed, and Miss Sharpe joined them. 'I'm just off the phone and bravo, Sophie, I believe another case has been wrapped up.'

'Oh, they've found the body?' Sophie said clapping her hands in delight. 'Gerard will be pleased.'

Jack frowned. 'Sounds gruesome.'

'A very old cold case,' Sophie assured him.

'Indeed, they have found a body, plus a knife and clothing in the wall. That was my contact in the police department,' Miss Sharpe confided. 'She often rings with a bit of news, and there was a reward for information regarding the disappearance of Abigail's mother all those years ago. You've earned that too. It's not much but will keep us in tea bags.' Looking pleased, Miss Sharpe clasped her hands as if the matter were settled and another job done.

'What a good morning's work for all of us,' Sophie said.

'How did you do it?' Jack asked. 'Did you get the villain to answer the right questions?' He spoke with a touch of drama in his voice and waved a hand around theatrically.

Sophie grinned. 'Actually, I saw a ghost. He told me all about it. I don't usually see ghosts, although in one of my first readings I saw a shadow flitting around that helped me find something the client wanted, but this was a full-bodied ghost.'

'Yes, your aunt could occasionally see the strong ones too, but only if she was wearing the glasses and it was very relevant to the case,' Miss Sharpe added.

'Amazing, and he was quite pleasant, despite having murdered his wife... so I guess he hadn't always been pleasant,' she said, reconsidering her comment. 'Can we break for morning tea?'

'You've got my vote,' Jack said, rising.

As Sophie rose, she noticed Miss Sharpe looking at her intently before leading the way to the kitchen.

'Are you alright, dear? Is Murdoch?' she asked in a low voice. 'I sense you are feeling a little flat.'

Sophie gave a gentle sigh as they all came together to make a pot of tea and Miss Sharpe put some of her recent baking efforts—jam drops—on a plate.

'I was a little hard on Murdoch. Don't worry,' she added hastily, 'he didn't come here in person. He said he wouldn't. But I dismissed him out of hand with the whole Venetia drama. I didn't sleep last night thinking about it and I feel terrible this morning. I have to learn to control my temper or ego, or insecurity... pick any one.'

Jack gave her a smile. 'Ah, you're not the only one, don't worry.'

'Oh, I am sure he has held no affection for Venetia for many, many years.'

'A century or more,' Jack added.

Sophie frowned. 'Everyone knows so much more than I do.'

'When you choose to accept and understand all your history, dear, it will come back to you more readily,' Miss Sharpe said and added almost wistfully, 'sometimes it's nice to be anew and be free of the past.'

'You can choose that?' Sophie asked.

'Of course. Murdoch has done that several times, but once he accepts his role, he remembers his past.'

Sophie looked at the ceiling and spoke to her deceased aunt. 'I'm sorry Aunt Daphne, but I'll get up to speed, I promise.'

Miss Sharpe and Jack chuckled.

'There's no hurry,' Jack said. 'History is not going anywhere.'

'Jack is right. Don't fret, Sophie, dear,' Miss Sharpe said. 'As for Murdoch, I suspect if he was very angry and upset, it's because he's not used to being denied. He has waited for Elsopeth's return most patiently.'

Miss Sharpe's words made Sophie feel even worse for being so heartless.

'He'll calm down as you did, dear, and you can both talk through it, don't fret.' Miss Sharpe patted her hand. 'Look, here's a nice gift for you now.'

Sophie looked up surprised, expecting Miss Sharpe to hand her something, but a voice called from the outside doorway and when they stuck their heads out of the kitchen, a delivery man stood bearing the most enormous bouquet of white and yellow roses.

Alfred saw Lukas approaching and with a glance at his niece, saw the grin she could not contain. Orli couldn't resist teasing her cousin as he entered the *Optical Illusion* store late that morning.

'Here's our model, back from his shoot.'

He cringed at her words. 'Yes, straight from the catwalk,' he responded drily.

'When can we hope to see the photos, lad?' Alfred asked, explaining to a client he was serving that Lukas had just become engaged and had a photo taken this morning to prove it, resulting in the customer profusely offering her congratulations as well.

Lukas thanked her. 'They'll be online this afternoon, apparently,' he said with no enthusiasm.

Suddenly Nikolas appeared, walking up the small path beside their store. He had arrived unconventionally and landed at the back of the store.

'It's Nik,' Orli said, surprised. She moved closer to the gift counter. 'Uncle, let me finish assisting Mrs Waugh. I have the perfect gift box for that figurine.'

Alfred was grateful for the tactful release from his customer and he thanked Mrs Waugh and Orli. He headed to the door and, without saying a word, told Lukas via mind-speak to stay put. A glance at his grandson's frown confirmed he got the message. Alfred exited and closed the door of the *Optical Illusion* store behind him.

'Playing safe with the entry again, Nik?' Alfred greeted him, trying to diffuse the tension that emanated from Nikolas.

'Thought you might have a customer,' he nodded to the lady at the counter inside, 'not to mention that damn curse Orli puts on the glass.' He cut to the chase, 'He's here.'

'Who? The Raven?'

'Yes.'

'Is Venetia?' Alfred asked.

'No.'

'Ah, it's alright. I visited the detective with our suggestion. He might be here to let me know he has spoken with Venetia.'

Both men looked to the opposite side of the road, where Murdoch alighted from his car. He didn't cross the road, waiting for the two men to join him on the footpath under a large maple tree.

'Mr Lens,' he greeted Alfred. He turned to Nikolas. 'Took you long enough to get here,' he stirred him.

'The car metal and glass slow down—' He stopped, realising he shouldn't be admitting that to the Raven.

Murdoch grinned. 'I'll bear that in mind.' He turned to Alfred. 'I've spoken to Venetia. She won't return here now that she has found me. We have agreed that there is no future for us in this generation.'

'Thank you, detective,' Alfred said, exhaling with relief and using Murdoch's professional title. 'I appreciate you dealing with the matter in such a timely manner.'

'Does she know Sophie is both the cursed and Elsopeth?' Nikolas asked, abrupt and tense.

'I didn't mention it nor did she,' Murdoch responded in a contrasting relaxed manner. 'I don't know what the consequences of that will be if any.'

'None of us does as yet,' Alfred agreed. 'But hopefully, if she is not pursuing you, Detective, she won't be concerned with who you see, be it Sophie or anyone else. I hope the decision was mutual and caused neither of you distress.'

Murdoch gave a nod of thanks to the stately older gentleman with impeccable manners. 'Thank you, Mr Lens, apparently it was mutual. She has transferred her affections to someone else, at last.' Alfred could sense Murdoch's relief at not having to go into battle.

'Lukas,' Nikolas muttered under his breath.

Both Alfred and the Raven snapped to look at him.

'—Our Lukas?' Alfred asked.

'—Lukas Lens?' the Raven asked with a glance to the store where he could see Lukas through the windows glaring at him.

'One and the same,' Nikolas said, looking less than pleased.

Alfred watched Murdoch to gauge his reaction. Was there going to be trouble? The young detective didn't look pleased, no one did when their former partner moved on, even if they didn't want the relationship. But Murdoch's countenance gave nothing away.

'Are you okay with that?' Nikolas asked Murdoch.

'I don't have much choice, and she can date whomever she likes,' Murdoch said, looking less than impressed. 'As can I.' Delivering the address directly to Nikolas.

Nikolas bristled and Alfred stepped in.

'Thank you, Detective, for letting me know. It was good of you.'

'No problem, Mr Lens. I have to get back to work,' he said and the men watched as he walked to his car. They were still there when he departed.

'Did you sense Venetia was interested in Lukas when she was in the store?' Nikolas asked.

Alfred shook his head. 'I could sense her attraction to him, it was mutual between them. I try not to read Lukas unless his thoughts invade mine, and I confess I wrote it off as Venetia toying with him, which she does quite skilfully.'

'That she does,' Nikolas agreed.

'Lukas's mind was full of annoyance about his photoshoot with Lucy, although he has been thinking of Venetia's timepiece. How long has it been going on then?' Alfred asked Nikolas.

'It hasn't started. But when she appeared when we were training the other night, they had a connection,' Nikolas said and lowered his voice as if Lukas might overhear even though Lukas's skills were not that good as yet. 'Their heart beats synced.'

Alfred inhaled sharply.

'Should we try and stop it?' Nikolas asked.

'That would only increase their attraction,' Alfred said. 'There is no reason for concern that I can readily think of, but I need to speak with Orli.'

'Except that when Venetia finds love, she finds it for eternity, and Lukas has just got engaged.'

'Except for that,' Alfred agreed and sighed.

CHAPTER 24

Sophie could not help but look at the flowers, again and again. Her eyes drifted to the window in which they sat framed by the curtains, the light of the garden behind them. Yellow and white, Elsopeth's favourites – she remembered that from Elsopeth's diary. And so many, two dozen in total, all long stemmed with their deep green waxy leaves intact. They were breathtaking, and she was drawn to their beauty.

Jack interrupted her train of thought.

'Your client has just arrived, Sophie, and I've narrowed the requests for appointments this month down to twenty for your consideration. Not an easy task.' He puffed out a breath. 'There's everything from "please help me find my missing canary" to a student asking should they study law or dance?'

Sophie laughed at the thought.

'You'll be pleased to know I've eliminated both of those from the list. Once the cold case you've just solved hits the news, we'll get a fresh range of the weird and wonderful,' he said with a chuckle.

'Thank goodness for you, Jack,' Sophie said giving him a smile. 'Miss Sharpe and I would be overwhelmed trying to respond and reject politely.'

'Here's Mr and Mrs Veroni coming up the path now. I don't think they'll be too challenging but you wanted to keep spaces open for Daphne's former clients,' Jack said under his breath.

'I do. They're a nice old couple,' Sophie said watching Mr Veroni offer his arm to Mrs Veroni as they made their way up the stairs, both with white hair and the stoop of the aged. She rose to greet them as they came up the hall, knowing she could make short work of their visit.

'Oh my, those roses! Look at those roses,' Mrs Veroni proclaimed.

'Someone loves you, young lady,' Mr Veroni said teasing Sophie.

'They are apology flowers more than love flowers,' Sophie told them in good humour and invited them to take a seat while Miss Sharpe came from the other room with a cup of tea for the pair, in the manner which she remembered they liked.

'Oh yes, I remember apology flowers,' Mrs Veroni said with a sly glance to her husband. Now I get offered a cup of tea instead.' Lifting the tea cup she received from Miss Sharpe with a small laugh.

'I was keeping the florist in business,' Mr Veroni explained.

'Go on you two,' Sophie laughed and put on her glasses. After helping the couple decide if Mr Veroni would remain in good health for a cruise before they booked it, and if Mrs Veroni would become a great-grandmother before she died or if her grandson was going to date forever, Sophie saw them to the door.

'Come see this,' Jack said beckoning her with excitement as she re-entered the room.

She leaned over his shoulder and gasped. The online news site was splashed with photos of Sophie, the cold case outcome, the arrest of Abigail's husband, Steve Middleton, detective Gerard Oakley at the scene walking a handcuffed Steve to the police car, and a very early and charming wedding photo of Abigail's parents before the murder.

'I feel sorry for poor Abigail. She's been dealt a double blow,' Sophie said sympathetically. 'Oh look.' She pointed to the bottom right side of the screen where a small photo featured Lukas with his arm around Lucy. It was a glamorous couple photo and a heading 'Model engaged'. The pain hit Sophie fast and hard and disappeared just as quickly, time was healing.

She returned to her desk to read both stories, keen to drop into *Optical Illusion* to congratulate and tease Lukas about his model shoot, but she couldn't yet, she promised Nikolas she'd stay away, and she didn't need Nikolas and Murdoch mad at her. As if he heard her thoughts—and she hoped he couldn't—Nikolas appeared in front of her.

'For the love of God,' Sophie said, jumping a foot high in her chair and placing her hand on her heart.

'Sorry,' Nikolas said with a chuckle. 'I'll zoom into the hallway next time and knock on the door.'

'That'd be appreciated,' she said drily. 'What's wrong?'

'Nothing. Why does everyone assume I'm coming to deliver bad news?' He turned and looked over his shoulder. 'Hi, Jack!'

'Hi Nik, all good?'

'Never better.' He turned back to Sophie. 'See, never better. Just thought I'd let you know that the Raven has spoken with Venetia and you are out of danger. She's not interested in him.'

'Is that so?' Sophie asked surprised and then felt sorry for poor Murdoch. 'He's not having a good week, is he?'

Nikolas chuckled and saw the flowers.

'Wow, who are they from?' Then he frowned and added quickly, 'don't tell me the Raven sent them.'

She nodded and said, 'The Raven sent them.'

He shook his head. 'Remember my warning.'

Sophie gave him a salute. 'So can I go visit the *Optical Illusion* store now and do some reading and congratulate Lukas?'

'Permission granted,' Nikolas said, 'but be cautious.'

'Why?' she asked, frustrated that more barriers were being put in front of her.

'Because Venetia seems to be fascinated with Lukas and his timekeeping skills, and even if she's not interested in the Raven, there's no need to flaunt yourself in front of her.' He lowered his voice. 'We don't think she knows that the cursed and Elsopeth are the same and trust me, there's no love lost between the two historically.'

'You talk about me as if I'm not one of them, like I'm not here,' Sophie scolded him.

'You are very much here. I am not,' he said with a smile and vanished.

'Men,' she said and rolled her eyes, getting a chuckle from Jack. So, she was 'free' again. She knew she should thank the Raven for his flowers, manners dictated it, and it gave her a good excuse to make contact. Sophie swallowed her pride, and ignoring Nikolas's warning, she picked up her phone and messaged Murdoch. And then she waited.

'Looks like I'm the star of the station,' Detective Gerard Oakley said to his partner as he gloated over the photos online.

Murdoch smirked at him. 'All hail you,' he joked.

Gerard laughed. 'Tell you what, she's good your young lady, isn't she?'

'She's not mine,' Murdoch answered too quickly, too abruptly, and Gerard held up his hands in surrender.

'It's not for lack of trying,' Gerard said, 'I've given you my best dating advice. She really does have a gift thought. We'd never have solved that. The drop-kick son-in-law would have got away with murder and poor old Abigail's mum would have remained buried in that backyard until someone decided to renovate.'

'That'd be a grisly find if all you wanted was an inground pool to take a dip,' Murdoch agreed. His phone pinged with a message and against every fibre in his being, he didn't grab it as much as he had wanted to, hoping it was from Sophie and hating himself for hoping it was from her. He casually reached for it and felt a rush of relief as her name appeared. Feeling Gerard's eyes on him, he looked up and said, 'So you want to know what I found out in my interviews?'

'Can you tell me over lunch? Solving that cold case has left me starving,' Gerard said and chuckled at his own humour.

Murdoch nodded, distracted. 'Sure.'

'Give me a minute to check messages and we can go grab a pub lunch,' Gerard said. 'In the old days, you'd get messages delivered on a piece of paper by the sergeant. Now, the bloody inbox is full of crap.'

Murdoch had heard it all before and he ignored his partner as he unlocked his phone and thumbed to read the message from Sophie.

'Thank you for the beautiful roses, they are breathtaking. I'm sorry about last night. I overreacted. Sophie x.'

He looked at the 'x' for a kiss. Does she put that in all her messages? He stared at the phone, an uneasy feeling welling inside him. Murdoch had waited all night and day for a message from her and it had weakened him. Now, the anger swelled inside him; the ball was back in his court and he didn't like being played. Elsopeth would never have done that; it's the actress in Sophie. The thing he least liked about the Elsopeth of this generation – her dramatics. For years he had worked successfully with Sophie's Aunt Daphne, keeping the cursed near but never having his wrath stirred. She was a good person, well-meaning, and she willingly helped him, even liked him. But Sophie was not her aunt.

He did not intend to tell Sophie, but Murdoch had gone to some of Sophie's theatre productions when Daphne had told him of them. He sat in the back and watched her on stage. She was okay, not the best, not the worst, but had she asked for his thoughts, he would have told her she was the shining light on the stage. It made him think of Elsopeth when she took up painting and was rather terrible at it, but he would never have told her that. He smiled at the thought.

But Sophie loved the drama. Is that why she asked him—the Raven—to protect her? Did she do it for effect? To shock everyone and to give her centre stage? She accused him of using her but was Sophie using him, toying with him? His rage burnt, eyes flared black, and the lights flickered.

'Bloody hell, not again,' Gerard said as his computer went to black and then whirred back to life. 'Forget it, let's go to lunch.'

Murdoch stood, grabbed his coat and followed his partner out. The sooner he got out of the building and distracted his mind, the better. Tonight, he knew what he needed to do. He had to catch up with his own kind. He had to put some distance between himself and Sophie, at least until he could control his anger and whatever the result of that might be.

Alfred Lens looked up from putting away the store's most valuable items before locking up for the evening. He saw Lucy approaching.

'Ah, here's your lovely fiancée,' Alfred said to his grandson. He watched the young woman crossing the road. She was beautiful and still wearing the make-up from the model shoot today, but Alfred sensed all was not well with Lukas. He didn't believe Lucy was the one for the lad, but he would never interfere or say so. Who was he to talk of love? Since his wife had passed—Lukas's grandmother—he had not dated once, and Miss Sharpe had been the one that got away. Perhaps if he had tried harder, not been so noble, convinced Miss Sharpe...

The little bell rang over the door and Lucy entered, her eyes seeking Lukas and then Alfred.

'My, don't you look lovely,' Alfred said and Lucy laughed.

'Thank you, Alfred, but you always say that.'

'It must always be true then,' he said and Lukas shook his head at his grandfather.

'He'd charm the birds out of the trees,' Lukas said, rising to greet and kiss her.

'Did you see our story?' Lucy asked Lukas.

'No, is it up?'

Lucy rolled her eyes at him as if it were the most important event of the day and in her world it was. She grabbed her phone, opened the news site that took the photo and showed him.

Orli appeared from the backroom where she too had been preparing to depart, and waving her iPad and greeting Lucy at the same time, exclaimed, 'I have it.' She joined her Uncle Alfred to show him the images.

'Well, that's absolutely lovely,' Alfred said studying the photos and looking at his handsome grandson with pride. 'I'm going to order that photo and frame it. We'll make a model of you yet, lad.'

Lukas groaned, embarrassed by the images. 'I look ridiculous.'

'You do not,' Orli scolded him. 'I wouldn't be surprised if we lost you to the modelling world now.'

'At least he has a career to fall back on,' Alfred said to his niece.

'You two are hilarious,' Lukas said drily and chose to ignore them.

'But look at this,' Lucy said steering him back to the front page. 'Sophie's cold case is the main story.'

Lukas stood straighter with interest and returning to his work area reached for his laptop. 'I've got to see this, wow!' He sat and logged in, oblivious to the displeasure of his fiancée but Alfred could sense it. He and Orli exchanged a glance and resumed their locking up duties, preparing to leave the young couple alone.

'This is amazing. She not only solved the cold case but one they didn't even know about. Wow... the house was sold. Imagine buying that not knowing you had a dead body in the backyard.' He looked up at his grandfather. 'And she solved the case with Detective Oakley, not Murdoch,' he said pointedly.

'Good,' Alfred agreed.

'You're missing the point,' Lucy said and impatiently drummed her fingers on the countertop.

'Am I?' Lukas frowned. 'Sorry, what's the point?'

'Look at the size of Sophie's story and our story. Hers is an old case that no one gives a hoot about.'

Lukas gave a small shrug. 'True crime is pretty popular right now from what I've read, and no one knows me from a bar of soap.'

'But I have over 30,000 followers who would click on this link to read our story and that increases the newspaper hits, but look where they've stuck us!'

Alfred cleared his throat to get their attention.

'Well, I'll be leaving for the evening. Lovely to see you again, Lucy. Lukas will you lock up?' he asked not waiting for Lukas's reply. Orli joined him.

'I'm off too. See you both soon,' she said and exchanged air kisses with Lucy.

Alfred debated whether to send Lukas a message or not and decided to do it regardless of whether his grandson saw it as interfering. He channelled his thoughts.

'Might be best not to praise Sophie, lad,' he transmitted and saw Lukas look up at him and give a small nod of understanding. All was not well with the pair and Alfred knew it was only a matter of time before something had to give.

CHAPTER 25

LUKAS LIFTED HIS GAME. 'Well, despite me being in the photo, you look beautiful; at least no one will notice me next to you,' he joked.

Lucy smiled at him and shook her head. 'Don't be crazy, we both look great... the photographer is one of the best.' Lucy cocked her head to the side as she studied the picture with affection. 'Orli is right you know, you could model if you wanted to get into it. Wouldn't it be amazing if we modelled together as a couple? It could be our thing, and raise our profiles.'

Lukas grimaced at the thought and closed the laptop in front of him.

'You're the model in the family, I couldn't do it. I like to work with fine machinery – the watches, the clocks, restore life to history and maintain it.'

She turned up her nose. 'Those stuffy old things. I would have thought you'd be bored stiff looking at the inside of a watch all day, especially when every piece is like the other.'

'But they're not. I just had in the most glorious—' He stopped, Lucy didn't care, why bother telling her. 'Anyway, let's see how many new followers this brings you,' he said moving back into Lucy's world.

They spoke for a while longer, and then Lukas saw Lucy to the door and locked it behind her. She made the excuse of catching up with a girlfriend tonight; he knew it wasn't true. His reaction to their photos and Sophie's story had disappointed her, again. Lukas had been good at that of late, and he had increasingly become aware that their initial attraction to each other had masked the fact they had little in common or saw life in the same way.

Lukas also knew her ex-boyfriend was back on the scene and that Lucy had considered a life with him. He could smell the deceit on her as clearly as her perfume. His grandfather, Alfred, had powerful skills, several of which Lukas envied, but this was a skill unique to Lukas. As well as hearing heartbeats in sync with his timepieces, he could smell deceit and fear, and several other human reactions, and Lucy reeked of it. He'd been foolish, he knew it. The thought that she might leave, made him want her and need her more, and propose long before he was ready to do so to keep her happy. But it was a false front, like a storm that blows in but does little than rattle the windowpanes and leaves without its promised rain. In his heart of hearts, Lukas knew this wasn't the real thing. But what to do now?

If he was honest with himself, he would acknowledge his own interests were distracted by another. Lukas had thought about Venetia a thousand times since he saw her at Nikolas's house. He felt her loss when she left, her timepiece's ticking fading away and her heartbeat falling out of sync with his. It felt as if he had lost a little bit of himself; Lukas was yet to fully understand it.

A sharp rap on the glass-framed door gave Lukas a start, and he looked up in annoyance especially since the closed sign was evident. A smile lit his face.

Sophie.

Opening the door, she hurried inside, her blonde hair free and wavy, her eyes full of life. He missed her.

'Hey you,' she said. 'Don't worry, I saw Lucy was here and waited until she drove off.'

Lukas breathed easier. 'Sorry about that.'

'It's not your fault. You look like you've had a hard day, everything okay?'

'Sure.' He gave a small shrug. 'Got time to have a drink with me? I've got a cold Sav out the back'

'Twist my arm. Pour away,' Sophie said, and followed him to the back room, taking a seat while Lukas poured them both a glass of wine. They clinked glasses, had a sip and then Sophie asked, 'So, were you happy with the shoot?'

He appreciated she didn't give him a hard time about it; besides, there were friends he hadn't spoken to yet who were bound to stir him, not to mention Nikolas, Jack, and anyone else he was yet to encounter.

'I hated every minute,' Lukas stated outright. She didn't laugh as expected, but gave a solemn nod.

'I get that. It's funny, I loved being on stage and acting, but when I had to pose for photos, I was so wooden and I had this frozen smile thing going on.' Sophie tried to imitate the look, making them both laugh. 'It's a skill, and Lucy is very good at it.'

He nodded. 'Grandpa will be sorry he missed you.'

'He's not upstairs?'

'No. It's his bridge card night. They're a bunch of card sharks, you wouldn't want to take them on.' He shuddered at the thought with exaggerated dramatics.

Sophie laughed and relaxed, breathing out with a small sigh. 'So, we're safe again. I hear Venetia has lost interest in the Raven.'

'Who told you that?' he asked a bit too quickly and then tried to mask his reaction with a casual shrug. 'I was hoping to tell you in person about the engagement and to be careful coming here.'

'Nik told me. The Raven told him.'

'Oh yeah, the Raven came here to tell Grandpa and Nik arrived, sensing him.' He cleared his throat. 'Can I ask you something, you don't have to tell me if you don't want to, but I figure your loyalties might have changed...'

'Sure, ask away,' Sophie said and took a sip of her wine as if to fortify herself for the question.

'I know Lucy's ex is back on the scene. I know she was thinking about going back to him...'

'Did she tell you that?' Sophie asked, surprised.

'No. But I knew she was seeing him at the same time as me.'

'How?'

He waved his hand casually. 'It's a thing I can sense.'

Sophie grimaced and he grinned. 'Yeah, makes it tough for future partners if they are thinking of having a bit on the side. I just wondered if she spoke with you about her decision to choose me?' he asked and sat back, toying with the wine glass in his hand.

'It was why we fell out,' Sophie said. 'Lucy told me Anders was back and, with their long history, she had to consider if it was worth another try. But she couldn't decide and insisted I read her and tell her.'

Lukas gave a surprised grunt. 'But you saw us together from the start, at your first reading... you told me.'

'I did. But I wouldn't read her because as I told her, all I would see is who she chose, not who might be best for her. But she insisted I could see ahead what life would be like with her choice. I didn't think I should do that.'

'Makes sense. So why did you fall out?'

'She didn't care about any of my reasons or warnings, she wanted me to tell her anyway,' Sophie said and gave a small shrug. 'Lucy booked an appointment under a false name and when she arrived, insisted on the reading.'

Lukas shook his head. 'Wow, that's full-on.'

'You bet. And then the weirdest thing happened. I could tell her in all honesty what I saw because I couldn't see anything! All the men in her images were blurred – you, Blaine, Anders, anyone male.'

'Ah, a forced reading reaction.'

Sophie nodded. 'You know about that? That's what Miss Sharpe said too. That under duress, the cursed can't read or provide the information. I bet that's helped and harmed in the past in equal measure, especially if my ancestors were predicting for royalty or powerful figures in military times.'

Lukas sipped his wine and sat thinking, eyes narrowed. He realised Sophie was studying him. At least she didn't have her glasses on.

'You're wondering if you really did go ahead and marry Lucy, aren't you?' she asked.

Lukas nodded. 'Don't worry, I won't force you to answer,' he said with a laugh.

'I could try. At least I won't be influencing your choice since there's only Lucy.'

He looked away. That wasn't quite true and if she could read his thoughts, Sophie would know there was someone else. But he softened and looked at her with affection. 'Thanks. I appreciate that you'd even try, but no, I'll sort it out. What about you? Is there anyone of interest in your love scene? I hear Jack is sharing your office space.'

'Jack is so lovely and Mel is making cow eyes at him,' Sophie said and smiled. 'That would be a great match.'

'Wow, didn't see that coming. And Murdoch?' Lukas asked and saw Sophie stiffen, a mask dropped over her thoughts and features.

'It's complicated.'

'It always is with the Raven,' Lukas agreed.

'When was the last time the Raven actually hurt a cursed descendant?'

'I know that one,' Lukas said and grinned like he had passed a test. Sophie laughed.

'There were two incidents,' Lukas continued. 'One was about 200 years ago and wasn't a surprise. The cursed was male and arrogant, and so was the Raven. No surprises that it wouldn't end well.'

'Did the Raven kill him?' Sophie asked, surprised.

'Yes, and sadly the protector too. Nasty business.'

Sophie gasped. 'I never really thought it would go that far or that you or Nik would be in any real danger,' she said, her blood chilling at the thought.

'It's rare these days. Most times it feels like we are all dealing with a hangover curse from a time gone by, but still, you don't want to play with fire,' Lukas said. 'The only other time after that, and the last time it happened, was a different Raven and a different cursed... a female. She survived. They all did; it was about 150 years ago. I'll photocopy it for you and you can read the account tonight.'

Not long after, Lukas saw Sophie out the door, the journal pages tucked under her arm. It was like old times; he had missed her coming around and had told her so. Now alone, Lukas decided he would do what he needed to do, what had been pulling at his insides all day. He wanted to visit Venetia and feel his heart sync with hers again.

As darkness fell, Murdoch could not lodge the feeling of disquiet in his chest. This was a new sensation to him, a dark feeling he hadn't experienced before, or at least for as long as he could remember. He wanted Sophie, he wanted to call her, see her, message her... anything just to see Sophie's face, read her name or hear her voice. The need to touch her almost overwhelmed him, but no sooner had he started that train of thought—and making love to her was never far from his mind these days—a wave of swelling anger beset him.

Why?

So they'd fought... but it was more than that, he knew it. She, the cursed, had dismissed him. Had she asked to be alone or for time out, or said she was not well, it might be different, but to tell him to go as if he was at her beck and call... the cursed does not get to do that. Anger flared again.

He needed to visit his kin. He left work and drove to where he would be accepted for who he really was amongst his blood relatives. It had been well over five months or more since Murdoch had been to his brother's home at the birds' nest – the affectionate name the family gave to the large house surrounded by trees in the leafy suburb of Mount Hope.

The street backed onto a reserve, like the protector's home, but Nikolas had remained rural so he could run when he needed to shift form. Murdoch's clan did not need to do that, they weren't wild animals, although no one had ever tamed a Raven.

His brother's home at Mount Hope sat in a green belt – the homes had become smaller, the block size reduced and the suburb more crowded, but the large trees surrounding the house created the perfect feel of the home being a birds' nest.

Allanon Ashcroft came out on the front stairs, recognising his brother's car. A smile spread across his face, he raised a hand in greeting and then ran it through his dark hair. The resemblance was striking, although younger, Allanon was bigger in build than his brother. Beside Allanon, two cousins—twins, Jordan and Joshua—appeared, crossing their arms across their chests like bouncers. They were lodgers that never seemed to move out despite all encouragement. Murdoch grinned at seeing his family; it had been too long.

Before he could greet his brother and cousins, Murdoch was assailed by his two young nephews and a niece, Allanon's wife, and the cousins' girlfriends. There was much berating for the length of time between visits, hugging, holding and telling him how handsome and drawn he looked. Allanon rolled his eyes, eventually rescuing his elder brother of two years.

'You'll stay for dinner,' he said, as if it were an order. 'Lose the coat and tie.'

Murdoch opened the car door and threw his coat on the seat, followed by his tie. He rolled up his sleeves and appeared more relaxed.

'Come on then, let's have a drink,' his brother said, clasping Murdoch's shoulder. 'Let me read your head.'

'Have the night off,' Murdoch told his counsellor brother. 'I'm here just to be with kin.'

He saw Allanon did not look convinced and then his brother said in a low voice so only Murdoch could hear, 'you have raw energy coming off you in waves.'

Murdoch avoided eye contact and followed Allanon to the firepit at the back of the property where it was cool and dark, the exterior surrounded by tall trees and the sound of the city far away. The flames burning in the pit and a wan moon were the only sources of light. He sat on one of the timber logs near the fire and accepted a beer; in the company of the men, Murdoch relaxed.

'You look fit enough,' Jordan said, giving Murdoch a chin-up movement. 'Doing some exercise then?'

'Running, crunches, that's about it,' Murdoch said.

'How many crunches?' Joshua asked.

'Not as many as you,' Murdoch said drily, looking at his beefed-up cousins and getting a laugh from the men.

'What's up, big brother?' Allanon cut to the chase. 'You haven't been to the birds' house since Christmas. Anger is radiating from you.' Allanon made a snatching motion in the air and a small spark sizzled and died.

Murdoch frowned. 'Sorry, I don't mean to bring my work home.'

'You don't need to be sorry. You're safe here in the family nest, and I'm guessing it's not work that's got you riled up.' Murdoch felt his brother's hand on his shoulder again and resisted brushing it off. Murdoch was the elder and had always been the strongest, but Allanon was his match physically these days. He was not, however, connected to the curse that Murdoch had inherited by birthright as the eldest.

'It's her, isn't it?' Jordan asked, his voice low and curious, with a hint of a sneer. 'The cursed woman.'

'Sophie is not just a cursed woman,' Murdoch snapped, his eyes blackened momentarily; his fierce expression was dark and raw.

'Holy crap, I'd heard that happened but never seen it,' Joshua said, leaning back a bit on his log seat as if Murdoch was about to shoot daggers his way.

Murdoch self-consciously ran a hand across his eyes and straightened, looking away. He heard his brother tell his cousins to leave them for a moment, and the two young men did, reluctantly. He could feel Allanon's eyes searching him.

Murdoch leaned forward, his elbow on his knees, cradling his beer. 'Something's going on. I'm not in complete control.'

'I know. I can sense it. It's unlike you... you're usually so put together.'

Murdoch nodded. His shoulders, his expression, his jaw, everything tightened.

'Tell me everything from the start,' Allanon said, 'and don't worry, you can't do any damage here.'

Murdoch hoped that was true.

CHAPTER 26

LUKAS WAS NOT ONE for being out late at night; it was not instinctive to his nature but tonight he felt quite at home, even pleased to be by the waterside, with the lighthouse nearby sending its beacon of light across the sea and the nearby hotel with its enormous clock tower. Dressed in a pale grey suit that he had worn to work that day, it was a warm night, not requiring a jacket, but he was grateful for it nevertheless as he felt the cool breeze coming off the water.

Lukas could not explain this attraction to Venetia, or the need to see her tonight but he was on his way to where she stayed. He walked along the lit path towards the hotel, offering a greeting now and then to the evening walkers or young lovers wanting their space and privacy and having no place of their own to go to.

Then he felt it, his heartbeat quickened, changed and fell into step again. It startled him for a moment like he was having irregular heart rhythms. It was Venetia's watch, she was nearby.

Lukas stopped and looked around and saw a woman at the end of the jetty. Her dark hair moved gently in the breeze, she was beautiful in a light flowing white dress, looking out to sea like Neptune's angel. He smiled, remembering the same name given to the women carved of wood that graced the front of ships.

She must have felt the connection and turned suddenly, looking straight at him. Lukas smiled and raised a hand, relieved she looked pleased to see him. He waved her to stay there and increased his stride to reach her side, entering the jetty and walking hastily towards the end to meet her. Lukas could not remember the last time he felt such a rush and desire to be near a woman, in truth, he never had.

'You came,' she said and extended both hands to him. He took them in his instinctively.

He drew her closer, looking into her distinct green eyes and felt a sense of relief at being by her side, as if he was where he should be.

'What is this?' Lukas asked, his voice low.

'I don't know,' she said and smiled at him. 'Maybe love. A timeless love.'

Sophie prepared for her nightly read, opening the photocopied pages Lukas had given her and admiring the old handwriting, she began to read:

The history of the glasses

An entry by Hannah Shelby. Written on this day of 24 September, 1879.

This tale does not end well, but fear not, dear future reader, I and my protector are safe, but take this as a warning. I have angered the Raven and paid the price. 'Tis my own doing and if I had not overstepped my mark, I would not have put myself or my dear protector at risk.

I will say in my own defence that it was an error born of naivety more so than intent. I have recently come out into society and attended several balls amongst our intimate circle. Some of the young women gossip terribly and the men seem to be either rakes of the worst order, awkward and unable to converse, or very flirtatious. At one such ball, while standing with several ladies who also were introduced to society at the same time as me, one of them pointed out a most sophisticated and beautiful lady. I was surprised to find she was not yet wed, as she would have been five-and-twenty or more. Her name was Miss Venetia Cawthorn.

No one could compare. She was beautiful, sophisticated, and elegant, and I was in awe of her. And then I saw him, the Raven, and so did she. He came straight to her side as if she were there with him all along. They were beautiful together; you should have seen how they moved when dancing as if they were one. I was not the only one staring at them.

But not long into the evening, another young lady arrived who was also new to society this year. Oh my, I felt quite dowdy in her company, but she was introduced to my circle of friends and was most charming. Miss Elsopeth Rayne was her name and there were whispers that she was... well not cursed like me or from a witch like the Raven, but that she was not completely from our world, that she was half spirit, half human. Silly really, but to see her, you would understand. She had this ethereal quality to her and then my friend nudged me and pointed out the Raven. It was like Miss Cawthorn was no longer in the room, and the Raven and Miss Rayne could not tear their gaze from each other.

Even if he is the enemy of my line, the Raven was the most beautiful man present and we girls retired to supper, speaking of them in silly whispers and giggles, of how romantic it was and how beautiful they were together. I did not realise that Miss Cawthorn had soon arrived behind us when I joined in the frivolity, and we offended her with our idle gossip. She knew who I was and that the Raven was my enemy, and perhaps as I was the only lady whom she knew in my party, she sought to punish me for our indiscretions.

Today on my walk, the Raven appeared. I got such a fright. He was there in front of me all of a sudden and I barely had time to cry out before he became a murder of crows, all flying at me. In between my cries, I begged forgiveness for my indiscretion, but still, their black wings beat against me, their becks pecked at my head, through my bonnet and drew blood threw my gloved hands. Such fear I have not known and while it seemed to last forever, my beloved protector appeared, sheltering me. The ravens dispersed and my protector saw me home.

I was bloodied, scratched and bruised, but fortunate to be standing and to have not lost my sight or use of limbs. It was a hard lesson to learn, and a mistake I won't make again. I just hope

that was punishment enough and he won't seek
to harm me again.

Sophie put the article on her bedside table and lowered herself amongst her blanket and pillows. It was frightening, she couldn't imagine the attack of such wild birds and it made her a little more fearful of Murdoch. Could he do that to her? Would he?

She recognised the name of the cursed writer, Hannah Shelby, the author of the diary entry, and one of her Great-Aunt Daphne Shelby's relations. Sophie picked up her phone and checked her messages again.

Why hadn't Murdoch responded to the message thanking him for the flowers? She mused. *Was he still angry* about *being sent* away, *or was he teaching me a lesson in his own way?*

CHAPTER 27

MURDOCH WOKE UP WITH a start and quickly looked around. In his professional life, as a detective, it didn't pay to wake up in strange surroundings, nothing good ever came of that.

'It's okay, you're home,' Allanon said in a quiet voice. Murdoch could just make out his brother's silhouette in the dark, sitting in a winged-back chair near the window. Murdoch threw off the blanket that had been placed over him, swung his legs off the couch, and sat up with a groan.

'I'm great company,' he said, running his hands through his hair and Allanon laughed.

'You're exhausted.'

'I didn't mean to keep you awake,' Murdoch said. He rubbed a hand over his unshaven face.

'I'm a light sleeper.'

Murdoch glanced at his brother, and Allanon smiled. 'And I wanted to make sure you were okay. Occupational hazard.'

'How many of your patients spend the night on your couch?' Murdoch asked and Allanon chuckled again.

'Only the special ones. I've given your predicament some thought.'

'Thanks. Did you come up with a solution?' Murdoch asked, sitting back, and wincing as Allanon opened the curtain behind him, letting in the morning light.

'Maybe. You have loved Elsopeth for as long as I can remember, and now Sophie as her reincarnation. Understandably, there are some teething problems that come with every generation. Remember Grandma's iron?'

Murdoch took a minute to catch up and then laughed.

Allanon continued, 'Grandfather would not let her avail herself of a steam iron because water and electricity together do not mix.' Using his grandfather's stern voice. 'Grandma had her work cut out bringing him along into a new century.' He smiled with a shake of his head.

'I miss them,' Murdoch said, uncommonly sentimental.

'Me too. My thoughts...' Allanon gathered a breath to continue.

'Am I paying for this session?' Murdoch said in jest.

'One way or another,' Allanon assured him with a smile.

'Go ahead, Anon.' Murdoch used his brother's nickname. Allanon could not abide by any other shorter version of his name.

'Brother, there are people who would give their life to have one great love, and you have found that. As have I, and we know how hard that is to find. So, you need to work together to know your boundaries now, in this time, in this generation. But I accept you are worried while you do so, your Raven side may overtake you and as she is the accursed, you might lose control and harm her.'

Murdoch nodded. 'I can feel it in here,' he rubbed his chest, 'stronger than it has ever been for any other of the accursed, well... for some time, anyway.'

'Find a potion maker. Someone who can quell the fire until you and Sophie find your boundaries. It won't take away your powers, just still them until you feel in control again.'

Murdoch looked at his brother as if the idea was preposterous, but Allanon did not speak, allowing Murdoch to work through the idea in his head. After a minute or two, Murdoch said, 'It may just work. I actually know a potion maker, she lives with Sophie, if I can get to her without Sophie's knowledge.'

Allanon nodded. 'No, I will go... a twofold mission. I will visit the potion maker and see if she can assist us, and I will pay your beloved a visit.'

Murdoch went to protest and Allanon held up his hand, asking for his patience and continued, 'I will explain to Sophie your concern, how she might consider adapting in the modern time if she wishes to see you, and that you will be in touch once you feel under control.'

Murdoch frowned.

'I assure you, Brother, I will be the master of diplomacy,' Allanon said with a smile and a roll of his eyes as if he had to convince his older brother that he was all grown up.

Murdoch smiled. 'I've no doubt you will be, you have a lot more experience with people than I do. I tend to only see them at their worse times. But you might encounter the wolf.'

'Why? Who is the protector this time around?' Allanon asked.

'Nikolas Saggers.'

'Is that so? The accountant's nephew,' Allanon said with interest. 'Don't worry, his dog smell only affects you, not me. But speaking of that, one small matter...'

Murdoch braced. 'Mm?'

'The kids want a dog or cat. Every day, day after day, the same request. A pet is good for a family,' Allanon said.

'Then get one, of course. Why have you not before?' Murdoch asked but he knew the answer.

'I know you will react to each other. Until now, I've told the kids you are allergic and that Uncle Murdoch couldn't visit if we had a pet, but given you come around so seldomly,' he hurriedly added, 'but don't let that be an excuse for not coming around!'

'Thanks, you're a good brother as brothers go,' Murdoch teased him. 'Get the kids a pet, but do me a favour? Make it a small dog if you go that way. At least I won't be hunted then.'

'Done,' Allanon agreed. 'I've got a spare razor, I imagine work beckons.'

As the brothers rose, Murdoch added, 'Anon. Thanks.'

'For you, my brother, anything.'

The pain in her chest—or was it in her heart—annoyed Sophie as much as Murdoch's avoidance of her. After all, they had been through already in such a short time... solving cases together, his history with her aunt, favours done, the time spent in each other's company, and their two intimate nights in the dream world together, he was going to be this petty? And for how long?

No!

Sophie wasn't always the first to admit she was in the wrong, but she had overreacted out of jealousy or embarrassment or both. But if Murdoch thinks being the moody stand-off type is going to work with her, he's got another thing coming. Or worse still, if he was the type who deserted every time the going got tough, then she definitely didn't have any time for him, even if it was sensible to keep your enemies close.

Feeling better and stronger for her stance, Sophie rose, showered and donned a red fitted dress. She slipped nude heels on her feet and felt better already with her fresh appearance. Next, to check her daily calendar with Jack and Miss Sharpe and as soon as time permitted, Sophie intended to visit the detective at the police station and deal with the matter head-on, so to speak. And hopefully the earlier the better.

Dressed and ready for work, Sophie entered the kitchen to make a coffee; Mel bound in after her.

'Morning. What is going on? It's so very quiet around here,' Mel said.

'It's early... no one has arrived at work yet,' Sophie pointed out the obvious and Mel laughed.

'Not that kind of quiet... magic quiet. I haven't sensed a presence here for a couple of days. I hope I'm not losing it,' Mel pondered. 'Is Murdoch away?' She sidled a mug next to Sophie's on the counter.

Sophie drew a sharp breath at the mention of his name. Damn him that he could cause her this much pain. 'He's mad at me, so he's brooding. He does that very well.'

'It does suit him,' Mel agreed. 'No Nikolas either?'

'Well, there's no call for Nik to come unless it's the monthly accounts meeting, which we don't need either, but I think he likes to get out of the office, and Miss Sharpe makes him lemon cakes.'

Mel laughed. 'He's lovely.' She looked coyly at Sophie. 'You two would look great together.'

'Hmm, protector and cursed romances are not uncommon, apparently.' She did not elaborate but studied her housemate as Mel took over making them both a coffee. 'You're up and at it early, working on something... like a love potion?'

'Never, love must come naturally,' Mel said in all seriousness. 'But I've been in my potions' lab for the last hour. I only get time to play there before and after work and I've had very good sales this month. If I could count on that every month, I could work in my business full-time. It is so good helping people and doing what I love.' Her voice brimming with excitement.

'That's wonderful,' Sophie said and clapped her hands together. 'Good for you.'

'Thanks! The online sales are picking up, and there's another one of those fairs soon, so I've booked a stand to display my potions. Jack's coming to help and to do some of his own magic. You're welcome to join us.'

'Is he now?' Sophie said, teasing Mel. 'My, you work fast.'

'Not fast enough,' Mel assured her.

'Well, thanks for the invitation, I'll think about it. All those witchy types in one room freak me out,' she joked.

'Funny, that's where I feel most at home.'

An hour later, with 'permission' to be out of the office for no longer than ninety minutes, Sophie headed to the police station, finding a park and paying for an hour's worth of parking. Her business with Murdoch wouldn't take that long. She was more determined now than before.

Sophie was recognised the moment she entered the station; she felt the stares and whispers. Several of the officers and staff greeted her by name or congratulated her, others just checked her out like she was the weird clairvoyant that had solved a few cases.

Arriving at Murdoch and Gerard's office, she thanked the receptionist for showing her through and walked in. Sophie saw Murdoch's eyes widen with surprise, then what looked like displeasure. His eyes narrowed and his jaw locked before she had even uttered a word of greeting.

'Well, if it isn't the lovely, crime-solving Ms Carell,' Detective Gerard Oakley said, rising from his chair to welcome her and putting an emphasis on the 'Ms' to show he could move with the times.

'Good morning, Detective.' Sophie turned and smiled at him. 'I'm not crime-solving this morning, well, I am looking for a missing detective,' she joked.

Gerard laughed. 'Agh, like that, is it,' he said with a nod.

Murdoch rose from behind his desk.

'I'll leave you two to talk then,' Gerard added.

'Stay. You don't need to go, this is business,' Murdoch said.

Sophie gave him a confused look, but two could play at this game. 'Murdoch's right, don't leave on my account,' she said to Gerard. If Murdoch wanted her to say her piece in front of his partner, well she would oblige.

Sophie saw Gerard look from Murdoch to her and back to Murdoch, and grabbing his phone, moved towards the door.

'I'll be back in five then, just checking on something,' he said and ducked behind Sophie, leaving the tense room.

'You need to get out of here,' the Raven hissed, not moving from behind his desk. 'Call your protector.'

'We need to talk,' Sophie said firmly, coming a few steps towards him, confusion sweeping over her face as he took a sharp step backward.

'Now! Call Nikolas. Now!' the Raven demanded in a voice too loud for a work environment.

He startled Sophie, and she stepped back. Then she saw his eyes flare black.

'Nikolas!' she called in a halting voice, not taking her eyes off Murdoch who had reared back against the wall as far as he could go in his office and looked dark and menacing. Nikolas appeared in seconds.

'What is it?' he asked, looking at the Raven and his surroundings for danger.

'Get her out of here,' Murdoch hissed. 'Hurry.'

Nikolas strode to Sophie's side, wrapped his arms around her and they were gone in seconds.

CHAPTER 28

MURDOCH SLUMPED. HE CLOSED his eyes and exhaled. She looked so beautiful, he knew her so intimately and had been deprived of Elsopeth for so long. Just when he had her back in his life and in his arms, he was close to attacking her, he knew it, felt it, along with a rising tide of loathing at himself at his almost loss of control.

What the hell was going on, he struggled to define it, but he must.

It was cruel... hard to see her, inhale her scent and harder to order her away.

His partner, Gerard, re-entered and looked around. Whether it was the raw and wounded look on Murdoch's face or the hard edge of his Murdoch's jaw, Gerard refrained from saying anything for the first time in their long partnership. Murdoch righted himself, cleared his throat and schooled his appearance; he was not a man given to emotions despite how volatile they were at the moment. The pain flared and simmered, constantly, just beneath the surface.

'Let's go then. Haven't we got a crime scene to visit?' Murdoch grumbled and with a swift nod, Gerard grabbed his coat and followed.

'What the hell were you thinking?' Nikolas asked as he and Sophie arrived back in her office, startling Jack at his desk, who spilled his cup of tea and hurried to wipe it up.

She pulled out of his arms and straightened herself.

'I wanted to bring matters to a head.'

Nikolas threw his arms up in the air. 'Well, you did that alright. You nearly got yourself cleaned up.'

She huffed. 'Murdoch wouldn't do that.'

'Murdoch wouldn't but the Raven might,' Nikolas said. He paced across the front of the windows, running a hand over his jaw. Remembering Jack's presence, he turned to him.

'Hi Jack, sorry about that,' he said glancing at the spilled tea Jack was wiping up.

'No problem,' Jack assured him. 'I need to get used to odd coming and goings.' Jack chuckled as he wiped a paper towel over his pens. Nikolas saw Jack was keeping his head down, avoiding staring directly at them as if avoiding their tension. Nikolas reined in his frustration and turned to Sophie.

'I've never seen the Raven like that and I've seen him a fair bit over the years while looking after Daphne's business books. Something's going on and you need to steer clear of him.' He made sure he had her attention. 'Seriously, Sophie.'

She bit her bottom lip and nodded. 'Thank you for coming so quickly.'

He calmed down. 'You're welcome. What did you say to him?'

'Nothing,' she said defensively. 'I didn't get a sentence out. He freaked out.' Sophie breathed in and closed her eyes momentarily. Nikolas studied her; she was upset, really upset. 'What have I done?' she whispered.

'Nothing, maybe, something.' Nikolas waved his hand around dismissing her responsibility. 'I don't know yet. Are you okay if I leave? I need to speak to Alfred.'

'Shouldn't I come with you?' she asked.

'No.'

'Fine,' Sophie grumbled. 'My car is at the police station; I'll have to go back.'

Nikolas rolled his eyes. 'I can't drop you there in front of everyone and I don't have my bike.'

'I was just about to go to the post office,' Jack said standing behind his desk and reaching for his car keys. 'I'll give you a lift to get your car, Sophie, we've time before your appointment.'

'Thanks, Jack,' Nikolas said and disappeared.

Nikolas arrived in seconds and knocked on the back door of *Optical Illusion*. It was nearing 9.30am and the front of the shop was open for business, but he wanted a low-key entrance. He hoped to pull Alfred aside for a private chat. The door opened and Orli greeted him.

'Morning, Nik, you're early.' She smiled then frowned slightly. 'Is everything alright?'

'No one's been harmed, but something is going on. Can I come in through the tradesman's entrance?' he said with a teasing smile.

'Please enter,' she said and stood aside. 'Next time, try coming into the back room directly. I've worked on a spell that lets you and select others break through my protection barriers.'

'Is that so? Thanks, Orli.' He smiled. 'Let's hope it works,' he said cricking his neck and recalling his last encounter when he hit the glass.

'Lukas is with a customer and Uncle is on the phone, but I'll bring him in when he is free.'

Nikolas watched the beautiful Orli depart through the curtained doorway to fetch her uncle. She always stirred him – her fragility and beauty, he wanted to instinctively protect her. But he also knew she was stronger than he and Lukas combined. As he waited, he had to admit he was worried about how things were unfolding. Nikolas had never come up against the Raven and he didn't expect to in this lifetime. There had been no drama for over a century and to date, the Raven had maintained a cordial relationship with the cursed Daphne. In the spirit of honesty, he also wouldn't mind if the Raven and Sophie weren't close. He liked the way she felt in his arms and liked her smile. He also liked—

'Nikolas, good morning.' Alfred interrupted his thoughts.

'Alfred, my apologies for arriving so early,' Nikolas said clearing his mind of his slowly increasing amorous thoughts towards Sophie.

'No need to apologise, Nik, you are welcome at all hours. Can I offer you tea or coffee? I'm going to have one.' He indicated the pot of brewing coffee.

Nikolas nodded his thanks and gratefully accepted the strong, hot coffee moments later, wrapping his hands around the mug. By now Lukas and Orli had joined them, the store momentarily empty of customers.

'There's been an incident,' Nikolas said taking a seat opposite Alfred at the table. He told them how the story unfolded that morning, why he was summoned – of seeing the Raven pressed firmly against the wall, his eyes black, a deep timbre to his voice. When he finished all eyes turned to Alfred.

After a moment, Alfred said, 'It was good of him to protect her.'

'What? Why?' Lukas asked. 'He put her in danger!'

Alfred held up his hand to his grandson suggesting he calm down and think this through.

'Sophie went to his workplace, to his lair, uninvited?' Alfred asked and Nikolas nodded.

'The detective has been avoiding her these past few days so something has shifted in him. That is what has me worried.'

Orli spoke up. 'Nik, you said the Raven told Sophie to call your name, that means he doesn't want to hurt her.'

Again, Nikolas nodded. 'And, when I arrived, he looked straight at me and told me to get her out of there. Trust me, Sophie was in danger, real danger. His whole demeanour was threatening if he had let go...'

'How is Sophie?' Lukas asked.

Nikolas shrugged. 'Confused, frustrated, but not too worried. She doesn't think Murdoch will hurt her.'

No one said the obvious, that the Raven was up to the task.

'What now?' Nikolas asked. 'I wasn't expecting this and I'm not sure if I should be doing something. But what?'

Alfred gave Nikolas a small smile. 'You are doing a great job as Sophie's protector, Nik. But sadly, this is the curse. There is little that can be done to prevent it other than being cautionary, which Sophie is not used to being with the Raven. As we all know, this is unprecedented. The Raven's love has never been the accursed before. There is nothing in writing to guide us. So, I propose...'

A bell tinkered at the front door as a customer entered and Lukas swore under his breath, rising to greet them. He no longer had a role in Sophie's protection, but Alfred and Orli with their spells might be able to do something.

'This is what I think we should do...' Alfred began.

Alfred was grateful for the quiet morning in the store, and for Lukas and Orli stepping up to deal with the occasional customer while he put into action his simple plan. He believed simplicity was key at the moment – one step at a time. Finalising his brief note, Alfred sat back, read it one more time and looked at his grandson.

'Shall I read this to you?' he asked.

'Please,' Lukas answered looking up. His mind had been engaged elsewhere, with Venetia, which his grandfather had also unwillingly read.

'It might be best to read it silently,' Lukas said with a glance to the door given Orli was expecting a client to collect their glasses.

'I agree,' Alfred said, and looking at the brief missive in front of him, tapped into his grandson's mind, which he could do effortlessly, and read the note:

Dear Detective Ashcroft

Forgive this intrusion but this message serves two functions which I hope you will accept in good faith. Firstly, our thanks for protecting Sophie. It was considerate and appreciated. Second, it is not my place to interfere but as Daphne thought of you with kind regard, and I know of Sophie's affection for you, I hate to see young people suffer heedlessly. May I suggest that you appear to Sophie in a dream setting of past eras which may diffuse any unusual anger or sentiment you feel at present? There must be some incident you can recall historically when you and Elsopeth had a disagreement and if you could place yourself in that environment, you may have grounds to explain—be it through inference—your current feelings and situation. I have taken the liberty of asking Sophie's protector to brief her that you might

286

be able to undertake this mission and for her to expect you. I imagine it will bring her some comfort.

    Assuring you of my best intentions,

    Alfred Lens.

Alfred looked to his grandson who gave the smallest of nods and replied also without words. Alfred listened and then sighed.

'I assure you, lad, I am not being overly conciliatory nor pandering to the Raven. Let me ask you why it is that with several peaceful generations of co-existence, you are so ready to storm the fort?'

Lukas answered impulsively and out loud. 'Because it is so instinctive, I can't help it,' he admitted, a slight flush to his neck to admit his weakness.

Alfred nodded. 'I know. It is innate, I fought the same impulse for years.'

He saw his grandson's surprised look and the look of relief that also swept his countenance. Alfred continued, 'But surely you and Nikolas don't want to be feuding with the Raven and risking Sophie's life if that can be avoided? It seems so medieval.' He regarded Lukas, offering a small smile.

'It is,' Lukas agreed, 'but that is our world. Witches, spells, and curses, are all undercurrents in the modern era. Was it for Daphne or for the sake of your sanity that you kept the peace all those years that you were protecting Daphne and she was working with Murdoch?'

Alfred nodded. 'Both. It was Daphne's wish too, and there was genuine affection between the pair. It is more difficult with Sophie and Murdoch because of their history of intimacy.' He looked once more at the note he had written.

'It's a good note, more than the Raven deserves,' Lukas grudgingly admitted and smiled.

Alfred chuckled. 'Then I shall send it off now to him.'

'I'll call a courier,' Lukas said, picking up his phone to call the familiar number they used to deliver packages when a client requested it.

Little did Alfred know—given he now had no insights into the thoughts or fears of the protector as his role had been passed on—that Nikolas had no intention of telling or encouraging Sophie to expect her adversary in a dream. The last thing Nikolas wanted was to encourage their affection.

CHAPTER 29

MURDOCH ACCEPTED THE SEALED note from the receptionist and studied it with surprise. He turned it both ways, but it bore only his name and the station's address. Seeing his partner was occupied on the phone, he slit the envelope open and admired the old penmanship. His breath hitched on reading the signature – Alfred Lens. For a moment his anger flared and his jaw locked.

What do the Lens family want now?

He took a deep breath, knowing that was unfair and recalling his respect for the oldest and strongest amongst them. He scanned the contents and calmed himself.

Yes. It might work.

Murdoch felt a wave of gratitude for the senior diplomat of the Lens family. A good deed paid back. So, he could go back, to past days before she was the accursed and before his Raven side began to overtake him. When they were already a little heated in an argument, so he could suggest ways of moving forward in future disagreements. This had to work for now, until Allanon could see the potion maker or until he could work it out for himself, a solution to this rising dark side that was threatening to take him over.

Murdoch's partner hung up. 'We might have a case we could use Sophie's help with,' Gerard said.

'You'll have to contact her and work with her on it. I can't.' He let the statement hang in the air and didn't make eye contact but nevertheless, he could feel Gerard studying him.

'Can't or won't?' Gerard asked.

'Both. Don't worry about it, it's short-lived, we'll sort it out.' He looked up at Gerard. 'I can't explain, don't ask me to.'

Gerard shook his head and mumbled, 'You young people. I saw a story on her this morning, it's unfair, she won't be happy.'

'Where?' Murdoch asked his attention snapping to Gerard who grinned at him.

'I knew you had feelings for her.' He smiled as if congratulating himself on his fine detecting abilities and laughed at the smirk Murdoch gave him. 'It's online, someone challenged her.'

'Well, that's nothing unusual,' Murdoch said with a shrug, 'you felt the same way initially if I recall.' He had a good-humoured dig at his aged partner.

'This is different. Someone's tried to "out" her by saying she has no skills, all her power is in those glasses she puts on, and if she wasn't wearing them, she'd be nothing. Crazy stuff.' Gerard nodded at the screen. 'It's online.'

'You're kidding, right?' Murdoch mumbled, eyes glued to the screen searching for the story and finding it. He let a low breath out between his teeth. He bet he knew the source and the Lens men would not be happy.

Sophie looked up on seeing Miss Sharpe enter the room where she and Jack worked. Miss Sharpe always brought news and Sophie was hoping she would say Murdoch was arriving, but instead she was wringing her hands with concern. 'I'm afraid there's a story online that may call for a response,' she said looking less than pleased, and Miss Sharpe rarely looked displeased.

'Uh oh,' Jack said, waking his laptop and Sophie rose, joining the pair at Jack's desk. She gasped on seeing the headline. *'No glasses, no talent'*. They quickly read through it. A reliable inside source had told the journalist that clairvoyant, Sophie Carell, had no clairvoyant skills, and it was the glasses she wore that gave her insights into the other world. They went on to say that anyone who wore them would have the same skills.

'Sounds ridiculous, no one would take that seriously,' Jack scoffed, 'magic glasses, what next?'

Sophie smiled. 'True, at least we have that going for us, and thankfully—not that it was meant to be a good thing—the curse works no matter what glasses I'm wearing.'

'How do you want to deal with this, dear?' Miss Sharpe asked. 'I wonder who the *"reliable inside source"* is?'

'Not me, I promise you,' Jack said, earnestly.

'Of course, it wasn't you,' Sophie assured him that neither Miss Sharpe nor herself would have thought that. 'I know who it was, and I guess I've been expecting something like this.'

Both Miss Sharpe and Jack looked at her expectantly.

'Who, dear?' Miss Sharpe asked confused.

'Lucy.'

'Oh goodness,' Miss Sharpe said and Jack used a more colourful word and apologised.

Sophie continued, 'Lukas mentioned in passing that Lucy was a little upset about the size of their engagement notice story; Lukas was secretly pleased because he didn't like the limelight. It was the same day—'

'—that you solved that huge cold case and it was all over the news,' Miss Sharpe said with a curt nod. 'What a great shame that young lady would be so put out as to do this.' She glared at the screen. 'I must say, I am quite disappointed.'

Sophie bit back a smile at Miss Sharpe's restraint.

'So, we best address it then,' Sophie said and sighed at the nuisance of having to do so. 'I'm not concerned about the impact on the business. As Jack said, it does sound ridiculous, but I hope we don't get a slew of people trying to steal my glasses off my face!'

Jack and Miss Sharpe chuckled at her dramatics as Sophie acted out trying to protect her face.

Jack stepped up. 'Why don't I pen a few lines now that we supply to the journalist for immediate release? We'll say you wear the glasses because seeing people's features close up is really important to your process, but it doesn't matter if they are the cheap magnifying glasses you buy at any chemist or your own prescription glasses. Why don't we ask him to publish that now and in return if he should do so, offer him an exclusive segment he can film for online release of you using numerous pairs of glasses handed to you by him or a small panel he might like to put together to test you?'

'Brilliant, Jack, thank you, that should work a treat, especially if he thinks he's getting an exclusive,' she said, smiling and relieved, and he nodded pleased with himself.

'You are worth your weight in gold, young man,' Miss Sharpe said to him making Jack chuckle.

'I'll take it in lemon tea cake,' he said teasing her and Miss Sharpe looked delighted.

'It must be about that time, morning tea,' Miss Sharpe agreed.

Sophie smiled, relaxed again with Jack handling that drama, and then a figure outside caught her eye. Walking up the path towards them was a tall, dark-haired man with a goatee beard, wearing jeans, a grey t-shirt and a black jacket. Sophie saw him glance at her office sign and come her way.

'Uh oh,' she said and got the attention of Miss Sharpe and Jack. 'He doesn't look like a client but he's on his way here.'

'He's a witch,' Jack said.

'Nikolas!' Sophie called, on edge at the moment and not hesitating to protect herself, Miss Sharpe and Jack.

Nikolas appeared in seconds, looked to where Sophie was looking and announced, 'Allanon Ashcroft, Murdoch's brother – a harmless witch.' And disappeared again.

'Murdoch's brother,' Sophie whispered, and all three turned to face him as he came up the hallway to the entrance door.

Before entering the building, Allanon Ashcroft looked around the grounds of Sophie's business premises and spent a moment admiring the looming presence of the building. He liked a bit of Gothic; it reminded him of the old days. Coming back to the now, Allanon checked he had locked his car and, with the satisfying beep and flash of lights, pocketed his keys. With that, he took the steps to the front area, noting the signage to Sophie's office and entered the premises, stopping short at seeing three people facing him.

He announced himself. 'Allanon Ashcroft, Murdoch's brother.' He gave a curt nod as if bowing was still the done thing and then on seeing Miss Sharpe, smiled widely. 'Miss Sharpe, it's been a hundred years, figuratively,' he added with a charming smile.

'Mr Ashcroft, I confess I did not recognise you,' Miss Sharpe said, smiling and taking his offered hand. 'The last time I saw you, you were a young boy.'

'Yes, I remember! Murdoch was dropping me to football practice and he had to swing by and see Daphne—Mrs Shelby—on the way there. He'd just got his licence and was happy to drive me around until the novelty wore off,' he said with a chuckle reciprocated by Miss Sharpe.

'Yes. He wasn't a detective then. He was here at Daphne's unconventional invitation to meet her, the new accursed. As I remember, he couldn't find you when it was time to leave, then we saw you climbing up near one of the gargoyles,' she said with a laugh.

'I still love them,' he admitted with a grin.

'May I introduce you to Sophie and Jack?' Miss Sharpe did the formalities.

Allanon shook hands with Jack and was slow to release Sophie's hand. 'My you look like her.'

Sophie cocked her head to the side, a little confused.

'Elsopeth,' he said her name softly, then shook his head. 'I'm sorry, I'm tripping down memory lane. I was hoping I could have five minutes with you, I've come on behalf of my brother.'

'Of course,' Sophie said, keen to speak of Murdoch. She glanced at Jack.

'Go right ahead,' he said. 'You've got touch and booking day, so take as much time as you need.'

Allanon raised an eyebrow in surprise. 'Touch and booking day? Sounds intriguing.'

Miss Sharpe laughed. 'Sophie sits with Jack and works through the weekly requests he has narrowed down for consideration and booking, and then she touches several items hoping to help those in need.'

'It doesn't work too often,' Sophie shrugged. 'I really need to see people and ask questions.'

'Well, I'm glad the curse is working for you,' he said and felt the three bristle around him. Allanon raised his hands. 'I'm a psychologist, I meant that in a positive way... that you were able to make something good of what is meant to be a bad thing.' He noted their body language relaxed again.

'Shall we walk around the garden then?' Sophie asked.

'Or I can get out of here if you want some privacy,' Jack offered.

'No, you've got an important message to respond to,' she said, referring to the challenge from the journalist. 'Besides, there's no shortage of private rooms in this place.'

'A walk around the gardens will be perfect.' Allanon picked up on her first suggestion. 'Then I hoped to get a potion from the resident potion maker. Murdoch said there was one here?'

'Mel, my housemate! She'll be delighted to oblige.'

They departed and Allanon could feel Sophie studying him. He was pleased she did not bring her glasses.

CHAPTER 30

THEY MOVED SOME DISTANCE from the building and the tenanted businesses and avoided a couple of office workers sitting on benches in the gardens.

'You care for him a great deal,' Allanon said, watching Sophie, his hands clasped behind his back as they walked along a path. He was surprised at how distressed she was from Murdoch's absence.

'Can you read me?' she asked cautiously, looking up at him and squinting in the bright morning light.

'No, not in the way you are thinking, don't worry,' he said reassuringly as he walked comfortably beside her. 'But I can read the surrounding energy. It helps a lot with my occupation.'

'Ah.' She smiled. 'You've got your work cut out for you with your brother then,' she teased.

'You got that right, I've pretty much given up reading his head,' he agreed, and they both smiled at the thought of

Murdoch. He didn't speak for a moment, knowing the power of silence and allowed Sophie to mention that which might concern her before he relayed to her Murdoch's situation. It usually worked with his clients.

'I don't know my back history that well yet,' she began with a confession. 'I've started reading Elsopeth's diary but Murdoch and I have not engaged in anything... uh, romantic, in this generation, yet.'

Allanon read how awkward she felt discussing it and aimed to relax her.

'It's a lot to learn when you haven't come into it gradually and I understand your entry to our world was a baptism of fire.'

'To say the least.' She indicated a bench under a shady tree where they sat at a reasonable distance from each other to be able to turn and talk side-on. 'Partly my fault on that score, but I'm glad to be here now. Tell me, why is Murdoch avoiding me? I thought it was safe now he had spoken to V.' She assumed Allanon would understand her reference.

Allanon cleared his throat. 'You must know from what you've read, that for Murdoch, there's been no separation, only waiting. He has had some dalliances over the years of waiting, of course, but he loves you completely as if time had stood still.'

He saw Sophie flush at the thought but read her relief.

'Then why won't he see me or speak to me? He won't even let me apologise for pushing him away the other night – in my dream,' she added hurriedly.

'There's a complication which he's never had before, rather you two have never had before because Elsopeth has never been the cursed. But when you dismissed him—'

'—I hardly dismissed him!' she defended herself.

Allanon gave a nod, accepting her interpretation. He knew from years of counselling that everyone's perspective varied when it came to their role in wrongdoings, and he waited, letting Sophie tell her side if she wanted to do so.

Sophie softened. 'Maybe I did dismiss him. It's what I know, how I've always fought in relationships, I guess. I don't know what I did in the past because I'm not really channelling Elsopeth or feeling my history yet.'

'Of course, understandable. Murdoch needs to know that, and I know you tried to talk with him,' Allanon said holding up his hand before she jumped in defensively again, 'but the thing is, the Raven is not dismissed—nor will he ever be—by the accursed.'

Sophie gave Allanon a slow nod and drew in a deep breath. 'Ah, I understand. I have caused an unbalance, I've challenged him.'

'It's not ego,' Allanon assured her. 'It's instinct, inbred, innate, impossible to ignore. That's why he won't let you near him until he can control it.'

'He's hoping a potion might help?' Sophie asked putting it together – Allanon's earlier request to see the potion maker.

'It was my idea... I thought it might settle his Raven anger, enough at least so you could find some traction. But Sophie, I have to warn you, this could be something that will happen with regularity if the two of you intend to have a passionate relationship in this era, and I'm using the term passionate in the fiery, not sexual sense,' he clarified.

'Nikolas said it could be a very dangerous situation. He's my protector,' she added.

Allanon nodded. 'I know, and Nikolas is right. So, you and Murdoch either have to work out how you get around this, or it might be best not to have any contact at all, not even for work.'

'Does he want that?' Sophie asked too quickly, and he felt her pain.

'That's the last thing in the world he wants, but if it means protecting you, he may have to take that path—' Allanon stopped short of what he was going to say.

'Go on,' Sophie prompted him, 'I'm not frightened to hear it.'

Allanon grimaced. 'Not seeing you and not loving you, might not guarantee your safety. After all, in this century, you are enemies.'

Mel's eyes widened as she saw Sophie at her office door beckoning her outside. Mel excused herself from her work colleagues and came out to find Sophie with a tall, handsome man who looked remarkably like Detective Ashcroft. Sophie did the introductions and explained what Allanon Ashcroft needed.

'I knew there was a witch in the house.' Mel smiled. 'Thank goodness, it's been days.'

Allanon laughed. 'You are tuned in. Well, from one witch to another of sorts, can you help me?'

'It would be my pleasure,' Mel said and in her bright and cheerful fashion, invited him into her potions' lab. While Sophie and Allanon said their goodbyes, Mel opened her grandmother's book of potions and was ready for him when he turned. She saw Allanon's surprise at the ancient book laid bare in front of her.

'Wow,' he said, 'that's something.'

'Handed down in my family for generations,' Mel said proudly, moving her fringe of pink hair out of her eyes.

'I feel in good hands already,' he said, and she sensed him relaxing a little, as if she might be able to help after all.

'Then please tell me what you need and be as specific as you can be about the symptoms and the desired outcome,' she said, inviting him to talk. Mel had understudied her grandmother, asking that very same question for decades and interpreting the answers. She hoped she could be as helpful.

Allanon stood, hands in the pockets of his jeans, and rocking on his heels, he relayed as simply as he could what was needed, finishing with, 'So, you see, Murdoch is despairing. He needs to see Sophie, but needs to quell the anger.'

'Poor Murdoch,' Mel said sympathetically. 'It must be torture. I hope he doesn't lose his cool on the job and take out a baddie.'

Allanon chuckled. 'Well, that might not be such a bad thing.'

'True.' She grinned. Mel knew exactly the page to go to in the ancient volume that she had read cover to cover. Her fingers gently turned the timeworn and delicate pages until she found the potion. 'I have everything that's needed,' she said looking at the list, 'but promise me one thing?'

'Sure,' Allanon agreed.

'While my grandmother has made this potion many a time, I haven't. Can you test it out first before Murdoch meets up with Sophie, if he's going to? Maybe work Murdoch into a temper and see how quick he is to respond.' She gave a small shrug. 'Or something like that.'

'I'll do my best,' Allanon assured her, 'fortunately as his younger brother, I am quite adept at riling him.'

Mel laughed. 'I have a younger brother and it does seem to be a skill.' Narrowing her eyes at him and winning a grin from Allanon.

'I shall give you a dose and a spare. If you feel you need more, I'll include my card and just let me know. I can have it delivered to you.'

'I can send my bird,' Allanon said and Mel looked at him, determining if he was serious or joking.

'Really?'

'Really. If you are not scared of eagles.'

'I have no grounds to be. Ravens maybe,' she said with a smile, and Allanon laughed. 'But does your eagle not clash with the Raven?'

'Over the centuries, they have learnt to live together. Sometimes they are friends, sometimes enemies, but always in co-existence.'

Not long after, he handed over his payment and Mel saw him off with several vials of clear purple liquid in his possession. She watched him depart and sighed as she thought about the Ashcroft men. Complex. Interesting. Handsome.

Alfred Lens saw the story before his grandson Lukas, which was not unusual as Lukas spent most of his day buried in the fine mechanics of timepieces while Alfred was online to reply to emails and booking requests. He had adapted to technology as he adapted to everything, with grace and ease, brushing off the praise of his younger charges by telling them, 'In my day, we did many more difficult things than sending the electronic mail.' He knew the proper name but liked to let them think they had something over him. But Alfred's eyes widened at the challenge to Sophie and with a glance through the gap in the curtain to the room behind, he decided to run it by Orli before telling Lukas – a protection spell might be needed for all of the figurines in the store in case Lukas's anger overtook him, again.

'What's wrong, Grandpa?' Lukas asked, sensing the tension. 'I may not be able to read your mind, but I can feel the change in temperature.'

Alfred smiled. 'Well done, lad. Yes, just something a little concerning. But don't worry, I'll speak with Orli.'

Lukas stiffened with concern and curiosity. 'Are you alright?'

'Never better, you know me.' Alfred felt Lukas trying to read his mind, the mild tapping a good start but not for an experienced and aged force like Alfred.

'Alright, Lukas, I shall tell you, and good try,' he said tapping his temple lightly. He called out to Orli, 'Would you be free for a moment, my dear?'

She came out immediately. 'Of course, Uncle, what's the matter?'

'Can you just protect the glass in the store... all the glass, including the figurines?'

Lukas leapt to his feet. 'What is it?' He almost growled and Orli immediately waved her hands around the store, reciting a small spell and declaring the job done moments later.

Alfred thanked her and nodded to his laptop screen. 'Sophie has been challenged and I believe the source of that challenge might be close to home.'

Lukas strode across the room and Alfred moved out of the way, allowing room for Lukas and Orli to read the article. Lukas slammed his fist on the counter and spat out her name, 'Lucy!'

'Steady yourself, lad,' Alfred said in a calm voice, as he saw Lukas's body stiffen and shake, his eyes flared amber, drowning out his customary pale blue, and even Orli took a precautionary step away. The glass windows behind Alfred shook but stayed intact and while the figurines tottered, nothing broke.

Orli flinched. 'Speak to her Lukas, but do not assume or accuse, just ask first.'

He nodded, his jaw locked, and Lukas took the deepest of breaths.

'Perhaps calm down first,' Alfred suggested, and Lukas shook his head.

'No. This is wrong.' He waved his hand at the screen. 'This petty, stupid jealousy, stopping me from being friends and protecting Sophie, the stupid photo shoot...' Lukas shook his head. 'I need to do what I should have done some time ago.'

Alfred waited for a beat, letting Lukas gather his thoughts before he added, 'Take your time, think very carefully, lad, before you go to that extreme.'

'You're going to call off your engagement?' Orli asked, shocked.

Lukas looked at his cousin. 'Do you think we're suited? Do you think we'll last?'

Orli gave a little shrug. 'Who am I to say? Opposites do attract after all.'

'No,' Lukas said firmly. 'We got the attract right, but the rest has been need, fear, dependence, call it what you like.'

'And you've met someone who shares your passion,' Alfred said and saw his grandson's eyes widen at Alfred's understanding of his romantic predicament.

'I wish you couldn't read me,' he said.

'Me too, lad,' Alfred said, 'but rest assured, I do my best to turn you off.'

'Who are we talking about? I seem to have missed something,' Orli said, frustrated. 'I only had one day off.'

Alfred and Lukas chuckled at her expression, and the tension released a little.

'Venetia,' Lukas said.

'Oh, really?' Orli said, her eyes widening with surprise. 'Well, she is beautiful, timeless and... the Raven's, isn't she?'

'Not anymore,' Lukas said with a smile. 'Our heartbeats sync when we are together, she understands me and my work. She sees the beauty in it.'

Alfred smiled. 'Then go end your relationship, Lukas, and begin your new life. But if I may suggest, do so gently, carefully, and respectfully. You loved each other enough to consider a life together once, don't be too harsh.'

Lukas nodded, but looked at the story again. 'No, this is a low blow and I will be restrained, I promise, Grandpa, but I am not holding back on my disgust. It's a betrayal of Sophie and me. So disappointing.' With that, he grabbed his keys and phone from his desk and strode out the front door.

Alfred breathed a sigh of relief. 'We survived that outburst.' He turned to study Orli. 'Isn't it about time you found love, my dear?'

Orli gave her uncle an affectionate look. 'I'll begin looking immediately and you'll be the first to know.'

'Excellent, I look forward to that,' he said and looked up to greet a customer as the familiar little bell rang above the store entrance.

CHAPTER 31

IT HAD BEEN A day of great emotion, and as Sophie propped herself up in bed that evening, Elsopeth's journal by her side, she thought of Allanon's visit, of Murdoch's predicament and her ache to see him, and of Lucy's ultimate betrayal. She was grateful to her clique – protector Nikolas, office manager Jack, the guru of all things Miss Sharpe and housemate Mel. How good it was to have them by her side. What would she do without their love and support? Sophie made a mental note to tell them again tomorrow how much she valued them.

Her eyes flew to the window as the frames rattled, but no one was there; the wind was up and the moon was almost full tonight. Sophie could see it from her bed, and she had left the curtains open for now to enjoy the splendour of it. The second-floor location of her bedroom assured no one could see in.

Sophie didn't want to think about Murdoch; the last few days had been so draining that in truth, she wished she had feelings for someone less complicated. She thought that was Murdoch until he was outed as the Raven, and she became Elsopeth reincarnated, for the love of God! The pain, it was physical... when did it come to this? Maybe she should have wooed Lukas Lens before he lay eyes on Lucy and they partnered, now betrothed. She smiled at her choice of the old-fashioned words, *wooed* and *betrothed*. Maybe Elsopeth was emerging after all.

There was Nikolas, too, of course. Tall, mysterious and handsome Nikolas Saggers, who was good with the books and a closed book himself for that matter. She smiled at the thought of him. His walls were always up and not once had he opened up to her, she barely knew him. Maybe the cold front was best for the cursed and their protector. Or did he have something to hide aside from who he was and who he could be? Miss Sharpe said he was a shapeshifter and could be anyone he wanted, but what exactly did that mean? Would he be howling at the moon in the next day or so when it was a full moon? She'd like to see that, she painted the picture of his shifting in her head. It was nice in his arms, the couple of times she had been wrapped in them while he zoomed her in and out of places. He always smelled musky and sexy—more animal than nature—and his suits and shirts were crisp and expensive.

Sophie sighed. She had enough dramas without shopping around for lovers. Which made her think of Murdoch again.

'No!' she said firmly and reaching for Elsopeth's journal, she opened it, intending to read any entries she could find about the burgeoning relationship between Elsopeth and the Raven, and even better, any tension. Any learnings would be much appreciated, and thumbing gently through the pages, she found the very entry the cursed, Hannah, had written about in the photocopied pages Lukas had given her. This time it was from Elsopeth's perspective and in her young voice. Sophie read the earlier account.

'I was so excited to be at my first ball and everything looked so beautiful. I wonder if every girl here was as terrified as I felt. The dresses were amazing, the candle chandeliers were breathtaking and the men, my, how handsome the gentlemen look in their attire. My guardian introduced me to a circle of ladies who welcomed me, so kind, although I did hear whispers about me... they were calling me the spirit girl.

'And then I saw him. The Raven! He was at the ball and dancing with a beautiful, dark-haired woman. I felt myself flush with embarrassment.

To think that just because he saved me from falling and sent me flowers, I had created this romance in my head and here he was, dancing with this most sophisticated beauty. She was everything I was not. What a fool I have been... of course a worldly man like the Raven would have many lovers.

'I turned away to focus on my new friends and I quickly learned that girls are very strange creatures. In my short earthly life, I had grown up with very little female company, except for that of my mother. No sisters, no friends. Once I was reborn, my exposure to girls my age was also limited, and those I knew, like Charlotte, were sweet and kind. But goodness, these girls made such sharp observations and then befriended the very person they spoke about as if they were all the dearest of acquaintances. Most odd.

'The dance finished, and the Raven saw me. My human heart that still beat stopped, I am sure of it. It felt as if he reached into me and grabbed my soul while everyone else in the room disappeared before my eyes. I know I shouldn't have stared, that is not at all becoming, but I could not tear my eyes from him and then he approached, and I danced with no one else for the evening.'

Sophie smiled. *How romantic*, she thought, and thumbed through the entries, reading key sentences about the Raven as they caught her eye, moving from one entry to the next, and the next.

'I cannot bear to be without him and yet he has not visited for two days.

'He is insatiably jealous. No man may look in my direction without feeling the wrath of his stare.

'He is such a man of honour except when it comes to the accursed, how his eyes darken when he thinks of her.

'Lucia is angry at me. I believe she thinks I have designs on her man.'

Hold up! Sophie stopped page turning and returned to the name that had just caught her eye. Lucia. She scanned the page and went back to find Lucia in context. Elsopeth had met a lady at one of the dances by the name of Lucia and they had become firm friends, but then there was this:

> 'We were such good friends, but when the earl approached me to dance, Lucia was quite angry at me. It would have been rude to decline his request, but I have no interest in the man she has set her heart on.'

Hmm, Sophie mused. Lucia, Lucy, interesting. She sighed and placed the book on her dresser, and turned off the light, lowering herself to the bed. Sophie was lonely, she had to admit that her life was great in so many ways and she wouldn't change direction or go back to her acting days for anything, but she wanted love and a relationship. She wanted what was beginning with Murdoch. She doubted she would sleep, but

the tossing and turning from the previous two nights had left
her exhausted and she was asleep in moments.

Murdoch waited, grateful that Sophie had left the curtains
open. In his bird spirit form, he watched her reading the book.
Her hair spread out on the pillow, the bed lamp lighting her in
a manner that reminded him so much of Elsopeth. The potion
had worked, he felt calmer for now. He hoped Mel's potion
would retain its strength and longevity to let him do what he
needed to do – to visit Sophie in her dreams and to assure her
they would be together again as soon as he trusted himself, and
they had found a new way forward. That included what could
be said, what couldn't, and how to manage each other in this
modern age.

At last, she turned off the bedroom reading light. It was time
for action.

In his mind, he projected himself into the time of Elsopeth,
a time of finery and manners, of rules and ceremonies. His
clothing was tailored, expensive, and unfussy. Murdoch could
not abide by the dandy way of dressing or the flashy displays
of wealth. And he waited in the corridors of her dreams. It was
akin to dark hallways, some doors with slivers of light beneath

them, but none were the era he needed to be in. Her thoughts were all in the now and he stayed out of sight, not intruding in her dream but waiting and yearning for her to return to the past, hoping the book she was reading before slumber would help bring in those dreams.

More dark hallways, more dark entrances, and then, after what seemed like hours, she was there. In front of Murdoch was the ballroom and he could see Elsopeth standing with several other young girls, all dressed in their finery and accepting refreshments before the next set of dances began.

It was now or never.

The Raven strode towards her, heads turned, watching one of the season's most eligible bachelors enter the room and some of Elsopeth's friends shrank as he caught their eye.

She turned and saw him, looking surprised, which confused Murdoch. Alfred Lens said Sophie would be told of his coming. Had the protector not passed on the message that he would try to speak with her in the old world via dreams tonight? Anger stirred within him. Of course, he didn't. He wants her for himself. Nikolas Saggers was not going to push Sophie, or Elsopeth, into his arms.

But her smile diffused his distress and as he reached out for her, her gloved hand almost in his as she said his name in delight, her breath hitching with the thrill of seeing him.

'Murdoch, you have come.'

Suddenly Sophie was gone, and he was back in a dark hallway, scrambling, running towards the doors and flinging them open, but none of them led to her, none to Sophie.

Why? What happened? Come back!

He roamed anxiously for some time, but she did not return. Murdoch yelled in anger and frustration and left her mind, returning to the now. He flew into the sky. Fast, hard, feeling the strength of his wings soaring in the night, the black sky enveloping him like he was drowning in ink.

The Raven flew and flew until he had no strength left in his frame. Until he was so spent that he fell from the sky to the earth below.

CHAPTER 32

SOPHIE WOKE WITH A start and sat upright; a tall man stood at the end of her bed silhouetted in the moonlight. She gasped in fright.

'It's only me, you are safe. You called out the Raven's name, I came.' Nikolas's voice cut through the darkness and he raised his hands in a placating manner. He looked around her room, concerned.

'What? No! I wasn't in danger,' she exclaimed. 'I just saw him...' Sophie's eyes scanned the room, searching and confused. She pulled the blanket up to her chin.

'Your cold,' he said, grabbing a wool throw-over from a chair by the window and coming closer.

'I... I just reached out to him, in a ballroom, he was there,' Sophie said, disappointment trumping her emotions and she tried to keep the frustration from her tone.

Why did Nikolas wake her when at last Murdoch had come to her?

Nikolas wrapped Sophie's wool throw-over around her shoulders and he lowered himself beside her on the edge of her bed.

'Sorry, I thought you were in trouble.'

'Oh, of course,' she said with a slight shake of her head. 'It was good of you to come. It is always good of you to come, thank you Nik.' She felt embarrassed to be caught half asleep, half undressed and confused.

'It's my role to attend to you,' he said, his posture reinforcing his strength and presence, his deep voice reassuring her she was secure and safe.

'I know, thank you.'

'But I'd come anyway,' he quickly added. 'I'm happy to look after you.'

She exhaled and gave him a small smile, the best she could muster. 'Sorry, I'm just disorientated. I was sound asleep, deeply asleep, and then I wasn't sure what happened or where I was for a moment there. I'm sorry I pulled you away from your night.'

Nikolas rose, and leaning over, did something untoward and intimate – he placed a kiss on her forehead and disappeared.

Sophie dropped back onto her cushions and covered her face with her hands. She wanted to cry and scream and hurl something through the window in frustration. But she couldn't blame Nikolas. He was only looking out for her and if she had cried out Murdoch's name, the Raven's name, then of course he came... but she didn't think she had called it out. She had smiled in delight at seeing Murdoch and said his name with whispered breath.

It crossed her mind... *Did Nikolas have another reason for preventing her from meeting with the Raven? But what would that be?* Sophie dismissed the thought, believing his intentions were good.

Murdoch was there, so gorgeous, so close.

Could she get back there? Back to him?

Wide awake now, Sophie turned on the reading light and reached for Elsopeth's diary. If she read some more about the ballroom and placed herself back in the era, if it were the last thing on her mind before she closed her eyes, she might get back. Opening the volume to where she had left the small white ribbon in the pages, Sophie read on. Her eyes scanned through the words, searching for the Raven's name, page after page, month after month, every liaison, searching for references to their growing relationship, and then she gasped, her hand flying to her mouth.

No!

Sophie re-read the words again that Elsopeth had written with such obvious despair:

'I am sick of heart and know not what to do. I love them both, the Raven and the wolf, Nikolas. What shall become of us all?'

THE END

Next in the series... the fourth and final volume:

Fate comes to call in the fourth and final volume of *The Clairvoyant's Glasses*. For the first time in history, the descendant of a powerful witch and the cursed glass recipient are one and the same – Sophie – and her enemy, the Raven can't be with her, or without. But the Raven is not her only enemy, and not her only love.

ACKNOWLEDGEMENTS

MY THANKS TO...

Karri Klawiter, Art by Karri for creating the beautiful covers for this series;

Proofreader Crystal L. Wren, COL Proofreading Service;

And special thanks to the readers of paranormal fantasy/romance who found volume 1 and whose reviews inspired me to write volume 2, 3, and 4. I hope you enjoyed this latest volume.

ABOUT THE AUTHOR

Helen is a hybrid-published, Amazon best-selling author. After studying English Literature, Media, and Communications at universities in Queensland, Australia, and obtaining a Counselling Diploma, Helen has worked as a journalist, producer and marketer in print, TV, radio and public relations. Born in Toowoomba, she has made her home in Logan Village, Australia, with her journalist husband, Chris, and Boxer dog, Baxter. She is published by Next Chapter, Podium Entertainment, and her own imprint, Atlas Productions.

Connect with Helen:

Website: www.helengoltz.com

BookBub:www.bookbub.com/authors/helen-goltz

Facebook: www.facebook.com/HelenGoltz.Author

Instagram: https://www.instagram.com/helengoltz1/

Also by Helen Goltz

The Lady Mortician's Visions (historical mystery/romance/paranormal twist)
The Missing Brides
The Fake Child
The Dastardly Debutante
The Deathly Dolls
The Potent Perfume
The Watery Grave
The Vanishing Groom
More to come....

Miss Hayward & the Detective Series (historical mystery/romance):
Murder at the Carnival
The Artist's Missing Muse
Mystery at the Asylum

The Mortician's Clue (introducing Phoebe and staff from The
Economic Undertaker)
Murder in Bridal Lane

The Clairvoyant's Glasses (paranormal/romance)
Volume 1 – A vision unexpected
Volume 2 – Time has a shadow
Volume 3 – Love knows no bounds
Volume 4 – Fate comes to call
Volume 5 – The Raven's Son

The Jesse Clarke series (cosy mystery):
Death by Sugar
Death by Disguise
Death by Reunion

The Mitchell Parker series (crime thriller):
Mastermind
Graveyard of the Atlantic
The Fourth Reich

Writing as Jack Adams (mystery suspense):
Poster Girl
Delaney and Murphy childhood friends' series:
Asylum

Stalker

Cult

Hitched

Carnival.

Writing as Ally Adams:

The Saints team (contemporary romance):

Team Lucas

Team Tomas

Team Niklas

Team Alex

Stand-alone titles:

The House on Findlater Lane (mystery/romance paranormal)

The Forgotten House (historical romance)

Three Parts Truth (mystery suspense)

Morphers (middle grade fiction)

With journalist Chris Adams, the Grave Tales series (non-fiction) x 9 titles:

Grave Tales: Brisbane Vol.1

Grave Tales: Great Ocean Road – Geelong to Port Fairy

Grave Tales: Sydney Vol.1

Grave Tales: Bruce Highway

Grave Tales: True Crime Vol.1

Grave Tales: Queensland's Great South West
Grave Tales: Melbourne Vol.1
Grave Tales: Queensland's Scenic Rim & Surrounds
Grave Tales: Tasmania.
Grave Tales: Cold Cases (an amalgamation of stories from existing titles).